Worm

Worm

By Cindy Glander

Edited by
Michael Glander

iUniverse, Inc.
New York Lincoln Shanghai

Worm

iUniverse, Inc.

For information address:
iUniverse, Inc.
2021 Pine Lake Road, Suite 100
Lincoln, NE 68512
www.iuniverse.com

ISBN: 0-595-31542-9 (pbk)
ISBN: 0-595-66332-X (cloth)

Printed in the United States of America

"There is a time for each and every aspect of life, and time does go by too quickly. Slow down and smell the roses. And don't sweat the small stuff. Be more concerned with what you do with your 'today,' because tomorrow seems to take care of itself. This has been the way I have lived my life, thus far, and is the way I will continue to live my life."

—Cindy Glander
December, 1999

Foreword, by Michael Glander

The book you are holding is the culmination of a lifelong dream for my mother, Cindy Glander. Like Uncle Henry and Jake in the story of *Worm*, Mom kept a mental "to-do" list that included several goals she wanted to accomplish in her lifetime. One of those goals was to become a successful author, and I have no doubt that if she were only given more time, that goal would have been attained. She wrote this story in 1994, and planned to submit it for publication before life got in the way of her dreams.

Mom had a wonderful, vivid imagination, which is clearly evident throughout the tale of *Worm*. As a young child, I can remember playing games that she invented, and listening to stories she created off the top of her head. Though she was a perpetually cheerful person with an infectiously optimistic outlook on life, she had a curious fondness for the macabre. She loved to tell gruesome ghost stories and watch gory horror movies, and she took great pleasure in writing some of the gorier parts of this novel.

Her deep love and affection for all animals ("feathered, finned and furry") was hardwired into her personality. From the time I was born, our house was filled with pets of all shapes and sizes. Her love of animals is plainly evident in this story, as is her love of soap operas and Stephen King novels.

The pet store that serves as the backdrop for this story is based upon a real-life pet store (also named "Critters"), based in New Milford, Connecticut, which was owned and operated by my parents for nearly seven years before they sold the shop and moved to Florida. It was truly a family-run business, with my parents tackling the day-to-day operations while my brother and I worked the cash register, cleaned the cages and waited on customers. Mom once told me that some of the happiest times of her life were spent in that little pet store, working side-by-side with her family.

The characters in *Worm* are purely fictional, but they have been instilled with such depth and dimension that by the end of this story, you feel as if you've known them your whole life. People often said the same thing about my mother. A stranger could sit with her for five minutes and walk away feeling as though he'd been visiting with a long-lost friend. That was her gift.

Worm is a fun read, and having read this book many times over the years, I've grown attached to this story. It is a story that I believe deserves a wider audience than it has received so far. By publishing this book, I hope to share the knowledge of what a truly fantastic tale it is, and what a clever and talented person its author was.

CHAPTER 1

Sheila Bennett swung open the metal door to her trailer and two hyperactive hounds emerged soon after. Spotting the neighbor's cat hiding in the bushes, the dogs bolted out the door, nearly knocking Sheila off her feet, and were soon at full stride, chasing the panic-stricken cat into the woods nearby.

"Damn mutts," Sheila barked after them as she lit another cigarette and slammed the door to muffle the aggravating noises. As if it weren't bad enough when her no-good husband brought home the first one, now they had two. He claimed it would make hunting easier. All she knew was that she had to clean up after the filthy animals while he was goofing off all day, and she hadn't noticed a difference in the amount of meat on the table. Another three hundred bucks down the drain, thanks to his impulsive spending. *He* didn't have to be at home with them all day. *He* didn't care how many nice things they chewed up and destroyed. *He* didn't care how often she had to vacuum all the damn dog hairs or how many piles of dog shit she'd have to step in at two o'clock in the morning in her bare feet.

So, if he didn't care, she didn't care. She didn't care if those dogs stayed outside all day while he was at work. She didn't care when the neighbors complained about their endless barking or when they would get into their garbage. In fact, she thought it was pretty amusing when her husband had to bail them out a time or two from the dog pound and pay a hefty fine after they'd been caught running around without tags.

As for this so-called "rabies epidemic" she kept hearing about, she certainly wasn't about to stand in line at the clinic all day to get the useless mutts a shot. She had better things to do with her time. Hell, it would almost be funny to see one of the bastards bite the old man on the ass and watch him start foaming at the mouth. Maybe they'd have to cut the dogs' heads off. Isn't that what they do? Hell, she'd even volunteer to do the honors! With that, the old woman let out a cackle that morphed into a violent hacking cough.

Sheila often thought about killing the dogs herself, especially if they ever touched her precious "Tweety." She took a long drag as she savored that thought, then flicked the butt onto her dirt driveway and ambled back inside the trailer. She walked over to the high hung bamboo cage in the corner and whispered, "Good morning, darlin'," to the bright yellow canary sitting inside. Tweety was her little baby, and she never minded spending a little money on goodies for her baby from the pet store downtown because she always brightened her day with her song. Besides, she ate like a bird—not like those bottomless pits on four legs.

Finding his seed bucket a little low, she managed to scrape up just enough to top off his little cup. An exasperated sigh pushed out of her puckered mouth with the thought of having to go to town to buy some more. She wished there were another pet store in town because she didn't like the dumb broad that worked there. How someone with such a holier-than-thou attitude could ever be a responsible business owner escaped her.

All Sheila had wanted was a little casual chitchat with the woman and she received a half-hour lecture instead. Sheila didn't see what the big deal was with the rabies scare. Everyone was blowing it all out of proportion as usual. She let her dogs loose all the time and never once had a problem. Well, that know-it-all at the pet store just couldn't let it go. She just kept rambling on and on about symptoms and warning signs and the importance of keeping your pets indoors until this "epidemic" was brought under control.

"Whatever," croaked Sheila. "Just give me my damn seeds." She would never forget the look on that pet store woman's face. She was so condescending; so self-righteous. What a bitch.

* * * *

The two dogs stared down the brazen raccoon. In keeping with their training, they surrounded their prey both front and rear to prevent its escape. The August sun was hot, and the air was humid and heavy. A full day of running without water must have slowed their thinking, as they were unprepared for what happened next. The raccoon should have run away when he saw them approaching in the distance. Instead, he calmly stood his ground with a glazed look in his eyes. The feral animal seemed mesmerized by the snarling hounds and appeared to be frozen in its footsteps until it suddenly charged at one of them, tearing into the soft flesh of one dog's neck with a frenzy before turning to the other and continuing its assault. Dazed and wounded, the dogs scurried home.

Less than two weeks later, the dogs were let loose to run again. Their symptoms went unnoticed by apathetic eyes, but were discovered shortly after their attack on eight-year-old Bobby Moore, who survived the attack only to face six weeks of inoculations. The dogs were decapitated and the heads were sent to a local lab, which verified the presence of rabies.

Sheila ignored the whispering of the townspeople. Underneath, she was delighted to be rid of the worthless animals. Outwardly, she resented her husband for bringing the mangy animals home in the first place. She hated him for all the accusatory looks she was receiving around town, and for all the gossip, and for the lawsuit filed against her and her husband by little Bobby Moore's parents.

She also did not want any part of that pet store. The last thing she needed to hear was an "I told you so" from that haughty little bitch behind the counter. It was with that reason she took the initiative to find another pet store. It was a little out of her way, but it was worth it just to get away from the accusatory glares of all the finger-pointers in town.

She hopped into her old, rusted Chevy wagon, settling in for the long ride to pick up supplies for her Tweety. Putting her can of diet soda in the holder, she turned the radio up loud and rolled down the window a crack as she lit a fresh cigarette.

Sounds filled the car: the music, the singing, the hum of the air conditioner, the scratching and clawing of tiny little feet. Her mind wandered, propelled by the song on the radio, as she maneuvered the back roads of Sherman.

She did not notice the quivering body in the back seat. She did not feel the body lunge onto the back of her vinyl seat with sharply-honed claws; the fat, bushy tail whipping sharply from side to side, the pointy little ears twitching nervously. She did not see the eyes dilate with every street lamp the car passed, nor did she see the foam dripping silently but steadily from its fanged mouth.

It wasn't until Sheila approached the sharp turn, noticed the road sign reading, "Steep Grade," with the picture of the truck, lightly touched her brake, checked her rear-view mirror, and stared intently at the glowing eyes staring back at her, that she suddenly felt a sharp pain in her neck. She instinctively jerked a hand up to grab whatever it was that had a hold of her, but this succeeded only in provoking the animal further into ripping at her hands, neck, and face with jagged teeth. In the ensuing struggle to pry away the sinking teeth fiercely attached to her cheek, Sheila was momentarily aware that she was about to die.

With terror-filled eyes she watched herself lose control of her car as she sped over the embankment, slamming powerfully into a rock ledge.

When the passing motorist stopped to examine the wreckage, speculation was that the woman had died on impact and not from the ravaging of the rabid squirrel bouncing off the walls of her accordion-shaped vehicle.

* * * *

Excerpt from the New Milford Gazette:

> Richard "Dick" Williams, former owner of Horse Gate Farm, died last Saturday evening. His body was discovered by four local teens in the Lover's Leap Mansion. Police speculated the cause of death to be suicide.

* * * *

Rumor had it that Dick Williams was guilty, and deathly afraid of prison. Facing a host of charges from animal abuse to horse thievery—not to mention the lawsuits from irate owners against him—the coward hung himself. The well-publicized photos of emaciated horses with protruding ribs had repulsed and disgusted the entire community. Two farmers' horses, once assumed to have run off a while back, actually showed up in his rat-infested "boarding stable." Of course, Mr. Williams denied all knowledge and involvement in the charges of blatant neglect, and hired himself the top attorney in town to defend him. He must have been guilty, though, to have taken his own life in such a gruesome manner.

In the old days, death by hanging was the standard punishment for horse thieves. In retrospect, then, it seemed highly appropriate for Williams to have killed himself in such a manner.

One could almost say it was poetic justice.

CHAPTER 2

Worm
The Early Years

The man appeared to be old, but he wasn't. His face was lined with deep grooves around his mouth and webbed wrinkles formed tiny crow's feet around his eyes. The nape of his neck looked like tanned rawhide, and specks of gray dotted his jet-black hair around the temples. His plaid flannel shirt had seen better days, but it was his favorite, despite the hole in the elbow and the torn pocket. His low-riding jeans were faded, and badly needed to be washed. He had forgotten to wear his shoes despite the coolness of the air outside, but with the amount of beer he had consumed that night, his feet were impervious to the cool ground below.

With tin can in hand, he walked unevenly to the fence framing the barn and leaned heavily on it. "Daisy," the old workhorse, thinking perhaps it was feeding time, ambled over and nudged the old man's arm. Startled, he struck the horse's muzzle with a sudden right cross, then wiped wet spittle from his hand across his sleeve while the horse ambled off toward his stable.

"Goddamn horse…scared the shit out of me," he muttered to himself and kicked a bucket next to his foot. Shoeless, he split open the end of his big toe and a chain of rapid obscenities spewed from his mouth. This startled the large black dog lying nearby, which began barking. The man picked up a rock, threw it at the dog, and by the sheer luck of a drunken man's aim, hit him square on the head. The dog, a rather large shepherd mix, became agitated by this attack, and found cause to charge the man, whom he had never liked anyway.

With hackles raised and fangs exposed, the mutt was on his target in two bounding leaps. During this assault, the man spilled his beer, and from a leather holster on his waistband, drew his trusty pocketknife. Despite the onslaught of the ravaging beast, the man managed to separate the sharpest blade and with one deft, backhanded motion, slit the dog's throat.

* * * *

A moment earlier, a young child was startled awake by the barking of his pet dog. Hoping that "King" wasn't raiding his father's chicken coop again, the boy leapt out of bed and ran to the window. The last time King killed a chicken, not only did his trusty old pooch get a beating, but the boy received one as well. The old man's reasoning, of course, was that it was the boy's pet, and therefore the boy's responsibility. The boy would have gladly accepted the belt for the both of them. After all, he reasoned, King didn't know any better. He was only a dog, and killing chickens was what dogs do.

The boy pulled back the drapes and scanned the yard toward the sounds of the growling and cussing. Squinting his eyes, he focused on two shadowy figures scuffling near the fence. With his eyes widening, he fought back a scream with both hands to his mouth as he watched his father slay his beloved pet.

The drunken man stood silently on wobbly legs for only a moment, then retrieved his beer can from the ground nearby. Giving it a slight shake and hearing nothing but foam on metal, he angrily tossed it across the back lawn. Through tear-filled eyes, the boy watched as his father wiped the knife blade on his bloodstained shirt and returned it to its holster. A look down at the bulky body lying at his feet, with its head slightly tilted back at an odd angle, causing the tongue to fall out from the side of its gaping mouth, must have reminded the old man of a thirsty man who needed a beer. Giving the dog one last kick, he muttered, "Goddamn mutt!" then hobbled back to the kitchen to his endless supply in the refrigerator. Three cans later he was passed out in his favorite recliner, mouth gaped open in successive snores.

The boy continued to silently weep as he listened to the snoring emanating from downstairs, which signaled the end to that evening's nightmare. A full night's crying left his weary body drained, but sleep did not come that night. The boy crept down the stairs to the living room and he wished at that moment that the sleeping sounds would stop and it was his father that was dead and not his canine friend. If ever he had despised the man before—and there had been many times—it was nothing compared to the hatred he felt at that moment.

Two months later, when the boy's father died from a kick to the head delivered by his workhorse, Daisy, he did not cry. In fact, he felt the horse—a witness herself to King's murder that night—had served a strange type of justice. He believed Daisy was justified in administering the appropriate punishment of death to the man that had caused so much pain and suffering to the family through the years. He did not understand why his mother cried. He didn't miss the mean old monster. He certainly wouldn't miss the loud arguments or the beatings or the midnight massacres.

He hated having to wear long-sleeved shirts and turtlenecks in the middle of the summer just to cover up painful bruises and cigarette burns. He hated his round, thick, black-rimmed glasses. He hated the teasing from the other kids at school. He hated going to school, yet he hated to hear the dismissal bell ring, as he was afraid to go home. He would sometimes find odd jobs to do for his teachers—any means of postponing the old man's mood of the day. It was because of his unpopularity, his label as the teacher's pet, his black-rimmed glasses and his turtlenecks that he earned the nickname, "Worm." It was a moniker that his father thought was the most righteous thing he had ever heard.

Despite the teasing and name-calling, school had been his temporary haven from home. There, and at his Uncle Henry's place, where his mother would take him for visits from time to time. His mother's parents died in a car accident when she was a little girl, leaving Uncle Henry and Aunt Vera as the closest relatives she had. Worm loved Uncle Henry, who always had some new project in the works before he had completed the previous one. He had a laugh that made his mouth pucker and pushed his cheeks so far into his eyes that they became tiny slits in his round face. He lived in what appeared to be a well-kept Cape Cod with an inviting front porch surrounded by various well-manicured bushes and flowerbeds. A walk around to the backyard, however, revealed more of the man who lived there. Strewn with pieces of lumber, rusty old tools and cans, assorted used tires, and a weatherworn, dilapidated chicken coop, it was the magical playground for a retired man and a young child.

For everything Worm loved about his Uncle Henry, however, he was at a loss for any redeeming qualities in his Aunt Vera. A hulking woman with foreboding eyes who wore her gray-streaked hair pulled back into a tight bun, she seemed to wear a perpetual scowl on her face. She was a stickler for cleanliness, and spent most of her waking hours either cleaning the house or nagging Uncle Henry to do the same. The couple had drawn their boundaries years ago. Hers was inside, his was outside, and never the two shall meet. Aunt Vera had a quick temper, a swift hand, and a penchant for using common household utensils to keep young boys in line.

Visits to Uncle Henry's always meant a brief, but welcome, respite from his father's backhand, or his belt, or the lighted end of a cigarette. Worm's body read like a book of every wrongful act he had ever committed, intentional or not. His mind accepted the punishment. He recognized his ineptitude and clumsiness. The only person who never seemed to mind was Uncle Henry. Uncle Henry would let Worm help with his latest project without being critical. He'd pat Worm on the head and provide him with a needed source of encouragement to feed his pitiful self-esteem.

Visiting Uncle Henry meant fishing trips, hunting for pheasants, or an ice cream cone with sprinkles after errand-hopping around town. Worm felt proud to be in the company of a man who was so well known, and well-liked, around town. Everywhere they went, from the imposing town hall with the adjoining police station, to Wilson's Hardware with shelves full of promising new projects, to the pharmacy on the village green to refill Aunt Vera's nerve tonic, to the little pet store to pick up dog food and visit with the animals, Henry always seemed to run into somebody he knew and never forgot to introduce Worm as his favorite little partner.

Worm didn't mind waiting as his uncle bent the ear of several passersby on Main Street, except when they happened to run into Hank Beecher, the grizzled old cop. Worm was uncomfortable with the authority figure and the look the officer gave him, as if he were guilty of some terrible crime. He remembered one time when the cop had pulled Uncle Henry aside. Worm couldn't hear what they were saying, but from the way the two men eyed him, Worm thought he was in big trouble. After a seemingly long while, he saw them both smile and shake hands. The tall man in uniform touched Worm's shoulder as he left and told him to "keep up the good work." Then he saluted. Worm wasn't afraid of the policeman any longer.

The freedom he should have enjoyed with the death of his father was negated by the loss of King. Worm found he was lonelier than he had ever been in his short life. His mother was never happy, and for the most part she kept to herself. She cried when her husband was alive and seemed to cry even more often now that he was gone. Worm could not understand why his mother wasn't happy. She no longer had to tiptoe around the house all the time, afraid to upset the old man and receive another beating. He was glad there were no more arguments, no more beatings, and no more fear. He couldn't understand why his mother wasn't happy, too. He didn't understand why she had married him in the first place.

One night, his mother went out without telling him where she was going or when she'd be back. Soon she was out every night, coming home long after tired little eyes could keep open no longer. In the old days, he had King for company, to protect him from the bogeyman in the closet or from the monsters under his bed. Now the frightened little child had only his imagination to keep him company.

The mother he knew and loved was home all the time, hair in a ponytail and book in hand. This new mother wore her hair down, and always had to go somewhere really important. She wore bright red lipstick, leaving smeared blotches on his cheek as she ran out the door, giving instructions for the night's dinner. When she came home late at night, she acted like a completely different person. She stumbled around on wobbly legs. She spoke funny. She acted funny. She smelled funny. And in the morning, she would sleep in so late, Worm would be in charge of making his own breakfast, and cleaning up his own messes. Over time, his mother began her nightly excursions earlier and earlier. Pretty soon, the old mother he knew completely disappeared.

His life became one big daydream. He daydreamed about getting his old mom back. He daydreamed about his favorite teacher's praise in school. He daydreamed about his next visit to the old Cape Cod and Uncle Henry's next project. Worm had many other dreams as well—one of which soon became true. After a few months of living with his absentee mother, Worm came home from school to find a suitcase packed and waiting for him at the front door. His mother silently drove him to the house with the pleasant front porch, rang the doorbell, kissed him on the cheek, and quickly drove off with tears in her eyes.

It wasn't until much later, after a week or two had passed, that Worm realized his mother wouldn't be returning to bring him home. He had a new home now. He soon realized, however, that "new" did not necessarily mean "improved."

CHAPTER 3

Funny thing about spring: it came at the wrong time of year. Spring brought a reawakening from winter's sleep. The trees formed tiny sandman buds on once-naked sleeping limbs. Birds that had temporarily lost their voices suddenly found their song. Flowers, like the daring crocus, timidly prodded through earth's belly with green sensors, finding warm air and sunshine. Even humans felt the iron gates of their winter prisons lifted with the sense of freedom from bulky coats and heavy bills, rediscovering their senses of humor once again.

The calendar was all wrong. Spring should come at the first of the new year. It made more sense to begin January with a beautiful, blue-skied, spring day. Instead, as Sergeant Horace Beecher sat in his heated cruiser, he made these observations shaking his head at the three-foot snowdrifts and sand-covered roads outside of his window. He really hated the cold. Oh, he imagined, there had been a time when he got excited about the white stuff. A time when school would be cancelled and he'd spend the day sledding or ice skating or building a snow fort. He guessed most kids loved snow until they started to drive. Once they reach driving age, most kids rapidly learn how often snow tends to screw things up. Things like parties, dates, school plays, and dances. Parents were famous for taking car keys away at the slightest hint of a few falling flakes.

Sgt. Beecher, known to his friends as Hank, sat in his cruiser at the top of the town green waiting for his shift to end. It had been a slow day, thankfully. His parking place afforded him a good overall view of his little town. New Milford had been a small, blue-collar farming town for most of Hank's life. Geographically, it is among the largest towns in Connecticut, though it never felt that way to anyone who lived there.

On the outside, it hadn't changed much in his forty years there. He gazed down the long maple-lined green with its scattered monuments, the lime green army tank, and the staunch landmark itself—the domed bandstand. He imagined that if he had been sitting in the same spot a hundred years earlier, it wouldn't look much different.

New Milford had changed, though. He was witness to all of its growth and development. Civilization had intruded upon the peaceful serenity of its old-fashioned mainstays. The problem with small towns is that they are so attractive to people that are looking to escape from big cities. The more of these folks that flock to a small town, the more the small town begins to resemble a big city itself. Small, family-owned grocery stores get shoved out of business by giant supermarket chains. Condo units dot the landscape where lush cornfields once stood. The army-and-navy store downtown loses business to the new department store or strip mall. The quaint, old movie theater on Bank Street gets cut in thirds to allow more screens, while ticket prices double in size. A new high school is built to accommodate the town's ever-growing population of students. And each step along the way, the long-time residents of the town shake their heads in disgust. As with all small towns, change comes gradually and reluctantly. Those on the inside fight to keep the town small, while those on the outside fight for ever-increasing growth. In the end, growth always wins.

A snowball hitting the passenger window brought Hank's thoughts to an abrupt halt. Leaning forward to peer past the ice crystals on the pane, he managed to see old Fred Wilkins raise a mittened hand to wave; an impish smirk on his face, a fake shiver, and another flip of a wave good-bye. Hank half-waved back, but doubted the old man saw it. He had busted Fred at least four times in the past year alone for disorderly conduct, drunken disorder, indecent exposure (he had taken a leak in front of Casey's Bar), and a DUI. There had even been a report a month or so ago, from a very irate neighbor of Fred's, who wanted to press charges of cruelty to animals. Seems she witnessed old Fred feeding a kitten to his son's ten-foot boa constrictor.

Fred wasn't the only thorn in Hank's side. It was a family affair. Fred's three boys kept the whole department busy with charges of drug possession, suspected dealing, robbery and assault, speeding and reckless endangerment. Those Wilkins boys had seen more time in the jail cell than they did in their own living room.

The radio crackled and Hank looked at his watch. Shift completed, he put the car in reverse to head back to the station. He had already checked on Maggie earlier that day, and figured he'd stop by again on his way home. It had been his routine for almost three years now. He made it a point to swing by the store at least once a day. He had promised Sam he'd look after her, and he had, though admittedly it was an easy responsibility to fulfill. Maggie was like his own daughter. He knew her since the day she was born. He was proud to watch her grow into such a lovely and caring young woman. Passing by the hospital, with the cemetery situated ghoulishly across the street, Hank let his thoughts roam to his old friend, Sam, and the thoughts kept coming even as he pulled into the police station and changed into street clothes at his locker.

Hank and Sam McCarthy had been buddies since grammar school. They shared a love for baseball and fishing. They spent every season of every year together, enjoying the pleasures of childhood and the challenges of adolescence, high school, and relations with the opposite sex. One girl in particular, Allison, had been the object of both of their desires and was repeatedly pursued all through high school until Sam finally won her over during their junior year.

Teenage pranks and mischief back in those days were innocent compared to the kicks of youth today. Hank and Sam lit a few manure-filled bags on cranky neighbor's front stoops and toilet-papered their fair share of trees. Later, they advanced to more mature stages of mischief, including sneaking beer from their fathers, trying cigarettes, drag-racing on old River Road, and the most daring of all—breaking and entering the old abandoned mansion off of Lover's Leap bridge.

The ancient, decrepit old mansion stood at the top of a winding dirt road. Rumors of it being haunted were peppered with tales of murder, satanic rituals, and sadistic tools of torture. The house had been deserted for years and was completely run down. Huge "No Trespassing" signs lined both the dirt road and the front lawn. In the end, they served more as invitations to teenagers for a night's scare-fest and the temptation to defy authority was often too great to ignore. Many had been caught; all had lived to tell the tale. And for three people, on one warm summer night, the challenge set before them was too delicious to ignore.

Allison was with them that night. She was as jumpy and nervous as a mouse in a stare down with a cat. Sam had gone ahead to explore the cobweb-filled hallways, leaving Hank to calm the shaken girl. He looked around the room. It was empty, but not particularly scary. There was a strong, musty odor that smelled like something had died recently. A light breeze outside and a full moon caused long wavy shadows to play across the windows and walls, adding to the eerie effect.

"I want to go home," Allison whispered, as if speaking normally would wake the dead.

Her voice barely escaped from her quivering lips. Hank turned to face her. She was beautiful. Seventeen years old, the moonlight dancing through her long, blonde hair, which cascaded around her shoulders. He took a deep breath and fought off the desire to hold her, to protect her, to love her. She was his best friend's girl. He watched her tremble slightly and her bottom lip pout as she attempted not to cry.

"Please, Hank, let's go. I'm afraid. I don't want to be here."

Hank slowly walked toward her and offered his hand. It both surprised and aroused him when she accepted it and gripped him tightly. He drew closer to her, inhaling the light fragrance of her perfume, and letting his heart seize control of his brain, kissed her firmly. To his utter amazement she returned his kiss, and they held their embrace until they heard Sam's voice echoing from another part of the house. What happened that night was never discussed by either party, though Hank would forever treasure that stolen moment in that old mansion.

Hank and Sam graduated high school, and were on a plane bound for Vietnam soon afterward. They served together, although in separate units, then Hank re-upped for a second tour of duty while Sam returned home. Throughout their time overseas, Allison had written them both, keeping them informed of local events, national war protests and town gossip. Sam's letters were more personal in nature than Hank's, of course, but he loved hearing from her nonetheless. Duty completed, Hank served as best man at Sam and Allison's wedding. He was little Maggie's godfather and was there for Sam when Allison tragically died in a car crash—the victim of a drunk driver.

Hank became a police officer while Sam became a small business owner. After their experiences in Vietnam, Hank enjoyed living life on the edge, while Sam chose to live a life of peaceful coexistence with the small, gentle animals in his pet store. Sam's little store was named "Critters," a term Allison borrowed from her Southern grandmother's generalization of all creatures great and small.

Sam found the all-American dream of being self-employed was not all he had imagined. However, through a lot of hard work, dedication, and a genuine love for animals, his business was successful. Critters specialized in down-home, friendly and honest service, and Sam was very proud of the reputation his business had earned. After Allison passed away, Sam's only employee was Maggie, who worked by his side since she was tall enough to see over the counter.

Sam's senseless death three years ago not only saddened the handful of relatives and close friends he left behind, but also a large community of townspeople whose lives he had touched with his unadulterated joy for appreciating all the little things life had to offer.

As Hank drove across town to the pet store, he wondered if and when the day would come when he would no longer need to check in on Maggie. Deep down, he knew that day would never come, both because of his promise to Sam, and the fact that he genuinely enjoyed her company. He could not imagine living through a day without seeing her smile. It was her smile that reminded him so much of Allison. She had the same hair, same slight body, same full lips and round, blue eyes. Sometimes when she tilted her head a certain way, lightly twirling a lock of hair, it was as if twenty-six years had melted away and he was gazing upon his high school sweetheart again.

* * * *

The next day, Hank heard a code over his radio signaling that another officer in the area needed backup. The caller's name was Kyle Wilkins, and Hank immediately wondered what trouble those Wilkins boys had gotten themselves into this time. Upon arriving at the scene, Hank found an ambulance and two police cruisers already parked out front. One officer stood outside collecting statements from the Wilkins brothers. When asked what was going on, the young officer simply shook his head and pointed inside the house.

Hank entered through the open door and followed voices to the basement stairs. As he descended, the familiar stench of wet blood and rotting flesh invaded his senses. The sound of a gunshot instinctively made him draw his pistol from its holster. He took a few hesitant steps down the steep, dark stairway. A lamp toppled over in the corner of the room dimly lit the grisly scene before him. There appeared to be the remains of a human body on the cement floor, its flesh shredded, its eyes removed from its sockets. There was a bloody, gaping wound where its nose used to be, and its cheekbones protruded from a lipless face. A pool of blood stained the floor and was strangely spotted with hundreds of tiny footprints surrounding the corpse. As Hank's eyes adjusted to the dim light, he noticed that numerous battered bodies of dead rats dotted the cement floor alongside the corpse. A young rookie, having been initiated into his first day of work, was standing to the side, his gun drawn and his mouth frozen in a silent scream as he watched the writhing body of the lone rat he had just shot.

Hank learned that the body was that of old Fred Wilkins. His boys had been out all night and returned home that morning to find their old man lying dead on the concrete floor of their basement. Dead, but slowly being devoured by hundreds of rats. Rats that had overpopulated small cages. Rats with long, hairless tails, coarse, smooth fur, and red eyes. Hundreds of rats left to breed, often neglected, as a constant food supply for a collection of snakes kept in makeshift glass tanks lining the basement walls. The boys had returned to find the rats' bulging confinements overturned with its wire doors opened. They ran upstairs to find loaded guns, and in unsportsmanlike joy, massacred the defenseless, starving rat colony, one by one. With each shotgun blast, each head exploding beneath a baseball bat, each neck severed by a meat clever, their insane laughter grew louder. Some of the luckier rats escaped to populate anew in the grassy meadows outdoors. The cold cement floor became a graveyard for many. As for the boas, pythons, and copperheads, they silently took in this scene from behind glass walls, uncoiled from their branches, tasting the glass with forked tongues. Such a waste of food.

Such the price for freedom.

CHAPTER 4

Worm
Age 15

Four summers had passed since Worm was abandoned on the front porch of his aunt and uncle's home. He had done a lot of growing, not only in stature, but also in his awareness for the cruel twists of fate that life presents. He learned his set of boundaries in his new home well. He learned why his Uncle Henry spent so much time outside, and why he only went inside the house to quickly eat or to sleep.

Each year brought added chores and duties to his role as member of the household, in payment for his upkeep. He never minded taking orders from Uncle Henry, who always seemed grateful to have a helping hand around the house. With Aunt Vera, though, he learned to do what she said, when she said it, or suffer another humiliating whipping with whatever instrument of torture she had handy at that moment. Though she could be downright sweet at times, she had a nasty temper, and would often explode in a fit of rage at the slightest provocation. Since it was difficult to predict what would trigger one of these explosions, Worm soon learned that it was better simply to keep his distance as often as possible.

His nickname had stuck with him through the years, and he now even referred to himself as "Worm," since he'd been named after his father and wanted no association with that son-of-a-bitch. Though the name was anything but flattering, being a worm had its advantages. Worms can be ripped in half, and each half can survive and go off in different directions. He would sometimes test this theory when he would mentally split himself apart and let one half suffer while the other half escaped to some far-off place in the sun where he could lie around in grassy meadows and stare at the clouds.

"You're not listening to me, young man," Aunt Vera boomed, her face growing red, with beads of sweat forming on her brow.

"You think you're too big to listen to me now? Is that it? Wipe that stupid grin off your face before I knock it off!"

Worm had almost forgotten what earned him this latest lashing, and then remembered something about tracking mud through the house. He and Uncle Henry had been in the middle of an important project when he had to use the bathroom. One more nail, then another, and pretty soon he couldn't hold it any longer.

"I said listen to me! How many times have I told you?" Another smack of the belt buckle.

"Stupid, ungrateful child." Arm raised high. Another smack of the belt buckle. He must have been stupid not to think of the mud that must have been on his shoes. It had been raining all morning.

"You never...(smack)...ever...(smack)...do that again! Do you hear me?" Another lash of the belt buckle. "You are just like your worthless father..."

The words cut through Worm's heart like a knife. Instantly, he felt a searing rage from within boil to the surface. He felt his face turn hot, and his hands tightened into fists. Aunt Vera's arm rose for one final whipping, but before she could follow through, Worm whipped around and grabbed her wrist. He must have had a wild look on his face judging by the disbelieving, astonished, and then terrified look on Aunt Vera's wrinkled old face. No one had ever dared to defy Aunt Vera. A battle of wills was fought in one long, anxious moment. Two warriors, head to head with arms raised and eyes locked, waiting for the next move.

It was Worm who finally conceded. Realizing the potential catastrophic consequences of his actions, he ran as fast as he could out of the room, out of the house, past his flabbergasted uncle, and into the field where he sat surrounded by the tall corn stalks of his neighbor's summer crop. With the vegetables surrounding him like a protective fortress, he sat there contemplating what means of retribution he'd have to face when he returned home. *If* he ever returned home.

* * * *

Some weeks later, as Worm carried out a load of sheets to hang on the line, Uncle Henry screeched to a stop in the driveway and jumped out of the old Chevy pickup. He was all excited about something and waved at Worm to come and take a look.

Putting an arm around the boy, he led him to the back of the truck where Worm spied wooden-slated crates with strange-looking beaks protruding through the slats.

"Ya know that old coop we been working on?" Uncle Henry asked. "Well, thought it was about time we had some tenants."

"But Uncle Henry, it's not finished yet. What if a fox comes? We didn't get the fence done."

"That's life, boy. Survival of the fittest. If the fox gets a couple, guess he has to eat, too."

And with that reasoning, Worm found he couldn't dispute it any further and helped to unload four crates of banty chickens and one tiny rooster he immediately named, "King George."

He hadn't had a pet since his old dog, King. He patiently listened as Uncle Henry explained the care and feeding of the chicken colony while Worm nodded his head in understanding, recognizing the responsibility to see that these animals had a good life. After all, they may be free to peck and scratch the ground, but in essence they were POW's in a human's prisoner camp. After all, that was the station in life for every domestic creature—to live and cope in a human environment.

The magnitude of a pet being so dependent and helpless struck Worm deeply. King must have been a superior animal to survive with a boy's inexperienced care. The old dog never complained—he even appeared grateful. He was the boy's best friend; a friend Worm missed. It was the type of friend Worm needed in his life.

Worm instantly grew attached to King George. The rooster strutted with a regal air around the small kingdom containing his harem. His bright red comb proudly stood erect on his head and the wobbly stuff under his chin tightened whenever he crowed, proclaiming his presence. Henry said soon they'd have fresh eggs for breakfast, maybe even a fried chicken dinner one night. Then he looked over at Worm out of the corner of his eye to get a reaction.

Worm's eyes grew large and he made an audible gulp.

"Please, Uncle Henry, we can't eat these chickens," he whined.

"Kid, as long as you don't name them, you'll be fine with it. You already blew that rule with King George over there. But don't worry. We need him to get all those hens goin'. Guess he's got a reprieve in just being a necessary link in our food chain."

Worm tended the coop every morning before school, every afternoon after school, and once again before bed. Day after day, one could see him perched on one of the fence posts, just watching the chickens hunt and peck. After his daily chores had been completed and his homework had been scribbled away, he found complete solace in watching those chickens live their simple lives.

Always at the center of attention was King George, whom Worm learned to respect from day one. The tiny, but mighty, rooster came heavily armed with spurs on the back of each scaly foot. Worm had only been speared once, while raiding the nest boxes. He hadn't bothered to find out where the mad cock was positioned. Henry warned him to make sure George was busy elsewhere when he did this. The pain shot up Worm's leg so hard and fast that a scream escaped his throat and his eyes teared as he looked around at the thing attached to his ankle. Perhaps more surprised by the attack than the actual pain itself, he fiercely shook his throbbing leg from side to side until the little rooster let go and bounced to the dirt. Ankle bleeding, he got a look of "I told you so" from Uncle Henry and a few swats from Aunt Vera for disrupting her during her soaps to apply iodine to his wound.

* * * *

School had once been Worm's haven; his solace from an often abusive world. Upon entering high school, however, he discovered that much had changed since the eighth grade. School was no longer a haven. It had become just another place from which he wished he could escape. Another excuse to split himself in two.

He had been content to be the outsider, the brunt of jokes, the "necessary link in the scheme of things" as Uncle Henry would have put it. He didn't belong to any clubs and he didn't have any good friends. He merely drifted along from class to class like a ghost—invisible to all of those who passed him in the hallways. The only contact he had with his classmates was when a group of jocks would occasionally taunt him in the hallways, knocking his books out of his hands or calling him names. He was an easy target for ridicule. Overnight, it seemed, he became a little too tall and a little too skinny. He seemed to be perched on legs that reminded him of King George's, and his face didn't sprout hair like some of the other boys—just pimples.

In addition to his own changes, he began to notice changes in the opposite sex as well. Seemingly overnight, they had developed breasts and curves and giggly little laughs that always seemed to trigger a raise of their hands to their mouths.

One girl in particular—Maggie McCarthy was her name—was the prettiest girl in school in his opinion. She was probably the most popular, too, though she didn't flaunt it like most of the snooty girls who turned their heads or giggled when he walked by. Maggie was the only person on the football field that day to stop the pushing and shoving and spitting he endured when the "jocks" decided to have some fun. Worm had been lost in his thoughts, carrying an armload of books. So lost in thought that he temporarily forgot that football practice was about to begin when he decided to take a shortcut across the field after classes. Six large young men, led by a bully named Frank, took him by surprise as they surrounded him, shouting such intellectual nuggets as "no geeks on the turf." Realizing he was in for another episode of name-calling, Worm just kept walking, preparing to split himself in half and tune it out as usual. But this time, it was different. This time his acceptance of their ridicule wasn't satisfying enough. His books were snatched from his arms and tossed into the mud, and they knocked his glasses right off his head with the first powerful shove. He was thrown from outstretched arms back and forth like an object in some demented human pinball machine. From behind, his pants were yanked down around his ankles, and he was shoved to the ground as he frantically bent over to pull them back up. The taunting and cackling echoed in his ears, and he curled into a ball with his hands over his head.

Witnessing this unprovoked attack from across the field, Maggie left her fellow cheerleaders and sprinted toward the circle of cretins. She shoved her way into the middle of the crowd and yelled at Frank to knock it off. She helped Worm up, wiped the mud from his glasses, gathered his books, and asked twice if he was okay. Then she smiled a sweet smile and walked away.

CHAPTER 5

There's a saying in New England: if you don't like the weather, just wait a few minutes and it'll change. One evening, Frank Wilson was sitting on his front porch in shirtsleeves waiting for the coming of spring. The next morning, he was shoveling several inches of snow from his driveway. Snow always cramped his style the older he got. Snow was one of the reasons he left New England after graduation to seek his fame and fortune in Florida. Having a scholarship to the University of Miami was a minor incentive as well.

His alarm had already awakened him from a delicious dream involving a keg party and several half-naked cheerleaders. He tried to recapture the dream after hitting the snooze button, but to no avail. As he padded down the hallway to the kitchen to fix himself some java, he heard the familiar noises from above that reassured him he wasn't the only unlucky bastard forced to wake up so early. The best thing about having the bottom-floor apartment was that one didn't have to step lightly out of consideration for those below. Not that old man Haggerty followed such rules of courtesy. His footsteps were always loud and heavy, and sometimes sounded like an approaching linebacker.

This analogy to the game he loved forced Frank's mind to wander. Frank had been an all-conference quarterback in high school and the captain of his team. His name and face appeared weekly in the local newspaper and he became somewhat of a local legend in New Milford. It was his prowess between the lines that landed him a scholarship to the University of Miami. It was a blind-side tackle in the backfield during the last game of his high school career that permanently ended his football career and gave him the limp that now distinguished his walk. That limp allowed passersby to easily pick him out of a crowd and say, "Hey, isn't that Frank Wilson, the all-state quarterback who blew out his knee? Too bad. He could've been somebody."

Frank often found himself drifting into the past, playing the "what if" game until he got so mad he'd have to hit something. In this particular instance it was the ceiling of his one-bedroom pad as he yelled at old man Haggerty to pipe down.

The stream of hot water ran over his head and down his face as he leaned into the shower's spray. As the waves of water flowed down his body, nostalgia once again flowed into his brain. With his good looks and status as captain of his high school football team, Frank never had any trouble finding dates on Saturday nights. He dated the most beautiful and popular girls in school, but for all of his conquests, there was one in particular who always seemed to elude his natural magnetism. Her name was Maggie McCarthy. She was like forbidden fruit—something he had to taste, but was always just out of his reach. There was something about her that said, "hands off," and unlike most of the other swooning babes who would faint at the chance to wear his letter jacket, he respected her. She intimidated him. She was beautiful, but she didn't seem to realize it. She was popular, but he didn't think she dated much. In the classroom, she was intelligent and carried herself well. She participated in several activities outside of the classroom, including a brief stint as cheerleader her freshman year. But for some reason, she gave that up. It's a shame, he thought, because she would've looked great in that uniform as a senior.

Frank found the nerve to ask out Maggie only once, when he asked her to be his date to the junior prom. He had approached her when they were among a group of mutual friends. He made a big production out of his request, presenting her with a red rose and dropping down to one knee. She had no choice but to accept. They made a fine couple, and Frank was never more proud than to be seen walking arm-in-arm with her into the grand ballroom. It was almost as if the music stopped and every head in the room turned to look at them.

Maggie looked absolutely stunning that night—easily the most beautiful girl in the room. To the surprise of no one, Frank and Maggie were named King and Queen of the prom. They danced under the watchful eyes of their classmates, and for a moment it felt as though they were the two most important people on earth.

The night went downhill from there, though. Frank had a little too much to drink at the after-prom party, tried to put a move on Maggie, and she bolted for home. They didn't speak again until years later.

A sudden burst of cold water streaming through the nozzle jolted Frank back into the present. He started to jump to the other side of the tub toward warmer ground when his knee gave out and he landed hard onto the porcelain floor. A bolt of pain shot through his entire nervous system as he desperately tried to shut off the water. After shouting several obscenities, he managed to towel-off enough to maneuver toward the medicine cabinet for his painkillers.

The pills his doctor had prescribed years ago led him to believe that if an ounce was good, a pound was better. He thought that if he took enough, he might still be able to play. He was wrong. A new set of friends showed him how euphoric life could be under the influence of drugs and alcohol. He tried them all, beginning with pot and graduating to cocaine and heroin. Money sent from home to a successful, loving son was a major source of support for his growing drug habit. Receiving the money was sometimes a problem as his address continually changed with new host families or new girlfriends. Finding girls in college proved to be just as easy for him in college as it was in high school, despite the loss in status. He didn't care what they looked like or where they had been as long as they had money or a place to stay.

Years of abuse to his body and mind eventually caught up with him. Despite his full scholarship, Frank never did graduate from college. By the end of his third semester, his grades were so poor he was placed on academic probation. Rather than continue the charade, he just dropped out of school. He never cared for the academic life, anyway. He roamed from place to place and drug to drug without a care for his future. He became a bitter young man with a death wish, and it was around that time that he opened the door to his latest crib and found his father looking at him disappointingly on the other side. Despite his protests, he was taken back to Connecticut and placed in a rehab center where he was weaned off of his habit little by little until he was eventually clean again. The painkillers in the medicine cabinet were a necessary evil, but one he now knew better to take in moderation.

Gingerly pulling on his blue jeans, Frank realized he hadn't heard a sound from upstairs in a while, and hoped that Simon Haggerty had finally knocked himself out. The man was an asshole. Even Maggie thought so, as she remarked recently while working at the pet store. Haggerty had recently been brought into the police station for questioning, after it was reported by a neighbor that he had drowned several kittens. Though he owned just one cat—a female—there was no evidence to support the charge, other than the anonymous neighbor's testimony, and he was let go. Frank was convinced Haggerty was guilty, and he told Maggie as much. Maggie was furious that anyone would ever do such a thing, especially since Critters would have been happy to take the kittens and give them away for free, as they had done several times in the past.

Frank looked in the mirror and thought to himself how funny it was that he came into his latest job. After returning to Connecticut, Frank held several part-time jobs in order to pay the bills and keep himself occupied. In addition to his job as manager of his father's hardware store, he had a landscaping job in the summer time, mowing lawns and doing landscaping. In the winter, he would plow driveways and do assorted handyman work indoors. Years ago, he purchased a fish tank, more as an excuse to get reacquainted with Maggie than for his love of tropical fish. But to his shock, he discovered he actually enjoyed caring for the little guys. It was relaxing to sit in front of the aquarium at nights, just watching them swim through life. Pretty soon, he purchased another tank, then another, and before he knew it he became pretty knowledgeable on the subject of tropical fish. One day, after fixing the store's filtration system as a favor to Maggie, she offered him a job. Since he needed the extra cash and was enthralled with the idea of working side by side with his old crush, he accepted.

He was convinced that all those years of playing the perfect gentleman would someday reap its benefits. Respecting her hands-off attitude, operating at arm's length during their infrequent get-togethers after hours, business always the main subject of their conversations, it would all pay off in the end. His patience was wearing a little thin, however. Perhaps it was time to speed it up a little. She probably wanted him to, anyway. Probably wanted him as much as he wanted her. One day she'd realize all he'd done for her, all his thoughtful actions would be recognized, and she'd willingly fall into his waiting arms.

"Yeah," he said aloud, as he looked into the mirror. She would soon give herself to him out of gratification and appreciation. It didn't matter why. "She's mine."

Chapter 6

The pond was blanketed with green, slimy scum that floated on the surface of the murky water like a patchwork quilt. Amy thought of it as a pretty cover to keep the fish and frogs warm. She and her friend, Patty, often went to the pond after school because all the seasons made the little patch of water so interesting. In the winter, it made the perfect ice skating rink. They would often go there and pretend they were Olympic athletes, usually falling over when the stupid boys would get carried away playing hockey and trip them with their sticks. In the spring, they would usually find a mess of pollywogs, and watch them turn into frogs. In the summer, they could reacquaint themselves with Moby, the goldfish they had put in there years before when he had outgrown his bowl. Autumn was a time for skipping stones and saying good-bye to Moby until next year.

This particular day, Amy and Patty had stopped by the pond on their way home from school because the ice had just broken through, and they were hoping to catch a glimpse of Moby. As Amy stood by the water's edge, Patty offered, "Oh, by the way, my brother said to be careful down here 'cuz there's giant water snakes way down deep in the middle of the pond."

Amy turned to make a face at her friend. Patty may be in the third grade, but even a second-grader knew there were no such things as water snakes.

"He said not to make too much noise or throw a rock that's too big or you'll wake them up," Patty continued.

"Patty, don't be such a sissy," Amy said, "There's no snakes down there. Everyone knows snakes don't hibernate in water." With that said, Amy inched toward a clump of weeds near the edge. In the sunlight that reflected off the still water, an object just below the surface glistened and caught her eye. Being extra careful not to get her new sneakers wet (or wake up the water snakes), she found what she thought was solid ground was actually marshy seaweed. She congratulated herself for catching her balance before she slipped down into the wet mud. She could still see something shiny and metallic right under the floating scum.

Patty heard the faint gasp and stopped her search for Moby long enough to ask Amy what was wrong.

"Nothing's wrong," she said. "I just slipped a little bit. Stupid mud. Do you see that thing over there?" she asked, pointing to a spot about six feet from where she was standing.

Patty squinted, but all she saw was mud and a bunch of dead leaves. She shook her head.

"It's over there," Amy pointed again. "Never mind. See any long sticks? I bet it's some kind of treasure. Maybe a jeweled crown or something. Help me get it out."

A quick scouting job produced a pointed stick with two split branches. A couple of slugs were hastily and abruptly removed from their home, and Amy proceeded to stab the water surface, slightly stirring the green slime.

A few more prods of the stick and Amy did get her new sneakers wet as her footing gave out in the soft, thawed earth and she fell backwards onto her back side, causing Patty to laugh hysterically. Undaunted, the impact only served to further her convictions to claim the sunken bounty. She now had a better angle anyway. After several more attempts she finally was successful in hooking one of the antlered tips onto the shiny object.

A lift upward didn't budge whatever the snagged thing was and Amy yelled to Patty to grab the stick in the middle and heave. The result was raising a shiny gold object from the murky depths—an object attached to a giant, gray water snake. With a chilling scream the two girls dropped the mossy stick and ran all the way home.

Of course, there are no such things as monster water snakes, at least not in tiny New England ponds in the middle of March. This was verified when Amy's father was dragged to the pond's edge to investigate the monster at the pleading of his daughter. And upon arrival, Mr. Cranston discovered that the gold object was in fact a gold watch—attached to the arm of a very dead Simon Haggerty.

* * * *

At the scene, Hank ran his fingers through his hair and looked around at the other cops to get their reaction to this bizarre occurrence. He looked over to Jake, dog leash in hand, talking to Officer Reilly. Lieutenant Granger and Captain Esposito were to his right, examining some report on a clipboard. Beanie, otherwise known as Officer B.J. Bean, helped a paramedic pull the bloated body from its murky grave.

People died all the time, young people and old people alike, for various reasons. But this latest string of deaths in this small town seemed to be more bizarre than usual. They were all freak accidents, more or less. A woman was bitten by a rabid squirrel and was driven off the road. An alleged horse thief apparently hung himself. Another man suffered a heart attack, bringing down an aquarium full of rats in his fall, and was subsequently eaten alive by his own rats in the basement of his own home. And now this.

A witness driving by late last night saw a man walking near the edge of the pond, peering into it as if he were examining something. A second driver said someone seemed to be wading in the pond under the dim light of the street lamp. For whatever reason Simon Haggerty had found to take a midnight dip, it apparently ended with him slipping in thawing mud, hitting his head on a rock, and drowning in the cold, still water of the pond.

CHAPTER 7

Worm
Age 17

At seventeen, Worm was becoming a young man and his aunt both recognized and feared this. Her control over him was waning and she could sense that he knew this as well. It was becoming increasingly difficult to keep him in line and she became increasingly frustrated finding new ways to do so. She crushed her cigarette into the bottom of the ashtray and immediately lit another one. She slowly rose from her recliner to clean out the ashtray in the sink. Peering out the window, she looked revoltingly at the cluttered backyard. All that litter and pieces of useless garbage piled on top of each other made her stomach turn. Worst of all was that damn smelly chicken coop. All those dirty animals waddling around with fecal droppings mushing between their toes. Oh, the eggs were nice, as well as the occasional roasted chicken, but her love for the birds stopped there.

With the cigarette dangling from the corner of her wrinkled mouth, she walked outside, the screen door banging shut behind her.

"Useless animals," she muttered to herself as she ambled toward the coop, "That stupid old man never finishes a damn thing he starts. He was supposed to fix that fence of his, but instead went out and bought all these damn animals. Pretty soon, he'll go on to somethin' else, and all we'll have then is a bunch of chicken shit..."

At the same time she noticed her sheets on the clothesline gracefully skimming the ground in the light wind, corners dragging through green manure, King George noticed an intruder in his kingdom. Spurs drawn, he plunged them into the unsuspecting giant and held on to protect his numerous wives and children. Momentarily stunned, Aunt Vera fell backward into the green slime, her bathrobe covered in mud and filth. She angrily grabbed a two-by-four Henry had left behind from one of his forgotten projects, and with a well-toned and muscled forearm brutally knocked King George into the air. For good measure, once he lit, she hit him three or four times more, just to teach him a lesson.

That evening, a feast was prepared consisting of mashed potatoes, black-eyed peas, peach cobbler and fried chicken. She watched out of the corner of her eye and smirked an evil grin as Worm enjoyed his meal. She waited until he had finished before she levied her most creative punishment to date. She asked Worm to take out the leftover corn to feed to his chickens.

* * * *

Worm didn't sleep much that night, or any night thereafter for several weeks. When he did sleep, he'd often have the same dream where King George had risen from the dead to take his vengeful justice, just as King did the day his spirit took over Daisy the horse. And each morning, he rose to face the enemy for a hurried breakfast before dashing out the door to school.

It was bitterly cold outside. Snow was knee-deep in some places, and the wind howled through naked trees. Worm hated winter more than any other season because it took his and Henry's playground away from them. Forced to stay inside the prison of the Cape Cod, he stayed mostly in his room while his uncle tried to keep busy in his workshop in the basement.

From time to time, he'd run errands with Uncle Henry downtown, and was grateful for the opportunity to do so. On one of those lucky days, Uncle Henry came to his room and asked Worm to help him load some junk in the truck for another trip to the town dump. The old vehicle rode closer to the ground with each heavy load added to the truck bed. The last box of old newspapers loaded, Worm ran up to his room to retrieve a few more items for the trip.

Henry patiently waited in the heated cab of the truck, listening to an old Glenn Miller tune, which reminded him of the high school dances he and Vera used to attend. Worm appeared soon thereafter, bearing a large cardboard box, and heaving it into the back of the pickup, hopped into the cab with Henry.

An hour later, their job completed, they rounded the corner leading to the house and spied several fire trucks scattered around their front lawn. Dark wisps of black smoke billowed upward from the old house as red-helmeted men scurried to extinguish the flames. Leaping from the truck, Henry and Worm ran toward the house, dodging fire hoses and firemen impeding their path to the front door. They were stopped by a burly policeman just yards from the door, and they noticed two men in white uniforms descending the stairs carrying a stretcher.

"I'm sorry, Mr. Allen," the cop said, "We did everything we could, but it was too late by the time we got here."

Worm later learned that Aunt Vera had apparently been smoking in bed and had fallen asleep, carelessly dropping the lit cigarette onto her blanket. The paramedics didn't think she had suffered much, as the inhalation of smoke probably claimed her life before her body had been completely burned.

Worm watched intently as the men pushed the wheels up and rolled the stretcher into the brightly lit ambulance. His feet seemed frozen to the spot on the porch where he stood. He didn't hear the muted voices of the small army of firemen. He didn't feel the numbing cold creep into his hands and feet. His smell was desensitized to the aroma of burning wood and plaster. He didn't notice Henry, staring blankly into nothingness. His focus was on that lumpy old blanket sitting alone in the rear of the white ambulance. In the magnitude of that moment, his senses temporarily shut down. As he stared at the mass under the blanket, all he could hear inside his head was the crowing of a rooster.

CHAPTER 8

The rain began to fall, and tiny raindrops gathered and trickled down the windowpane. From the outside, as Maggie stood looking out, it appeared she was crying. The shadows played across the front lawn like school children frolicking in the dark. The streams of water before her face distorted these images in a way that invited her subconscious to emerge from its hiding place.

Rain always reminded her of her father, who loved to lie awake in a dark and quiet room, listening to the sound of the rain drops hitting the windowsill. He loved this sound so much, in fact, that he once installed a metal awning above the windowpane outside his bedroom window in order to amplify the sound.

She pictured herself as a small child, joining her father for a twirl in the rain. The two figures danced and smiled, holding hands while the rain carelessly pattered off their bodies. Her teeth biting her bottom lip, she looked back into her own eyes as she slowly leaned forward, resting her forehead on the cool glass. And now, if anyone happened to walk by at that moment, with the rain rolling down the window and the slight figure huddled against itself, one would surely see that she was in indeed crying.

The thoughts of her father still fresh in her mind, Maggie plopped down on the couch, stretched out her legs, and fumbled for a pillow to hug. A few years ago, memories had haunted her mind and soul with such frequent occurrence that she found strange comfort in them even when they often brought pain. As time passed, she allowed them in by invitation only, at times when she felt she could handle them without fear. Lately, though, especially on rainy nights such as this, these thoughts invaded her privacy with such overwhelming presence that it made her uncomfortable, as if she had lost control.

A cold shiver brought her legs up under her body, and she reached out for a ratty afghan on the back of the couch. The rain outside grew heavier. She turned to watch rushing rivers of black water stream down the glass, and flinched a little when a shot of lightening lit the room in an eerie yellow glow. She leaned her head back, closed her eyes, and mentally counted to herself before hearing the clap of thunder in the distance. She kept her eyes closed for a moment afterward, having convinced herself if she opened them she might actually see him standing there. She brought one hand up to massage her temples. There was nothing supernatural going on here. She had, a long time ago, dealt with the loss, the grief and the despair. It was clear she had invited the ghost herself this night, ultimately asking to be haunted by sitting in a darkened room, alone, during a thunderstorm.

She thought she had overcome the bitterness and anger she felt toward the armed addict who senselessly robbed her father's life during a hold-up of the store's register three years ago. But she still felt the anger bubble inside her—anger not only toward the crack addict who pulled the trigger, but also toward her father for leaving her alone.

Throwing the afghan aside, she strode into the kitchen, snapping on the light. A steaming cup of hot chocolate would help rid the chill. The warm mug cupped between her hands, she resumed her position on the couch. If memories were to flood over her on this dark and stormy night, at least she'd be comfortable.

Looking across the room to the collage of photos hanging on the wall, Maggie's eyes rested on the picture of the three of them together: herself, her mother, and Sam. It seemed like yesterday that picture had been taken. She was ten years old at that carefree Fourth of July picnic. It was the last family photo ever taken before her mom passed away.

Her mother was a beautiful woman. People said Maggie looked a lot like her mother, and Maggie always smiled at that. The love between her parents was evident to all who knew them. Allison was the root that held together their little family tree. She could always bring out the laughter, and turn bad times into good ones. Some of Maggie's fondest memories were of simple times when the family would be together at the pet store, laughing, talking, and enjoying each other's company as they worked through another day.

Maggie grew up surrounded by love and caring, a way of life that her parents extended to all living creatures. Even a bee, trapped inside a house struggling and crashing against a windowpane, would be wrapped in tissue and released outdoors. The menagerie of pets in their tiny shop was treated like children. Her parents felt it was their duty to provide extremely good care for all of their livestock before shipping them off to strangers, for once they left that store they couldn't be sure what kind of life the animals would have. It was their duty to make the animals' temporary housing as comfortable, safe, and healthy as possible. And no animal—furry, finned, or feathered—left the store without explicit instructions given to their new owners about proper care. It wasn't beyond Sam and Allison to pass up a dollar if they didn't feel comfortable with handing over one of their wards.

The store was Maggie's second home. As a small child, she would chase rabbits and kittens throughout the store as her parents waited on customers. As she grew older, and more and more responsibilities fell her way, she began to feel useful and important. Oftentimes she would get upset when one of her favorite pets left the store with a customer. Sam told her the secret was to never name any animal, and that way she wouldn't become so attached. He followed his own advice with the exception of Rocky, a feisty yet beautiful Blue-fronted Amazon, full of mischief and antics.

Rocky had been purchased with the intent to sell, but after endearing himself to Sam and the family, he became the store mascot, the store trademark, and the object of much laughter and amusement to all that visited. Maggie was secretly amused her father would break his own cardinal rule and allow Rocky to touch his life in such a way. She found it strange that he chose such a rascally character over all the other creatures that passed through their door. She recognized, however, her father's soft spot for the one that could never find a good, permanent home because of its challenging personality. She supposed it was one of the things that made Rocky so endearing.

The store eventually moved and expanded, drawing a greater flow of customers and a healthier profit as word spread throughout neighboring towns. As she entered high school, Maggie had her hands full with her studies and an after-school activity or two, but still found time to work at the shop on evenings and weekends. She never seemed to have enough time in the day to do everything she set out to do. She had no time for boys, and was pretty sure they weren't interested in her anyway. A quick check in the mirror told her her lips were too full, her eyes too big, and her breasts too small for any boy to notice her.

Her father admirably filled his dual role as father and mother to Maggie, as well as his roles as guidance counselor, love advisor, and leading antagonist to her inferiority complex. He always made sure she had everything she needed, whether it was advice or answers to her questions or money for the latest style of clothing.

On her sixteenth birthday, he gave her a journal to record her daily activities. He told her to address each page with the salutation, "Dear Mom," so she'd have a woman with whom to confide her darkest secrets.

Her pet cat, Apollo, decided to intrude upon her thoughts, and with a cat's stealth pounced onto the couch beside her. He rubbed his massive head against her leg, and Maggie responded by scratching him behind the ears. She looked down into her lukewarm cocoa and smiled faintly.

After high school, Maggie continued her education at a local community college, allowing her to live at home and help out the stubborn old man at the pet store who wouldn't hire any help. Upon graduating, her father gave her a plane ticket to Mexico, where she stayed with her aunt and uncle.

"It's time you saw that there was a little more to this world than New Milford," her father told her. "Take as much time as you want. Decide what you want to do with the rest of your life. Oh—and have fun."

Maggie quickly became absorbed in the culture of Mexico. After meeting her aunt and uncle at the airport in Mexico City, Maggie enjoyed a wild ride through the winding roads of the ancient city. Her eyes took in all the local color, from the cactus-strewn landscape to barefoot natives and thatch huts. In the hour it took to arrive at her relative's home in the tiny village of Tequistiapan, her eyes and mind had been widened by this completely different world.

She spent the next week taking in the sights and sounds around her. Poverty was rampant. Makeshift houses under open skies in cactus fields were shared by three generations of family members, their loyal cow, goats, and chickens. Their marketplaces were outdoors or in buildings with open spaces where flies and cockroaches played. Dirty little children sat by their pitiful, pregnant mothers, begging with outstretched hands. Women did laundry in muddy streams—the same water they used for bathing and drinking.

Conversely, Mexico also had many wonderful and beautiful sights to offer, from the ancient pyramids, to the stucco-walled houses and elegant pools that adorned her uncle's neighborhood, to the handsome American man with the black, wavy hair and the dark, haunting eyes whom she met while roaming the marketplace during a weekend in Acapulco.

Together, they enjoyed a night under the Mexican moon and stars, with the sounds of strolling mariachi bands and the taste of soothing sangrias. It was a magical night filled with dancing, laughter and romance. It was a night where they shared soft, sweet kisses that moved from her cheek to her lips to the nape of her neck. A sleeping beast awoke within her that night, and she found herself drowning for desire for the man named Jake. But it was not meant to be, for in the heat of the moment, he pulled away, stroked her hair, and held her face in his hands.

"I'll be right back," he lied. He gave her one last kiss, and without any explanation disappeared into the night. Two days later, she returned to her father a different person. She felt more mature, more confident, and more ambitious, ready to face the world.

Getting up from her spot on the sofa, Maggie set her full mug of hot chocolate on the table and walked to the other end of the room. Walking over to the picture, her finger lightly traced her father's face, and then slowly moved to her mother's. She glanced to the picture of Hank, standing arm-in-arm with her in front of the store she inherited, and considered herself lucky to have a guardian angel in him. Hank had always been there for her, through the toughest times and the best. In a way, he was like a second father, and he made her feel truly protected and loved. Maggie smiled. A muffled yawn accompanied a stretch to the ceiling with both arms. It had been a long night, and she finally felt tired enough to fall asleep—probably as soon as her head hit the pillow. Apollo concurred, and ran to the bedroom, leapt onto the bed, and curled up on the thick comforter.

CHAPTER 9

Worm
Ages 18-20

As his high school graduation drew near, Worm began to think about his future. There wasn't a lot of money available for college, and Worm had no marketable skills that would lead to a promising career. Henry fished around in his shirt pocket for a crumpled piece of paper, and putting his reading glasses on, began to read off a list of possibilities for the boy's consideration. With each line read, discussed and scratched off the list, it was determined that the best course of action for Worm's future would be to join the army. There, he would not only learn new skills, but grow and develop his badly-shaken self-confidence and mold himself into the man he always knew he could be.

Along with the changes that occurred within him, Worm also made an important outward change during this time. He decided to no longer call himself Worm. Instead, he went by his given name, John Paul, and took his uncle Henry's last name, Allen. Since John was also his father's name, he opted for the nickname "Jake" instead.

Mr. Jake Allen's mind flourished with the regimented routine of the military. His soul flourished with the camaraderie of his unit. His body flourished with the rigorous workouts and training. His acne disappeared, as did his thick glasses, which were replaced with contact lenses. No longer was there a need to wear turtlenecks in the dog days of summer. Only a few scars remained from all those years of abuse at the hands of his father and Aunt Vera. The mental scars took much longer to heal, but with each passing day of donning his U.S. army uniform, decorated with shiny metals of honor and achievement, those, too, disappeared.

Two years into his service, Jake applied for a transfer to the K-9 unit after watching training sessions with a buddy of his. He was intrigued by the power the instructors had to control the behaviors of such intimidating beasts. With each short German command, the dogs went from playful pet to sentry on alert. From a warning bark, to an all-out attack on the padded arm of a posing intruder, the transformation was simultaneously frightening and fascinating. The assault was halted as abruptly as it began with the issuance of another simple command. The dog then received an appreciative pat on the head, a tussle of his massive neck, and once again became man's best friend.

There were times when Jake would look into a mirror and see Worm looking back at him with haunting little boy eyes, still frightened and confused. Sometimes, even after splashing cold water on his face, he would look up and that little boy was still watching him, droplets of water caught in his lashes like tears from a time passed. The mirror served as a constant reminder of the power he had in the past—a power he had tried to forget. It was the power to separate himself into two halves: Good Worm/Bad Worm, Good Times/Bad Times, and now Worm/Jake. Sometimes he could shake the ghosts away with a slap or two to his cheeks. Other times he chose not to look in the mirror at all.

There were times, sitting in the barracks, when conversation would turn to family picnics and all the great times that were had with their families during various leaves of absence. Jake would just listen silently, unable to share his own happy family experiences. He would forever recall, however, one particular experience when he used one of his leaves to visit Acapulco with some of his buddies.

There he was, sitting in that little cafe one night, laughing it up at a table in the corner of the room, when in walked a stunning blonde who seemed strangely familiar. Although the night had just begun, and the *cervezas* had not had ample time to take effect, he could have sworn that the girl was Maggie McCarthy. Surely, the coincidence was too great. This woman walked like Maggie, moved like Maggie, and smiled like Maggie, but there was just no way it could be her. There was only one way to find out. Jake excused himself from the table and walked across the room to the woman on the other side.

He introduced himself, and she invited him to join her. There was no doubt about it. It was indeed Maggie McCarthy. She was a bit older, a bit tanner, but it was unmistakably the same girl who saved him from the thug jocks that day on the football field six years ago. Although her invitation was gracious and her smile was genuine, he expected a more enthusiastic welcome, considering the fact that they both grew up together. Aside from that encounter on the football field, however, Jake figured the two of them never really spoke to one another. In fact, it was quite possible that since they never really spoke, and since he felt he had changed so much since graduation, that she did not recognize him at all. He was on the verge of exposing his identity when in mid-sentence he noticed that Maggie was looking at him in a way she had never done so before. Somehow, he thought, "Hi, Maggie! Remember me? Worm? Yeah, the kid you saved from drowning in spit in the middle of the football field a few years back?" would not be the wise thing to say at that moment. So instead, he was content to leave his former self behind and capitalize on his status as a stranger in a strange land.

From the cocoon of adolescent uncertainty to his metamorphosis into adulthood, Worm had become the new and improved Jake while Maggie had stayed the same sweet girl he always knew—only more beautiful and desirable. Their conversation was relaxed, and slowly their chairs were drawn closer in order to hear themselves over the rhythmic music of the mariachis. Finding the cafe sparsely populated now with vacationing tourists immersed in their own intimate chatting, Jake asked Maggie to dance, finally holding her in his arms as he did in his imagination many times before.

She was lithe and delicate and conformed to his body following his deliberately slow lead. He did not speak, as he was consumed by the scent of her hair, the feel of her heartbeat, and the way her smooth satin skin seemed to glow by the light of the dim oil lamps and candles that rested on the tables. Her face upturned to his, just inches away, her warm breath against his face and neck. As he drew her closer, her chin to his shoulder, he kissed her lightly through her hair. Another soft kiss was delivered as he drew back her hair to expose her exquisite, lilting neck. Her breath matched his own and she turned her head slowly to face him, eyes closed, lips slightly parted, a slight tremble to her arms around his neck. All sound filtered out of the room, and for the moment it was just man and woman, sharing a lonely dance by the moonlight. His mouth gently searched around her cheeks, her nose, to the corners of her mouth. The soft touch of her lips upon his sent fantastic chills through his body, awakening long-dormant feelings and desires.

As suddenly as his arousal had begun, however, his conscience took over. Feelings of doubt and insecurity that had been tucked away re-emerged, and he wondered if this facade could last forever. Soon she would discover his true identity, and his world would crash down around him. It would be foolish to start something he could not finish. It would be foolish to elevate his hopes and dreams when it was obvious that this beautiful woman would never have him. Not knowing who he really was.

With that, Jake pulled away from her. He wanted to tell her all his insecurities. He wanted to confess his true identity. He wanted to explain to her why they could never live happily ever after so long as Worm was still a part of his life. Instead, he simply excused himself and never returned.

* * * *

He left Mexico and his elusive fantasy the next day. He returned with his buddies and served another year in the military before he was honorably discharged with the rank of E-5 sergeant. Armed with confidence, discipline, and skills, he returned to the old Cape Cod.

Jake discovered upon his return that his once lively uncle had become a fragile old man in his absence. It was as if the life had been drained from him. For reasons Jake could not understand, the death of Aunt Vera had been very difficult for the old man to accept. She had never been very nice to her husband as far as Jake had witnessed, and she certainly wasn't nice to him. As morbid as it was, Jake actually felt a heavy weight lift from his shoulders when the miserable old lady died. He never understood Uncle Henry's reaction to her death until the night the two sat together around the kitchen table. Jake found the courage to confront him with the issue, and Uncle Henry explained through glassy eyes how his wife had once been a very pleasant and charming woman. Jake knew that Uncle Henry and Aunt Vera once had a son that died before Jake was born, but he never approached the subject with either his aunt or uncle. There were no photos of their son in the house, and no one ever mentioned him by name, so Jake assumed the subject was off-limits. On this night, however, seated around the kitchen table, Henry spoke openly about his son for the first time with Jake.

Years ago, Henry explained, the couple's only son asked permission to go to a party with some of his friends. Aunt Vera vehemently disapproved, as the weather was very bad that night, with the roads icing over after a midday shower. Uncle Henry tossed the boy his keys, though, and told him to drive safely. Later that night, they received word that their son had careened off the road, over an embankment, and had died upon arrival to the hospital. Aunt Vera never forgave her husband, and Uncle Henry never forgave himself. This, he explained, was why he never questioned her methods of discipline.

"She may have been harsh on you, Johnny, but she was a good woman. And she was just doin' what she thought was best." He excused himself from the table and retired for the evening. The next morning, Jake discovered that Uncle Henry had died in his sleep. The old man's last words to him were, "I'm proud of you, son." That was all Jake needed to hear.

He stood at the steps of the Cape Cod, and just as all the damage from the fire had been patched up so, too, he felt all the bad memories of this place had been covered up. His first act of independence was to build a ceremonial bonfire in the backyard. All the old hand-me-downs he used to wear as a boy—the long-sleeved shirts with turtleneck collars—were tossed into the flames one by one. All the report cards and memorabilia of a childhood best forgotten were consumed by the flames, instantly turned into ashes. Only the most prized of possessions, symbolizing the few happy moments of his childhood, were kept, locked in an old toolbox once belonging to Uncle Henry, and tucked away in the attic.

Uncle Henry's funeral service was very well attended. Jake was impressed by the turnout of so many to honor a man that had been a friend to so many beside himself. He recognized many of the faces, though many did not recognize him. One couple stood out among the rest: a man and his daughter, who walked toward him to extend their sympathies. Jake recognized the man as Sam McCarthy, owner of the town's pet store. The woman needed no introduction.

At first, the look on Maggie's face was one of vague recognition. It soon morphed into one of complete shock and disbelief. Jake didn't hear a word of what Sam said to him, as his full concentration was focused on Maggie, whom he hadn't seen since he left her sitting alone in that bar in Acapulco. Sam departed, leaving Maggie and Jake alone.

"My, my, what a small world," she said in a deadpan voice. It was hard to get a read on her.

"Maggie, I want to apologize for running out on you that night," Jake replied. "I know how angry you must be with me."

"I'm not angry, Jake. I'm just a bit surprised to see you here. I had no idea you were related to Henry. Do you live here in New Milford?"

"I do now," Jake answered. A long, uncomfortable silence followed.

"Well, I'm sorry to hear about your uncle," Maggie offered, finally.

"Thank you," Jake said, as he began to fidget nervously. "Again, I'm sorry about what happened in Acapulco. I hope we can still be friends."

"Friends," she repeated with a crooked grin. "Sure, Jake. I think we should start fresh from the beginning." She then extended her hand. "Maggie McCarthy. It is very nice to meet you."

* * * *

Finding himself alone in the Cape Cod that had once terrified him, and later comforted him, he was unsure of his next steps. The idea of starting fresh with a new identity in a new town appealed to him greatly. But the town of New Milford had grown on him, and the prospect of getting to know Maggie intrigued him. He had inherited the house from Henry, and owned it free and clear. He could easily sell it and use the money to start a new life, but he would feel guilty doing so. The house had been Henry's gift to him.

Along with the house came a tin box containing neatly-folded stacks of letters addressed to Jake from his mother—letters Jake had never known existed. The postmarks originated from several different states throughout the country—the last of which was stamped, "Bethesda, Maryland," more than eight years ago. Jake found it odd that these letters had been kept from him all these years. He surmised that it was Henry's way of protecting him.

The tone of each letter was a bit impersonal, not to mention a bit incoherent, and the content was disappointing. There was no mention of any regret over having given up her child, no apologies, and no begging for forgiveness. Just a simple recap of her life and vague promises of some future visit that he knew would never come.

Applying the advice of Uncle Henry from years ago, Jake's front pockets became mini file cabinets where lists of things to do were carefully stored. First on his list was repairing the old house. His goal was to customize the house to his own tastes, which included the construction of a small kennel out back to house the German shepherd puppy that would be arriving soon.

He named the puppy "King," in honor of a friend long gone, and the two of them spent many hours together in rigorous training sessions, balanced with plenty of "play time." Jake stayed primarily in the background, away from townsfolk and the general public eye. His sole companion during this time was his dog.

Eventually, Jake mustered enough courage to visit the pet store, where he knew there was a good possibility he'd run into Maggie. Using the excuse that King could use a new collar, he pulled up to the front of Critters Pet Store. Sam appeared to be alone as Jake opened the front door. He was sitting on a stool at the front counter reading a magazine.

The familiar, friendly face of Maggie's father greeted him with a hello and a large smile. There was no sign of Maggie. With a quick scan of the shelves, Jake found the section devoted to dog supplies and thumbed through the selection of leather and vinyl, all the while looking for Maggie out of the corner of his eye.

"Can I help you, son?" Sam inquired without rising from his perch.

"No, thanks," Jake replied, adding the standard explanation, "Just looking."

He tried to be casual, combing the field looking for her, but she was nowhere in sight. He eventually gave up, selecting a burgundy leather collar and a rawhide dog bone.

He returned to his car, collapsed into the front seat and handed the treat to his pet. Taking a deep breath, Jake pondered his next move. It had been a few months now since his return to New Milford. He had managed to keep a low profile, and had restored the old Cape Cod to his tastes. He had been living off of his share of Uncle Henry's inheritance, but he recognized that it was time to begin a career. Fate had always been his life's director. Fate had steered him from one significant change to the next. Some huge hand created him, molded him, threw roadblocks in his path, and often split him in two just to make things interesting. Fate made him Worm and Fate turned him into Jake. It was Fate that hurled him into the next life-altering change that would dominate the better part of the rest of his life.

It was on that morning, staring wide-eyed and bewildered at the morning paper, reading how Sam McCarthy had been slain in his own pet store, just hours after he had left the store, that Jake finalized his decision to become a police officer. On the same day as Sam's funeral, Jake applied for a position at the new, modern police station in town. He tried to avoid the cemetery, but found himself standing among the sympathetic mourners that had come to pay their respects. He stood in the background, getting a glimpse of the sad girl sitting in the front row, holding the folded American flag on her lap. He wanted to comfort her, to hold her, to tell her he'd always be there to protect her. Instead, he left without a word, unnoticed and unseen.

Eight weeks later, his training complete, Jake and his dog drove out of the driveway of police headquarters in a brand new Ford cruiser to begin his shift.

Chapter 10

New Milford had always been the kind of town where a person could recognize each and every face that passed by on Main Street. One could catch up on all the local gossip and politics with a quick visit to Jimmy's barbershop or a lingering breakfast at Al's coffee shop. No secret was sacred, no scorecard required.

People born in New Milford seldom left. Most who did leave eventually returned as if some supernatural power compelled them to do so against their will. Some outsiders settled there through occupational change. Others settled because of the closeness and hospitality small towns like New Milford have to offer. Still others came to escape a troubled past, to start over with a clean slate in a town where no one knew their secret.

With the influx of incoming strangers, it became increasingly difficult for even the "lifers" to recognize every face on Main Street, and to keep up with all the news of their small town. Along with this growth came the inevitable, yet disturbing, increase in crime that led most folks to lock their doors at night for the first time in their lives. The weekly police report had once been filled with overzealous drunks, free-spirited youths, a few disorderly conduct charges, and a shoplifter or two. With the subtle takeover, more sophisticated crimes and horrendous forms of human degradation became more commonplace. Crimes such as these often led the townsfolk to turn a deaf ear, a sign of rebellion against those who intimated that their town was decaying, an all-out denial that the times had changed their once-cozy environment into one of fear.

That's why he liked it there. New Milford was his home. He could choose to be recognized or disappear through a crowd of strangers. He could come and go as he pleased. He could become a shadow, weaving in and out of people's lives without arousing suspicion. The town provided him with a veil of security. He could proceed as planned without interruption or interrogation.

He liked to think of himself as a hero. He was a crusader, forced to mask his true identity to ensure the safety of his mission. He was the Justifier, the Protector. It was his duty, his responsibility, to fight the forces of evil that invaded the lives of harmless, innocent beings. The world was polluted with horrendous people who used and abused the weak and helpless. Fortunately, his assignment was to protect just one innocent being. It was his job to protect this fragile soul from all stress and worry, from those who threatened harm. And protect her he would, at all costs—even with his life. It was his duty, his responsibility, his addiction and his obsession.

Across the parking lot, he leaned against the cool wall, ankles and arms crossed as he breathed in the night air. It was a clear evening, with a night sky dotted with thousands of stars, and a new moon invisible against the darkness supplying his hiding place. It had been a long and busy day, and he could use the sleep. With the sounds of the store door closing, he crept further into the darkness and slid his body around the corner to ensure he would not be noticed. He watched her open the door to the SUV and load several boxes in along with her briefcase. He stood like a sentry at his post until the taillights disappeared around the corner of the building. He stayed a while longer, just in case she had forgotten something. And when he saw that it was safe to emerge into the light of the parking lot, he casually walked to the back door of the store, key in hand. His flashlight preceded his entrance to the back storage room, and he soon found what he was after. Finding nothing of significance, he breathed a sigh of relief. All was safe. He would sleep well tonight. Opening the door a crack, checking for witnesses, he carefully locked the door and retreated to his waiting vehicle.

CHAPTER 11

Maggie
Age 20

After hours—after the doors were locked, the lights were turned off, the animals were fed, and the open sign was flipped to closed—was Sam McCarthy's favorite time of the day. It was during these times that Sam would stand back and gaze around his little shop and congratulate himself for another day's job well done. Pride filled his heart with the fact that it all belonged to him, still somewhat amazed that he actually had succeeded in making his and Allison's dream come true.

Owning Critters, or any other business, certainly had its headaches. It came with the territory. But it also had its moments when it seemed like all that hard work paid off. It was during those times, especially, that he wished she were there to celebrate with him, to experience those ups and downs. She would be proud, too, to know that it all worked out. All the years of building inventory and customers, all the hours spent establishing the little store, all the money spent in supplies and advertising, the long wait to build up a solid reputation, had finally begun to pay dividends. Allison died believing the all-American dream meant being enslaved to a business that owned them, owned every waking hour of their lives, and owned every aching muscle in their weary bodies.

Sam closed the register and gave himself a mental pat on the back. The final tally showed that it had not been a bad day, considering the weather. He hated the summer season most of all. It was his slowest sale period of the year. In the fall, pets became rewards—or bribery—for good marks in school. In the winter, pets provided hobbies for those locked indoors by the cold winds. Christmas was the season of giving, and Easter was the season of bunnies and other furry animals. In the summer months, it was simply too nice out to stay inside caring for pets. People were content to maintain the pets they had, but didn't necessarily have a need for new ones.

Sam stuffed the register money into his briefcase and made his way to the back of the store. He had a nagging feeling he had forgotten something, but when he turned around everything looked in order. With a shrug, he turned back to lock things up for the night and get home to Maggie, who would have supper waiting.

As his hand reached for the door, that prickly feeling struck him again. He knew he had locked the front doors, but it came so automatic that he often felt the compulsion to check them one more time, just to be sure. Keys in hand, he set the briefcase down and, snapping on a set of aquarium lights, made his way back to the front of the store. As he passed by Rocky, one foot tucked and head buried in his back, he apologized for disturbing his sleep.

"Be outta here in two shakes, you old buzzard," he said. He often thought the sleeping act was halted the minute he left the store, as he often found evidence the next morning that suggested a small party had taken place the night before—books shredded, ornaments broken, and occasional droppings on the rug. When he returned in the morning, however, Rocky would always be stationed in his usual roost, right where he had left him, with an angelic look on his face, and a cheery "hello" as if nothing had taken place.

He approached the first door and, finding it locked, started toward the second door. His steps were interrupted by a strange sound coming from behind the counter. At first, he thought something had escaped its cage. Then he thought Rocky might be getting an early start. He approached the counter quietly on tiptoe, prepared to capture whatever critter had gotten loose. Hands on the shiny urethane counter, he slowly peered over the top, expecting to see a rat's tail or the bright blue eyes of a kitten. Instead, he was startled to discover the shadowy figure of a man huddled into a tight ball, squatting on the floor just below the cash register.

The intruder's cover had been blown. This had not been part of his plan, which was hastily formed after discovering the unlocked door to the darkened store. The plan was to hide until the coast was clear, then raid the register and take anything he fancied he could sell or trade for his next fix. The intruder's dealer was a snake fanatic, and there were a couple of nice-looking boas in the corner he imagined he could trade for a month's supply. Only that plan was spoiled when the old man made his U-turn. Now it was time for "Plan B."

The intruder stood, and Sam spotted the familiar gleam of steel and knew he was in trouble. The two men simply stood and stared at each other for a moment, contemplating their next move. Neither one had planned on the night's events unraveling this way. Sam was the first to speak.

"Now, just take it easy, son. Think about what you're doing now."

"Don't worry, pops. I know what I'm doing. Now here's how it's going to work. You're going to hand me the money, and I'm going to leave out that door. This will all be over quick and painless."

"There's no money here," Sam replied, motioning to the cash register. "You can check for yourself. The drawer's empty."

"Aw, c'mon, man. I ain't stupid. I know you haven't been sitting here all day without selling anything. Now I'm only gonna tell you one more time...give me your money."

Sam could see the gunman was nervous. The gun was shaking slightly, and he could tell just by looking at his eyes that the man hadn't done this before.

"Okay, settle down," Sam said calmly. "The money's in the back of the store. I'll go get it for you if you'd like."

The gunman studied Sam's face for some hint into his intentions. The old man could be telling the truth, he thought, or he could make a break for the back door. He stood silently for a moment, weighing his options, contemplating his next move.

He was about to speak when, from behind him on a perch high above, Rocky unleashed a deafening scream that, ordinarily, was an extremely common sound in that little shop. But first time visitors, such as the armed assailant, were often startled by such a noise. The noise surprised the gunman so much that his panicked finger convulsed against the trigger of the pistol that happened to be aimed at Sam McCarthy's chest.

Every passing second magnified, giving Sam the illusion that the world had slowed down. He slowly dropped to the floor, raw pain washing over his body, a pool of blood slowly staining the carpet. He could feel the life draining from his body as he pleaded with the gunman to phone for help. But the killer simply stood over him, motionless, smoking gun in shaking hand, unable to believe what had just occurred. Leaving cash and snakes behind, he hurtled out the door to the black Camaro waiting outside, and sped off in no particular direction.

The gunshot silenced the squawking birds and the bustling animals behind glass cages. It was still silent when Hank arrived after responding to the 1118 call on his radio—shots fired. Hank entered the silent domain to find his long-time friend in pain, the life quickly draining from his body. He attempted to apply pressure to the wound, tried to stop the endless flow of blood from his friend's chest long enough for the ambulance to arrive. Sam tried to talk, to explain what had happened. He found only enough strength to ask his best friend to watch over his daughter Maggie. And hearing the promise escape Hank's lips, Sam peacefully went towards the light surrounding his waiting wife, Allison.

* * * *

Hank held Sam's body until the ambulance arrived. He held Maggie's hand throughout the funeral. He closed the store for two weeks, stopping daily to care for the menagerie of pets. He looked in on Maggie as often as his schedule allowed, but was thankful that she had caring relatives who could look after her while he hunted for Sam's murderer.

Unfortunately, there was very little evidence to support his search. It would be impossible to differentiate the murderer's prints from those of the customers, salesmen and deliverymen that filed in and out of the store on a daily basis. Prints from the register were smudged—even a partial thumbprint on the register drawer. The owner of the video store next store phoned in the gunshot, but by the time he had reached his front door, all he caught was a quick glance at the killer's car exiting the parking lot. Hank tried to keep it all in perspective and treat this case like any other. But Sam was a good friend, and Maggie didn't deserve to lose her father this way. This case was personal.

He recognized that Maggie had become overwhelmed by all the decision-making that invaded her privacy after her father's death. She briefly contemplated selling Critters, but after a long talk with Hank, he convinced her that she had the knowledge and ability to run the business herself and keep Sam and Allison's dream alive. He also persuaded her to hire some help. It wouldn't be easy tackling a task such as this, never mind doing it alone.

Stacey was a long-time customer of Critters, and had previously expressed an interest in taking a part-time job there when Sam was running the show alone. She was friendly, outgoing, knowledgeable, and a perfect match for Maggie's needs. She eagerly accepted Maggie's offer and proved to be a very wise choice.

Frank had come along at just the right time. Though Hank sensed that Maggie and Frank had some differences in the past, they had apparently been buried long ago. The pet store needed a man that could help with the heavy lifting and provide some security, and Frank was extremely knowledgeable in the one area—aquarium maintenance and expertise on the store's complex filtration system—where the business needed the most help. Frank's troubles with drugs and alcohol were well known. There are no big secrets in a town as small as New Milford. But Hank was confident that those troubles were a thing of the past.

Hank immediately developed an affection for Stacey. She had a talent for endearing herself to people, and he could see that Stacey could become a much-needed friend to Maggie at a time when he believed her social life was severely lacking. As for Frank, Hank always kept a watchful eye on him. There was something about him he just didn't like. Something about the way he looked at Maggie made him uneasy, and he was afraid that under the circumstances, Maggie might be vulnerable enough to fall for him. Hank imagined himself as a father figure to Maggie, and envisioned a day when he'd give her away at her wedding, but it was now his duty to make sure that man she was marrying was worthy of her.

CHAPTER 12

He slouched in the driver's seat of his parked car, just across the road from her house, his left hand cradling his stubbled chin. He just sat there, the motor running, the radio turned down low, as if he were the getaway car in a crime. It was silly to feel nervous about knocking on her door. It wasn't as though he had never entered that house before. In fact, he had been a guest there several times. But each time he reached out to shift into drive, he quickly recoiled his hand and grabbed onto the steering wheel. Her driveway was just yards away, yet it seemed like miles.

Maggie had always been "just yards away." Her presence always close, but just barely out of reach. He felt that was her place, though, high atop a pedestal, immortalized in a museum for all men to admire. She was the epitome of purity, untarnished by the spawning sins of a crumbling society. A museum was the ideal place for her—a place where she could be kept under glass, to keep her safe. He shook his head, realizing the absurdity of the idea of Maggie allowing anyone to lock her up, to tie her down for any reason.

He admired the way she had handled herself since her father's death. In a way, his death had been the catalyst she needed to find some direction in her life. She had always been stubborn and adamant about her independence. If she knew she had a guardian angel like him, she definitely would not approve, but he knew he was doing the right thing. She deserved to be happy, and it was his job to make sure that she was.

His eyes fixed on her dimly lit house. His stare was rewarded by a glimpse of Maggie at her picture window. He slid further down in his seat, hoping that the darkness of the night would provide a sufficient blanket under which to hide. She stood at the window with her arms crossed over her chest and she seemed oblivious to all her surroundings but the moonless, starry sky. He sat idle, captivated by the surrealism of the sight. The scene before him reminded him of a painting hung in a posh museum: the portrait of a fragile, winsome young girl backlit by the soft glow of candlelight, framed by the molding around the windowpane. It was a priceless painting created on a warm May night for an audience of one.

As quickly as she appeared, she disappeared and the lights were soon extinguished. He blamed himself for not acting sooner, for now his chance to be with her was gone. She would have welcomed him inside for a cup of coffee and a little friendly conversation. But the opportunity had passed, and he reluctantly threw his idling car into gear and flicked on the headlights.

With Maggie safely tucked away for the night, he drove down the narrow street en route to his own warm bed. He veered into his driveway, but remained in the car with his foot on the brake. His mind filled with possible solutions in his quest to keep her safe and happy. Just as Maggie kept her wards at the pet store safe and comfortable in their environments he, too, had found a way to keep her safe and comfortable. Without her knowing, he had become her personal bodyguard, an undercover assignment undertaken by a party of one to protect his client in her best interests and for her own good. It was his duty. It was his pleasure. It was his destiny.

* * * *

How appropriate it was May. Not because Tucker Quinn appreciated the beauty of the flowers in bloom, the soft breeze wafting through the full trees, or the happy songs of little birds building their nests. Tucker associated the merry month of May with an old game he used to play as a child:

Mother, may I?

Mother, may I sleep a little longer?

Mother, may I have some dessert?

Mother, may I borrow the car?

Mother, may I take your gun and blow your fucking head off?

No jury would ever convict him. He could actually get away with it if he ever found the guts to do it. What was it called? Oh, yeah—"temporary insanity." That was what his mother said when she blew apart his dad with his own deer-hunting rifle. Sure, the old man was a scumbag who was sleeping around with his mother's best friend. But she didn't have to kill him. Tucker missed his old dad. He missed his old house, his friends, even his old school. It was his mother who uprooted the two of them and transplanted them in this little shit-hole town. And while he was suffering without any of his old friends around, his mom was getting banged by some local-yokel with two precious little daughters and they were all supposed to live happily ever after together. And if they couldn't do it together, then it would just be, "See ya, Tuck, nice knowing ya!"

He looked around his room, which had grown to resemble a jail cell lately. His stereo system blared hard rock from monster speakers stationed at all four corners of the room. It was his prized—and only—possession. It was a gift purchased for himself, by himself, as a reward for hours of backbreaking lawn mowing. The money had been stashed in a secret hiding place, away from prying eyes. After months and months of saving, the stereo system was his.

Standing in the doorway of the darling girls' room, he noticed it was stocked with all the perks and privileges of being the favorites. Lightly touching the matching pink comforters on their beds, Tucker scanned the room, noting the small color television with the video game system attached, the enormous collection of stuffed animals on each of their beds, the color-coordinated wallpaper, and the bed coverings that matched the lace-frilled curtains.

Those snotty girls had no idea just how spoiled they were. Tucker felt it was his duty to make them appreciate everything they had. Whenever the opportunity arose, Tucker would often sneak into their bedroom and destroy something they loved, so that they could feel the same pain that he felt on a daily basis. Their lives were just a little too perfect for Tucker's tastes. Watching them suffer was just about the only pleasurable aspect left in his life.

A squeaking noise emanating from the floor of their pristine bedroom diverted his attention for the moment. He lowered himself to his knees to watch the carefree guinea pig family merrily squealing for their daily carrot treats. A large tricolor father, his black and white mate, and three multi-colored offspring struggled to climb the bars of their rapidly shrinking confinement, forgetting they lacked the ability to do so. He noticed the pieces of feces and cedar chips stuck to their fur and the pads of their feet and, smiling wryly, decided they needed a bath.

The warm water filling the tub, the sixteen-year-old boy carefully lifted each family member out of its cage and placed him or her one by one into the water. Making sure the water level wasn't so high that they might accidentally drown, he watched them awkwardly attempt to swim around a while before he plugged the hair dryer into the socket. He flicked the switch to "high" and dropped it into the water. The smile grew wider across his face as he watched the bodies convulse and fry. He then stood in front of the mirror and practiced until he was satisfied he could produce a genuine look of remorse in the wake of this tragic "accident" he had caused by trying to do his loving sisters a favor.

For the most part, he had been successful convincing his mother of his story. And the look on the girls' faces when he told her was pure gold. He did all he could to keep from smiling or pumping his fists in the air. His victory dance was short-lived, however, as his mother immediately ordered him to drive the girls down to the pet store to buy two new guinea pigs, with the cost to come from his own pockets.

Ever the dutiful son, Tucker drove his step-sisters to the store as instructed, wearing a wide grin and keeping the radio uncharacteristically low so as not to drown out the girls' sobs. While the girls chose their new pets, Tucker chatted with a friend of his and, out of earshot of the girls, triumphantly bragged about the whole ordeal. Unfortunately, the bitchy owner of the store was in earshot, crouched in the aisle next to him, tending to a pack of gerbils. Needless to say, she refused to sell the animals to him, so he was forced to drive to the pet shop down the road where they were more than happy to accept his money.

A week later, Tucker found himself in an empty house once again. The mailman had delivered a letter to the lucky winners of a local contest. The prize of a trip for four to an amusement park was enclosed, and not surprisingly he found himself to be the odd man out.

He sat on the edge of his bed, contemplating his next move. Left alone in the house, he had free reign to do whatever his warped mind could conceive. Somewhere below the din of the music that blared from his speakers, he could faintly hear the sound of running water. But this was impossible—unless, of course, the family had returned earlier than expected. That thought was too painful to bear.

Tucker turned down the stereo and listened. The sound of running water was unmistakable now. Perhaps his mother had put a load of laundry in the washer. Or perhaps there was an intruder in the house. That theory, however, didn't make any sense. How many burglars break into a house to take a bath?

Tucker ventured out of his room and down the hall toward the source of the sound. He marched into the bathroom and discovered the tub was slowly being filled with water. The stupid-ass girls must have forgotten to shut it off after their baths. It would serve them right if he just ignored it and let his parents come home to find their darling little daughters had flooded the house.

A smug smile crossed his face with all the possibilities and ramifications at hand. At the same time, he felt his skull crack under a heavy blow from behind. Tucker awoke to find himself naked and lying in a pool of cold water in the bathtub. With blurry vision returning to his widening eyes, he watched with horror as the girls' small television set was dropped into the tub next to his protruding belly. He felt the jolts of electricity course through his body. His hair seemed to catch fire, and each pore from every inch of his skin's surface seemed to erupt with volcanic body fluids. Tucker thrashed against the porcelain sides, and small rivulets of blood trickled out of his bulbous nose.

Tucker Quinn was dead.

CHAPTER 13

Worm
Age 22

Jake recognized the familiar glazed-eyed look and the smell of marijuana the moment the driver rolled down his window. The driver's car had been pulled over after running a red light. Before approaching the vehicle, Jake had called in the plate number and discovered that the owner of the vehicle was out on parole after serving time for drug trafficking.

"Aw, come on, man. That light was yellow," argued the driver, before Jake had a chance to speak.

"Sir, please step out of the vehicle," Jake ordered, taking a step back with his eyes fixed upon the driver's hands.

"Step out? What the hell for? All I did was run a red light," the driver protested.

"I thought you just said it was yellow," Jake said with a smirk. "Step out here and we'll talk about it."

The driver shook his head slowly, then reluctantly stepped out into the cool night air. Jake ordered the driver to turn around and place his hands on the hood of the car.

"Come on, man! You've gotta be kidding me!" the driver protested once more, then begrudgingly did as he was told.

"Is there anything in your pockets I should know about?" Jake asked.

The driver exhaled loudly, shook his head in despair, then said, "You're probably gonna find it either way, man, so I may as well tell you about the joint in the front pocket of my jacket."

Jake removed the contents of the driver's front pocket and discovered the incriminating cigarette. He continued his pat-down, then asked the driver to place his hands behind his back. The driver complied, and Jake applied his handcuffs. He then reached into the driver's back pocket and extracted his wallet.

"Well, Mr. Garver, I thank you for your honesty," said Jake. "But it seems you've violated the terms of your parole."

"Shit, man. I can't go back to prison," Garver protested. "They'll kill me, man. I'm serious!"

"You should've thought of that before you decided to go on a joyride with a joint in your pocket." Jake led the perpetrator back to his cruiser and helped him into the back seat, where he sat beside King.

"He doesn't bite, does he?" Garver asked.

"Not unless you give him a reason to," Jake replied. "Anything else in your car that I should know about?"

"No, man. It's clean."

"You know something? I believe you. But if you don't mind, my friend and I are going to check it out anyway."

Jake led King back to Garver's car and let the dog sniff around the interior. After a brief search, King verified that it was indeed clean. On the ride back to the station, Garver continued to protest and plead for leniency. Then, he said something that got Jake's attention.

"Hey, listen, I've got some information for you. You know that murder that happened here in town a couple years ago? I just came from a party where a dude was bragging about killing that old man. I can take you to him."

Jake swerved to the side of the road and stopped the car so abruptly, poor King was slammed into the back of the passenger seat.

"What old man?" Jake asked, trying to keep his composure.

"The old man at the pet store," Garver replied. "This dude shot him. I know where he lives. I can take you to him."

"Not only are you going to take me to him," Jake said, "but you're going to help me get a confession out of him."

The following night, a surveillance team, led by Jake and Hank, sat in unmarked squad cars outside the home of James David Moore, waiting to hear the magic words. Inside the house, drinking, smoking and laughing it up with Moore, was Tim Garver, who was dutifully wearing a wire beneath his clothing.

After more than two hours of partying, Garver was able to coax Moore into retelling his story of the murder he committed two years ago. Once the taped confession had been verified, Jake gave the signal and five other undercover cops poured out of their vehicles.

For Jake, the adrenaline rush was almost too great to bear. He had dreamt of this moment since the day he put on a uniform. It was the reason he decided to become a cop in the first place. For Hank, it was a chance for redemption and closure, both for his fallen friend, Sam, and his honorary daughter, Maggie.

Jake motioned for two of his fellow officers to head around to the back of the house, then directed another officer to remain outside in front of the house. Hank and Jake stood poised at the front door, with guns drawn. Upon Jake's signal, the front door was kicked in, and Jake burst through the door, with Hank following close behind. As the officers at the back door gained entry to the home, a man streaked across the hallway between them toward one of the bedrooms. Jake sprinted toward the bedroom in pursuit. Disregarding all sense of personal safety, he bolted through the open door of the bedroom, spotted Moore frantically sifting through his nightstand, leapt across the bed and tackled him. Moore's head slammed against the wall so hard, it left a hole in the sheetrock. Jake wrestled Moore's arms behind his back and handcuffed him.

Later ballistics tests revealed that Moore's gun, found fully-loaded in the nightstand, matched the weapon that killed Sam McCarthy.

Later that night, Jake, Hank and the rest of the team celebrated at the local pub.

"You got that son of a bitch!" Hank said to Jake, pounding him on the back.

"No, *we* got him," Jake corrected.

"Always Mr. Modesty," Hank replied, shaking his head. "Why don't you stop by the pet store tomorrow morning and give Maggie the good news in person?"

"No, I think she'd rather hear it from you," Jake replied, sipping his beer.

"Suit yourself, buddy," said Hank.

* * * *

The next morning, Hank anxiously headed out the door. The news would certainly put her mind to rest. No longer would she need to feel threatened by being in the store alone. Finally, she could rest knowing the man responsible for her loss was behind bars where he belonged.

Sam would approve of the job Hank had done so far. Maggie had developed into a fine businesswoman; confident and headstrong. She learned to develop her weaknesses into strengths, and after only a short while she seemed as comfortable in the working environment of the store as she had ever been since he'd known her. He was proud of her. And he was sure that somewhere Sam and Allison were proud, too.

Hank veered into the parking lot, finding a spot just in front of Critters. He walked to the door and pulled, but it didn't open. A glance at his watch told him it was ten-twenty, and he tried the door again. Maggie always opened by ten o'clock, rain or shine. Customers expected consistency. He went to the front window and cupped his hands around his eyes as he peered through the glass. The lights were on, but there was no movement in the aisles. Looking deeper into the store, he could see that the aquarium lights had not been turned on yet, but there was a dim light emanating from the back room. He returned to his car and drove around to the rear of the store, discovering Maggie's SUV parked outside in its usual spot.

He was fully prepared to give her a hard time about her absent-minded preoccupation stealing valuable time and money from paying customers. He made a big production out of opening the unlocked back door and slamming it shut behind him, but his phony consternation disappeared from his face when he spied the pathetic figure of Maggie sitting on the cold cement floor. Tears streaked her sullen face as she raised her head to recognize the intruder, all the while cradling the lifeless body of her beloved store mascot, Rocky.

Hank knelt down beside her, old familiar words of comfort escaping his lips as he tried to console her. He listened as she finally managed to explain how she had come in that morning to find the Amazon lying at the bottom of his island. She quickly checked for vital signs and desperately tried to revive him, but it was too late. He was gone. She blamed herself, saying he must have been sick and she should have noticed earlier. Her father had trusted her with his love, and she had failed him. She had failed herself. Perhaps she wasn't cut out to run this business after all.

She rose from the floor, still cradling the bird in an old, tattered blanket, and placed the fallen creature into a cardboard box. She asked Hank to leave, as there was work to do, and she needed to be alone. Hank went home to an empty house—a house that had never been filled with a loving wife and the standard two and a half children. He had made Sam's family his family. Sam's wife had become his wife, and Maggie was as much his daughter as she was Sam's and Allison's. He made a mental note to check on her later. Perhaps then she would be ready to talk, and he would be there for her like he always was. Later, after she had calmed down, he would deliver his good news, and she would feel better. She just needed time.

* * * *

Frank reached for another tissue, adding to his collection in the wastebasket nearby. He hated being sick, and a beautiful spring day like today was no time to be in bed with a cold. He winced at the stack of papers piled on his desk in the next room and wished he could call in sick. Summer was the hardware store's busiest season, and if he didn't tackle that pile now it would only get bigger. He reluctantly rose from his dreary chamber and plodded toward his awaiting task. He neatly sorted a few purchase orders lying on top of the pile and stacked them to the side. As quickly as his work began, it ended with a phone call from Stacey from the pet store.

"Frank, you'd better get down here. The filters are clogging and Maggie's having a nervous breakdown. She just got the results of Rocky's autopsy back, and I'm afraid this is the last thing she needs."

Frank drew a deep breath, comparing the pile of paper on his desk to the volume of paper in his wastebasket.

"Can't you guys fix it yourselves? I've shown you a thousand times how to take care of those things. It's not that difficult."

"Nice, Frank, real nice. I'm glad you're so sympathetic. Just get down here."

And with those words, Frank was left to converse with a dial tone. *Sympathy,* he thought. *What am I supposed to do—buy a Hallmark card saying, "Sorry about your stupid bird?"* He never liked the bird anyway, ever since the thing bit him and drew blood while he was attempting to hold it down so Maggie could clip its wings. He had no use for any type of pet that didn't have fins and gills.

If Frank had one outstanding quality, it was his patience. He had been more patient with Maggie than any of his conquests, but he felt the end would soon justify the means. The progress was slow, as he let her dictate the speed of their relationship, fearing that if he pressed too hard, she would surely end it. He had been making progress, even taking her out on a few "dates," though their conversations tended to be anything but personal.

Lately, though, his patience was wearing a bit thin. Working at Critters gave him the opportunity to get closer to her than most people, and he could tell that he was beginning to break down the emotional walls she had built to protect herself. After Rocky died, however, she became more distant and somewhat preoccupied, declining offers to meet after work. Now, it appeared she was in need of some comfort and reassurance, and he would be the man to give it to her. Maggie was his. He had staked his claim to her years ago. Feeling a sudden wave of health come over him, Frank grabbed his coat and headed out the door.

* * * *

The cold, hard wind whipped against his face, making it difficult to open his eyes. The frigid gales blew with such force that his steps were labored and painfully slow. He slowly raised ice-crusted hands to his ears to cover his head, but snake-like tentacles of ice sprung from each narrow slit between his fingers. Without knowing why, he compelled his naked body forward, pushing inch by inch toward some unknown goal, his bare feet numb as they sank into the steadily deepening snow. Above the shrill howl of northerly wind echoing in his reddened ears, he thought he heard a woman's voice. A shroud of white surrounded his body, and still there was nothing visible to him as he pushed further ahead.

He fought the desire to lie down, to let the soft, white blanket warm his body. To sleep, for his legs were tired from their battle. Hunched over, head down, he plodded forward when he suddenly hit a wall. It was hard, but smooth to the touch, and he slowly ran his fingers over it, exposing a window. Scraping the frost from the pane with his fingernails, he peered through to the other side where there was a field filled with wild flowers, and a warm sun shining down from a beautiful blue, cloudless sky. In the center of the field, on a checkered cloth, surrounded by daisies and heather, sat an enchanting young woman with long, strawberry blonde hair. She held a single blade of grass to her porcelain cheek. Sitting beside her was a dark-haired man dipping a ripe, red strawberry into a bowl of fluffy whipped cream, and after feeding the woman, leaning over to lick off the excess cream from her sensuous smile.

The window iced over again, but when he began to scrape it off once again he heard that same familiar woman's voice, only this time much louder and more vivid. Recognition washing over his sullen face, he folded his fingers into fists as he heard his name repeated over and over.

Worm. Worm. Worm.

His fist pounded on the glass, each blow harder than the last, until the skin cracked, releasing tiny rivers of blood that plummeted to the ground below, forming patches of dark red on a snowy white landscape. The voice grew louder and more demanding, and the threat grew more intense. His two fists tried in vain to break the shield and he tried to scream at the people on the other side, but no words escaped his muted throat. As his pounding shook snow and ice from the invisible barrier, the frozen, tortured soul recognized the carefree man on the other side to be Jake. His voice finally returning to him, he managed a scream.

Which is how Jake Allen woke up that morning.

Splashing water on his face at the bathroom sink, he expected to look up and see Worm looking back at him from the mirror, with his empty dark eyes magnified by thick black-framed glasses. Instead, his stubbled reflection stared back at him and returned his silly grin.

Jake paused for a moment before applying the shaving cream, to see himself as others saw him. He had been successful in hiding his past. It had been easy to return home a stranger. With the exception of the dark eyes, which he feared betrayed his soul, he didn't look much like Worm anymore. Everyone in town had accepted him as the long-lost nephew of the late Henry Allen.

With each stroke of the razor blade, Jake removed not only whiskers, but also his self-doubt. His faded list of things to do was slowly being whittled away. Each item completed was victoriously crossed out. He had gotten his dog, King, who was out in the backyard living in the chicken coop that had been remodeled into a fine kennel. The old Cape Cod looked better than ever. The old interior was repainted, the damage from the fire had vanished, and nothing remained of the old couple that used to live there except Uncle Henry's recliner and a few mementos in the attic. His job on the force was rewarding and fulfilling despite the low pay and the long hours. He'd made a few friends, including Hank and Maggie, and earned familiarity and respect with the people in town. He had even made progress in his pursuit of a meaningful relationship with Miss McCarthy.

He had become a regular in the store, occasionally stopping by after work with the excuse of picking up some things for King. His visits were sometimes short, as Maggie would be busy tending to other customers, but often the two would just stand by the front counter and chat. For two long years, Jake was content with a casual friendship with Maggie, never over-stepping the bounds into something more romantic. He had a suspicion she might be involved with Frank Wilson, although he wished it weren't true. He remembered Frank from high school. He didn't like him back then, and his feelings for him hadn't changed.

He had received a strange call from Maggie earlier that day. Although she did not mention there was anything wrong, he could tell she was upset. She asked Jake to stop by some time that day, and since he was working a late shift, he decided to swing by the store on his way to work.

A few days earlier, he had received a warm hug preceding a brief smile through misty eyes, which meant more to him than the chief's citation. The arrest seemed to be the beginning of a new chapter in their brief history together, dampened only slightly by the sudden death of Rocky.

When Maggie learned of his part in the killer's capture, Hank drove her to the little Cape Cod. Hank waited in the car while she knocked at Jake's door and surprised him with a tight embrace. Jake tentatively returned her hug, then stepped back slowly when she whispered, "Thank you." He invited her inside, but she explained that she could not stay. They embraced again, and she returned to the car, where Hank sat behind the wheel, giving Jake a wink.

Realizing the time, Jake yelled to King out the back door. He did not want to keep Maggie waiting. Resting under the warm sun, the dog leapt to the sound of his name and bounded into the kitchen.

Walking through the back door to Critters, he came to an abrupt halt as he watched a furious Maggie stomping around the back room, her hands knotted into tight fists, her teeth clenched firmly, and a distant look of anger in her eyes. In the middle of her tirade, she must have felt his presence. The expression on her face was so unlike her that Jake hesitated to approach her.

"Damn it! Why?" she spat at him, drawing her eyes upward as if God might answer her. "I cannot believe it! How can there be such cruel and inhuman people in this world?" she asked, looking at Jake as a faint quiver invaded her bottom lip.

"Jesus...what happened, Maggie?" Jake asked, finding his voice. "What the hell is going on?"

The outburst by whatever demon had possessed this woman slowly began to fade, as anger drained from her body and sadness took over. Feeling it was now safe to approach her, Jake wrapped his arms around her as she began to cry. He gently stroked her hair and found it was damp against her neck. Whatever the problem was, it could wait until she was ready to tell him. He held her close until she took a deep breath.

"Thanks. I needed that," she said, "Glad to know there's a cop around when you need one."

"Just doing my job, ma'am," he returned her smile with a salute.

As the two of them stood on the concrete floor of the back room, Maggie surveyed the room as if composing her thoughts. She continued sweeping the room until they rested on an empty branch of the dismantled parrot island. A long, cleansing breath escaped from her lips before she finally met Jake's eyes.

"I got the autopsy report on Rocky yesterday," she said before diverting her eyes back to the empty branch. "It said he died from acute liver hepatitis." Her voice began to falter. Jake reached over to take one trembling hand in his own.

"The doctor said he found a toxic level of lead," she continued. "Rocky was poisoned. His liver just shut down. I've been here all night trying to find something—anything—he could have gotten into. I can't find it." Jake followed her gaze as he absorbed the news.

"I have checked, scraped, and swept this place looking for some sign, but I can't find anything. I was here all night last night, and spent most of my morning, and still nothing."

If there were any doubt the anger was returning, the swipe she took at the empty branch confirmed it.

"I think I finally figured it out. Since the poisonous substance did not come from this room, that means it must have come from the outside. And that only means it walked in with some customer who deliberately, or by sheer ignorance, handed it to an innocent, trusting bird."

For the next half-hour the two friends batted around other possibilities, but each time they reached the same conclusion. The poison had acted quickly on the body of the Amazon. So quick, he had to have ingested the substance within a few days of his death. Since birds mask their illnesses so well, they determined there was no way for Maggie to have known. The bird's death was beyond her control; much like outside forces had taken the lives of her mother and father.

Jake would be late for his shift, and Maggie still had much to do before opening the store. Making a date for lunch the next day, they each went their separate ways. King greeted Jake in the truck with almost angry licks to his owner's face—a little perturbed to have been left alone for so long. He gave the dog's bulky head a rough stroke and whispered into the dog's upright ear.

"Don't worry, boy. Nobody will ever hurt Maggie again."

CHAPTER 14

The diner was unusually busy for a Wednesday. Frenzied waitresses scurried from table to table, barking orders to the men in the kitchen. Every seat at the front counter was filled, and a parade of scrambled eggs and bacon passed by their eyes as they awaited their breakfasts.

"The Sox are playing way over their heads," Jake offered between sips of steaming black coffee. "They're just getting your hopes up now so they can rip your heart out in the end, just like they always do."

"Yeah, well, the Yanks can't buy their way into the World Series every year," Hank countered. "We almost had 'em last year. We'll get 'em this year. At least we have a little hope."

"No—at *most* you have a little hope," Jake beamed with a wink. "Ain't that right, Beanie?"

Officer Bean, hovering over a warm cup of his own and oblivious to their conversation, appeared to be startled awake by the sound of his name. He looked blankly at his co-workers for a moment then stammered about something totally unrelated to the conversation at hand. Hank and Jake simply nodded their heads and exchanged a bewildered look.

As Hank took another sip from his mug, he noticed Frank Wilson sitting at a table in the corner of the diner having an animated chat with an attractive woman wearing a two-piece tailored suit. He figured the woman to be a salesperson who was persuading Frank to purchase some hardware equipment by buying him breakfast, but Jake saw the scenario a little differently. He noticed the way that Frank would lightly touch the woman's hand to emphasize a point he was making, and their body language suggested that this was a little more personal than a business meeting. Jake wondered exactly how many women Frank was entertaining when he was supposed to be so taken by Maggie. Frank had gone out of his way not long ago to suggest that Jake remove himself from Maggie's life. "She's mine," Frank warned, as if Jake had a claim to her—as if *anyone* had a claim to her. Needless to say, he wasn't the least bit intimidated by Frank's pathetic threat, although he had to admire his boldness to stand up to a man in uniform. Or was it stupidity? Either way, he pitied the poor man. He could sympathize with any man that carried a torch for Maggie McCarthy.

Jake wished that Maggie would walk in at that moment to catch Frank at his best. Maybe then she'd see him as the two-faced con man everyone knew him to be. Unfortunately, as keen as Maggie was about certain affairs, she wasn't as sharp in her judgments of some people. She held the naive belief that most people were good by nature. She was sometimes disappointed, but then she would always find excuses to explain their behavior. Jake would love to hear Maggie's explanation of why Frank was now using his napkin to sensuously wipe his partner's chin. He got his wish when he heard Hank call out Maggie's name. Jake rose from his chair as Maggie greeted Hank with a hug. She flashed a smile toward Jake while Bean shyly watched from the corner of his eye.

"Hey, guys! What's new?" Maggie said, her smile warming the room.

Jake and Hank eyed each other, mentally agreeing to keep the latest police business between them. Maggie would soon find out for herself. No sense in starting off her day on a depressing note about some fat kid frying himself in his bathtub.

"Nothing much, Maggie. Nothing much," Jake said, ending the long pause.

"Nothing much?" Officer Bean blurted through a mouth full of toast. "Only if you don't consider that Quinn boy taking a bath with a television set to be nothing much!" The nasty glares by his two co-workers, along with the wide-eyed look on Maggie's face, led him to believe that might not have been the appropriate thing to say.

"Maggie, I'd like you to meet Mr. B.J. Bean," Jake said in exasperation. "Bean, this is Maggie McCarthy."

"Yeah, I know Beannie," Maggie said. "We go way back. We used to be neighbors."

Bean simply blushed and returned to his breakfast. Jake apologized for Bean's outburst. "I'm sure you didn't need to hear that news to start off your day," he whispered as they walked to the end of the counter.

* * * *

Maggie had been looking forward to having a wonderful day. She had contracted a belated case of spring fever, and had high hopes for a bright day ahead. Instead the name "Tucker Quinn" echoed in her brain—a name so familiar to her, yet she couldn't quite place it. There had been some gossip about Tucker Quinn molesting a ten-year-old girl a while back. The rumor mill said there had been other girls, too, but that their parents had not pressed charges, unwilling to subject their children to the horrors of a trial.

Tucker Quinn. There was something else in that name that hit closer to home. She heard he actually came close to being put on trial once, but he got a youthful offender status and received a slap on the wrist. *Tucker Quinn.* Something about the bathtub rang a bell. The fact that he had been electrocuted also danced on the edge of her conscience, tightrope-walking the thin wire of recognition. Then, suddenly, the ironic connection hit her. It was Tucker Quinn whom she heard bragging about electrocuting his sister's guinea pigs that day not long ago. The uneasy sensation in her stomach briefly turned to forbidden triumph before her guilty conscience admonished her for thinking such a thing. It served him right, though, killing all those innocent animals. No one deserved to die, of course, but she would shed no crocodile tears for this particular human being.

In the back of her mind, the vision of her father looked over her sternly, a look of disappointment in his eyes. In an attempt to avoid the ghost, she took the alternate route to the pet store, stopping by the post office to collect her mail. Perhaps there would be another one of those peculiar notes waiting for her. She actually looked forward to the notes, which were periodically sent to her from an unknown admirer. It had been almost a year since the first one appeared in her post office box. She hadn't a clue as to who had sent them, but she often let herself imagine it was her knight in shining armor, the one she had once believed in as a little girl. Of course, she knew it was probably somebody playing a joke on her, but she allowed herself the fantasy just the same.

The notes never came on a regular schedule, though always when she least expected them. They always cheered her up, putting a bounce in her step and boosting her fragile ego. Whoever wrote the letters was a flattering charmer, and a very fond admirer. Maggie knew it was silly. In the back of her mind, she also thought it could be dangerous. But her life needed a little excitement anyway, and her admirer seemed harmless enough.

This time, her mailbox contained only a few trade magazines, unwanted bills, and the usual assortment of fliers and junk mail. But no note. By the sheer anticipation of finding a note, Maggie had succeeded in regaining the good mood she had lost back at the diner. By the time she arrived at the pet store with donuts in hand, she was fully prepared to become "Ms. Proprietor" again.

Since Stacey arrived well before the store opened, the two women had plenty of time to talk. During their conversation, Maggie mentioned Tucker Quinn, and a horrified Stacey shared her eerie feeling about the whole situation. Stacey had witnessed several times the ranting and raving of her boss about the inexcusable destruction perpetrated by some of the degenerates that walked through her door from time to time. The unadulterated horror to which that Quinn boy subjected those helpless animals was inexcusable, and Stacey listened as Maggie vented her frustrations once again.

Stacey had proven to be a good listener, as well as a good friend. Her employment with the pet store was a coincidental instance of being in the right place at the right time. She had gone to the pet store that day to pick up some supplies for her children's rapidly expanding colony of gerbils—a trip she made at least once a month. She walked through Critters' door expecting to leisurely pay for her supplies and have her customary chat with the store's friendly owner. Instead, she found the owner on the floor, frantically mopping up overflowing aquarium water from the floor while several customers impatiently waited to be served. Having watched Maggie hundreds of times before, Stacey grabbed a net and a container and went to work, allowing Maggie to clean the mess and adjust the filter system in the back room. After the job was finished, and the satisfied customers had gone home, Maggie offered Stacey a job.

Leisurely enjoying their coffee and donuts before the hour hand had reached the ten, the two women discussed the death of Tucker Quinn. Debating the uncanny similarities between the boy's death and the death he had inflicted on his sister's guinea pigs, they soon found themselves sharing the very human defense mechanism of humor. Before long, they found themselves doubling over in laughter as theories of dead guinea pig ghosts haunting poor Tucker Quinn grew to ridiculous proportions.

The sound of Hank and Jake knocking at the front door momentarily diverted their laughter. Face aching and tears welling in her eyes, Maggie attempted to straighten herself up before answering the door. She hadn't noticed that the store should have opened ten minutes ago.

"'Bout time you opened!" Hank chastised jokingly. "Is this any way to run a business?" He looked at the two women desperately trying to contain themselves and soon found himself laughing with them without reason. "Wanna tell me what's so funny around here? I could use a good laugh."

"Nothing you men would understand, Hank. You know us girls, getting all giggly over nothing." She felt a small blush wash over her cheeks, either from guilt over making fun of the dead or the fact that Jake followed Hank into the store.

Stacey, eagerly trying to regain composure, then offered the men some donuts. Then, realizing the stereotypical connection between that particular pastry treat and that particular blue uniform, she burst out into hysterical laughter once again. Excusing herself, she went into the back room to tackle the grungy bird unit.

Hank took notice of the awkward smiles and sporadic eye contact being exchanged between Maggie and his partner of the day, and suspected they were more than casual acquaintances by this time. Neither one of them showed any inclination to confide in him about their romantic relationship, although he knew they had been seeing each other for some time. They both insisted, however, that they were merely friends. Whatever the case, Hank was glad that there was someone else in the picture to push Frank out of it.

"So, Jake," Hank said, seizing a golden opportunity, "Did you get a date for the captain's retirement party yet?" Receiving his angry stare and exasperated shake of the head, he followed, "Not much time left, you know. Pretty soon all the good ones will be snatched up." He then gave an exaggerated nod of his head in Maggie's direction, causing them both to blush like a couple of teenagers.

"Don't you have some protecting and serving to do or something," Maggie said, flashing an equally exaggerated furled brow at Hank.

"Okay, okay," Hank said, content that he had done his best as matchmaker for the day. "We're going...jeez what rude service this place has. See if we ever shop here again."

"We're trying to weed out all the lowlifes anyway," Maggie countered, then turned to Jake to ensure that he knew she was kidding. "Good-bye, Jake."

The two men walked out the door just as the first real customers of the day were entering. "Oooh!! Good-byeee, Jakey-pooh!!" Hank mimicked in his best Maggie impersonation, adding a jab to the ribs to his partner. He then gave a familiar wave over his shoulder, and the two men were off to begin their workday.

Maggie had told Hank before that she had no interest in attending the captain's party, although they both knew it wasn't true. Captain Esposito had been one of the original "Three Musketeers" (or "Three Stooges," depending on whom you talked to.) He, Sam, and Hank were the best of friends, members of the same V.F.W. lodge, and shared a hunting lodge in Vermont. Maggie grew up calling him "Uncle Dan."

She also knew she could use a little R&R. She spent far too much time wrapped up with her business that she could hardly remember what a social event was. Besides, how long had it been since she got all dressed up? If for no other reason, she wanted to attend just for the excuse of being with Jake in a social context—a "coming out party" of sorts. After waiting for so long, she even considered asking Jake herself, but in the back of her mind, that scenario did not play well with her deep-seated fantasies. It was getting to the point that she even considered reliving her prom by asking her former prom date, Frank. He could be a little rude and insensitive at times, but deep down she knew he was a good man, and he had always been there for her. In addition, she knew it would be an excellent way to get under Jake's skin. Just as the thought crossed her mind, Frank reported for work through the back door.

"Sorry I'm late," he said. "We got an early shipment at the hardware store, and my father needed an extra hand."

"Not a problem," Maggie replied. "Listen, Frank, I have a question to ask you."

But before she could utter another word, the cowbell over the front door rang, and Jerry Mitchell walked in. Maggie prided herself on being the type of person that is able to get along with everybody, but Mitchell was the type of person that made it impossible to like him. As Mitchell made his way to the back of the store, Frank volunteered to help him. He got no argument from Maggie. A flood of customers began filing into the store soon afterward, and by the time the flood subsided, Maggie had forgotten about her question for Frank.

The following morning, on her daily visit to the post office, Maggie found another note in her box.

CHAPTER 15

Jake listened as Lt. Granger recapped the month's open cases and arrests during Friday morning role call. In particular, he listened with interest that the case of Tucker Quinn had been closed. The contusion on the back of the boy's head was found to be consistent with the way his body had thrashed against the hard tub walls during his violent, jolting seizures. This conclusion eliminated any question of foul play, but it didn't answer why Jake heard the sound of the rooster crowing again at the scene of the boy's fatal accident. Something about the death of that boy just didn't add up.

He felt alone with his own uneasy suspicions. He was either going mad or Worm was trying to tell him something. These crazy thoughts certainly didn't help him concentrate for the approaching detective exam. Passing the exam would mean freedom to investigate these lingering thoughts. With an exasperated shake of his head, he silently admonished Worm to back off.

New business for the day included the anticipated seizure of illegal fireworks from private citizens celebrating the upcoming Fourth of July weekend. The evidence room was already rapidly filling with the confiscated items, although there were some cops who simply kept them for themselves. Oftentimes, off-duty policemen gave the best fireworks shows in the neighborhood. The room was given the standard holiday order to keep a close eye out for DUI's leaving picnics and parties.

Lt. Granger paused, then announced, "A warrant has been processed through the D.A.'s office to pick up Dennis Chapman…again."

The collective voices groaned in unison. The department had been after Chapman for ten years, from suspicions of his involvement in drug trafficking, to child pornography, to pimping and racketeering. Having ties to big-name New York organized crime, he seemed to infest the small town of New Milford like a silent, deadly disease. He always managed to evade the law through legal loopholes fortified by his tenacious, ethically-devoid lawyer, Paul Monsanto.

Hank and Jake were the lucky ones chosen to bring Chapman in once again. Each man had more than enough reason to lock the scumbag behind bars and throw away the key. Chapman was using bribery, coercion, and muscle to slowly take over the town. Stores allegedly approached by Chapman were quickly sold, while others lost merchandise in freak fires. Sam hadn't been immune to the pressure. He mentioned to Hank before he died that Chapman had threatened him, demanding that Sam pay him a fee for "protection." Hank couldn't shake the feeling that Chapman and his friend's untimely death were somehow connected. Recently, Maggie had been approached by Chapman as well. Though he could be a very persuasive man, Maggie refused to be intimidated. She suggested that if he didn't intend to purchase anything in her store, he should leave immediately before she made a phone call to her good friend on the police force. Chapman was persistent, biding his time, using his pet dog as an excuse to infiltrate her life with subtle threats.

Chapman's latest indiscretion included charges of rape and sodomy levied against him by a woman who had been admitted to the hospital the night before. She intended to make a positive identification. Of course, victims and witnesses always had a funny way of changing their minds at the last minute when faced with a court date against Chapman.

On the drive up Candlewood Lake Road, the cruiser was especially quiet except for the low panting of King in the back seat. Hank watched the scenic landscape roll by without his usual sense of appreciation, all the time thinking it could have been Maggie lying in that hospital bed.

Jake broke the silence. "We have to make it stick this time."

"That animal needs to be destroyed, not vacationing in some white-collar cell," Hank snarled.

Chapman's house was more like a mansion. After agreeing they were in the wrong business, they knocked on the door. Chapman graciously allowed himself to be arrested and handcuffed, and was placed very softly in the back seat so as to avoid a police brutality suit. Jake almost wished he had put up a struggle, so he'd have the opportunity to whack the guy and get that smug smirk off of his fat, pockmarked face. His lawyer was waiting for him at the station, and moments later he was waving to the arresting officers with that same pretentious smirk still in place.

* * * *

For a Sunday, and especially a holiday, Maggie noticed the traffic was light as she made her daily jaunt to the pet shop. She hopped out of her SUV, briefcase in hand, and took a moment to enjoy the fluid flight of sea gulls overhead. Almost reluctantly, she turned toward the back door and noticed a box tied with a red ribbon waiting for her at the foot of the door. She placed her briefcase on the ground and examined the box to find no label or card explaining its presence.

She had found many boxes outside her pet store over the years, always containing unwanted pets, but none so exquisitely wrapped as this one. Lightly tracing the bow, she picked it up and found it a little heavy, but there was nothing moving inside. She thought for a moment that it could be a gift from that admirer of hers.

She tore the wrapper like an excited child on Christmas morning, ripping the ribbons of gray paper hastily to expose a generic cardboard box sealed with masking tape. Using the nail of her thumb, she slit the tape and opened the flaps to discover the box was lined with white tissue paper. Carefully, she pulled the paper back and heard herself gasp with the shock of seeing what was inside.

The dead cat had its throat slit, exposing a pink tongue that hung out the side of its gaping mouth. The head was tilted back so far that it seemed to be unattached from its body. Surprisingly, there was very little blood. The eyes were open and glazed with a thin film covering them—the remnants of dried tears. The sight was so horrible and repulsive not only because the animal had died so violently, but also because the animal looked exactly like her cat, Apollo. It had the same orange fur, the same green eyes and the same long, bushy tail. At first, she even thought it was her beloved pet, but this cat did not have the same distinctive green collar with the gold tag. She knew for certain that her Tabby was safe at home. Whoever had committed this brutal, senseless act was truly sick and demented. The message was not entirely clear, however. Should she feel nervous, threatened or afraid? Or should she be thoroughly outraged at the senseless destruction of life in front of her? Whatever the message, the sender had succeeded on all accounts.

Trying desperately to contain her rage, she sealed the box and phoned Hank, but there was no answer. A similar call to Jake's desk produced the same results. In the back of her mind, she thought she knew it had to have been Chapman who left her this gift this morning. This was just another attempt to threaten her into selling out. By the time Jake walked through the door of the pet store, Maggie had convinced herself beyond a shadow of a doubt that it was, in fact, Chapman.

As Maggie described the ghastly scene she encountered that morning, she could sense the rage welling behind Jake's eyes. This time, he told her, Chapman had gone too far. He was always a nuisance, but now he was getting personal, and it was time to put an end to his games once and for all. It was time to pay Mr. Chapman a visit.

Jake tried to appear calm, to reassure Maggie that she was safe. He focused on the large display aquarium in the center of the store and watched the graceful motions of the fish inside. He assured Maggie that Chapman would be apprehended, that the police department would take care of the situation. Somewhere in the middle of his speech, however, he lost his focus. Withdrawing from the peaceful scene inside the tank, Jake stared into his own reflection and saw Worm staring back.

* * * *

Frank had been counting the days to the Fourth of July picnic since Maggie had agreed to accompany him. He looked forward to spending the entire day with Maggie outside of the work environment, and he hoped this would be the perfect opportunity to rekindle some of the old flames they had kindled back in high school. He had planned his strategy like a general going into battle. First, they would spend the day socializing, eating, playing lawn games and all the other corny things people do on that holiday. Then, he would take her for a bike ride on the back roads near his old house. A dirt path would lead them to a special place he knew where he used to take a lot of girls in the old days. It always worked like a charm, and it would surely work on Maggie as well.

When she arrived at his front door, she looked as though she was in no mood for frivolous fun. She explained to him how the gruesome package had been left at her back door that morning, and how Dennis Chapman was behind it. Frank was familiar with Chapman, as he had been one of his many landscaping clients. He had heard plenty of rumors about Chapman's involvement in the mob, but Frank had never had a problem with him. He tried to console Maggie as best he could, and eventually got her to smile by cracking a few jokes.

He had succeeded in taking her mind off the incident until Hank crashed the picnic, in full uniform, after hearing about the incident from Jake. He made his way through the crowd exchanging quick pleasantries, and found Maggie swinging in an old wooden bench swing with Frank. She smiled immediately upon seeing him, and rose from the bench to throw her arms around him.

"I heard what happened, Maggie," Hank told her, "and I want you to know the matter will be taken care of real soon."

"Thanks, Hank," she said, "I appreciate it. I really do. But I hope you don't take offense when I say I'll believe it when I see it."

Hank did, in fact, appear to be a little stung by her words, but kept his emotions in check. "Nah. I can understand that. Listen, I have to go catch some bad guys. You take care of yourself and drive safely—there are a lot of drunks on the road this time of year." And with that, he flashed a knowing glance toward Frank, still sprawled out on the bench with empty beer bottles surrounding him. Years ago, Hank had taken Frank in for DUI, and seemed to take extreme pleasure in administering the field test. Frank vaguely recalled slurring through beer-soaked lips that he could not walk a straight line because of his "trick knee." Of course, he had no ready excuse when he failed to recite the alphabet.

With a wink, Hank motioned toward Frank. "See you on Sunday, Frank," he said with a smile. Frank nodded, raising a soda to his snarling lips. As if it weren't humiliating enough getting nabbed by the old bastard, he also happened to be on his lawn-mowing route. There were advantages to being a cop, for sure.

Later that afternoon, Frank and Maggie hopped on their bikes and headed down the dirt path toward Frank's hidden alcove. Throughout their leisurely ride, Frank imagined the scenario that lay ahead. He envisioned himself unfolding a blanket at the edge of the lake, where he and Maggie would sit and watch the sunlight glistening off the water. He would then lean in and kiss her, and she would return his kiss with unexpected passion. She would confess that she had a crush on him since high school, and had been waiting for this day to come for years. They would then make love on that blanket in the shade, totally isolated from the rest of the world.

That scenario unfolded as planned, right up to the part where he leaned in to kiss her. When he did, Maggie recoiled with a look of surprise on her face. "What are you doing?" she asked.

"Come on, Maggie. You know you want it. Just give in to it." He leaned in once again, and she pushed him away.

At that moment, the thought crossed Frank's mind to force himself upon her. Deep down, he suspected that Maggie was just playing hard to get. He knew she wanted him. He could see it in her eyes. And if she didn't play along, he could handle that as well. They were all alone, hundreds of yards away from the nearest person. She could scream as loud as she wanted and it wouldn't make a difference.

He made another, more aggressive move toward her, and she held him at arm's length, saying, "Frank, think about what you're doing. We have a nice friendship, and a healthy employer/employee relationship. Let's not ruin that."

Frank hesitated for a moment, considering the ramifications of his next action. The humiliating prospect of being led away in handcuffs by Jake and Hank was enough to stop him dead in his tracks. Maggie was now standing, keeping a cautious eye on Frank while scanning her surroundings.

"I'm sorry, Maggie," Frank said, with a look of remorse. "I guess I just got my signals crossed. It won't happen again."

Maggie looked at him in a way that Frank interpreted as pity. "Let's get back to the picnic," she said, walking toward their bikes as Frank gathered up the blanket. They peddled back to the picnic in complete silence, each internally vowing to pretend the events of that afternoon had never happened.

* * * *

He sat in his car watching the darkened house across the street. It was an impressive structure, with its circular driveway, professionally trimmed hedges, and spiral columns, overlooking a gorgeous man-made lake. Hard to imagine one could afford waterfront property just by selling real estate. There was no need to check his source for this mission. This mission had come to him on short notice, but it would be easy. No need to be so creative this time, either. This assignment would be a breeze without the burden of schemes and cover-ups.

This particular piece of human waste was just another link in the food chain—a weak link to be eliminated for the betterment of society. Society was overflowing with these degenerates, and he would see to it that each and every one of them would perish. One by one he'd eliminate every evil being in the world, and pretty soon there would be no need for people like him. He was a human garbage disposal, ridding the earth of all the unwanted trash so that he and his beloved could finally live happily ever after. He was an evil necessity, but a necessity nonetheless.

He would gain access to the house by walking right up to the front door. He had been to the house before, and knew the layout of the place from the inside out. He would spend a few minutes distracting the victim with some conversation while he looked around, ensuring there would be no witnesses. The rest would be a piece of cake. Simply subdue the victim, slash his throat and clean up any trace of evidence. The entire job should last no more than fifteen minutes, tops.

A pair of headlights approached. It was time to get to work.

* * * *

At the Monday morning roll call, Lt. Granger addressed the troops.

"As some of you may already know, the body of Dennis Chapman was discovered early this morning in the living room of his home on the lake. His hands were bound behind his back with common clothesline cord. His neck was slit from ear to ear. It was a clean, professional, gangland-style murder. We are at this time inclined to believe that his death was tied to his underworld connections. We are in the process of conducting a full investigation."

His reply to the standard, "Any questions?" was a room full of suppressed celebration.

* * * *

The next note Maggie found in her post office box was so unlike the others that it almost took her breath away. She stared at the latest note, rereading each line as if she didn't comprehend its meaning the first time. She understood the meaning, all right, but she couldn't believe the same person had written it. She had always pictured the author as being a thoughtful, intelligent person who for one reason or another had trouble expressing himself verbally—a modern-day Cirano DiBergerac. The person who wrote this note, however, was no romantic. He was crude and obscene with his descriptions of her naked body and the strange things he wished he could do to her.

She crushed the note in her hand and put it in the front pocket of her jeans. Either she had two secret admirers, or her old admirer had a split personality. Either way, she found herself frightened by this latest note, and angry that she hadn't put a stop to this sooner. The game had lasted long enough. It was time to get a second opinion.

CHAPTER 16

Maggie received another note shortly thereafter. This time, the note was apologetic in tone, although it was impossible to accept his apology. The damage had been done, and the fantasy had been destroyed. At this point, there was no going back. Whoever penned these letters would eventually learn that she wasn't interested, and soon he would stop sending them. Although the previous letter had been incredibly crude, there was no evidence that the author was a violent man, and therefore no reason to bother Hank or Jake with more of her problems. They were busy enough with more important matters, and she was tired of taking advantage of their relationship. As long as her mystery man remained docile and apologetic, he would not be a threat.

Besides, there were other, more important, matters to deal with in her own life, beginning with the impending Captain's retirement party. After weeks of hesitation, Jake had asked her to accompany him during a routine visit to the pet store. Although he appeared nonchalant, she could sense that he had rehearsed the question several times before asking her. She gave him a bit of a hard time, playfully pretending that she had better things to do that night, before finally accepting. After two years of flirting, she sensed that the night of the dance could prove to be the turning point of their relationship.

* * * *

Jake sat at his kitchen table munching on a cold piece of dry toast, scanning the folded old piece of notepaper in front of him. His list of things to do had all been accomplished except for the two most recent entries. King rested his bulky head on Jake's knee and gave his owner a look that meant he needed to be let out. With the screen door opened, the burly shepherd trotted out to the wire gate of the elaborate kennel in the backyard. The dog waited patiently for his friend to catch up and open the gate, then sped directly to the first tree.

One item on his list had been so severely crossed out in red ink that he almost forgot what had been written underneath. However, upon re-entering his house he noticed an old tire just outside the door that had been converted into a plant holder by Uncle Henry. He kept that memento around to remind him of the good times he had with his uncle in the backyard of that old Cape Cod.

The red-streaked item on his to-do list was a reminder to seek the whereabouts of his mother. As the years passed, however, that connection seemed less and less important to him. Eventually, he crossed out that item altogether. He no longer cared to cross paths with his mother. His need for a family reunion disappeared when he joined the police force, and Hank had become the type of father figure he needed. He was always there for him to provide advice and guidance. He reasoned that if his mother really cared to reunite, she would have sought him out by now.

There were no regrets. Things had progressed nicely. Before the end of the month, he would be a full-fledged detective. He enjoyed his work, and imagined that there were not many people in the world who could make that statement. In a way, he owed a debt of gratitude to Maggie. It was, after all, her tragedy of losing her father that planted the seed that became his career. Maggie was the ideal choice for the penultimate item on his tattered list, "Settle down," and she would also most assuredly provide the missing link for the last item on his list—"Live happily ever after."

As much as he yearned to begin his life with Maggie, he could not bear to let her in knowing that Worm was a part of the package. Worm still held the power to come and go as he pleased, usually when Jake's guard was down. In addition, there was that rooster he heard echoing through his head from time to time. Without a doubt, there were still questions to be answered and ghosts to be exorcised before Maggie could ever be a part of his life.

Jake shook his head, folded the paper into its familiar position, and stuffed it into his shirt pocket. He had time for one more cup of coffee before heading to work. There was no need to tackle these issues now. In time, he knew all of his questions would be answered. In the meantime, he had two weeks to prepare himself for another slow dance with Maggie McCarthy.

* * * *

He had a hard time concentrating on his latest project. With all the interruptions, he found it extremely difficult to keep his train of thought. Of course, he did not have to follow any set schedule. The insufferable matter had been going on for months, yet he felt inclined to handle it swiftly and succinctly before any more harm could be done. He cradled his head in his hands, his fingers grinding against his temples. A passerby noticed his discomfort and offered some aspirin.

"No thanks," he said, "It's just one of those tension things everybody gets after working here a while." He pasted on an oft-practiced, imitation smile, and flipped a good-natured wave of his hand to send the Good Samaritan on her way. The smile bent into a sneer as he continued his business. It was so easy to fool people. Lucky for him, society tended to be gullible. It made his work much easier. Not that he was a villain by any means. In fact, he was doing them all a favor whether they realized it or not.

In his mind's eye he constructed several plans for his next attack. The Mitchells could be considered "Exhibits A and B" if society were on trial for cruelty, dishonesty, and greed, and lately they had become a major source of stress and unhappiness for Maggie. Clearly, the world would be a better place without them. The best approach, most likely, would be to eliminate them one at a time, although the job could also be accomplished by killing two birds with one stone—so to speak. Just then, an idea hit him like a bolt of lightening.

He was correct in his assumptions about the gullibility of people in general, and it would be a tragedy if he didn't utilize that knowledge in a practical manner. Jerry Mitchell would be putty in his hands—molded and smashed by the day's end. Maria Mitchell would meet her maker shortly thereafter. Maybe she and Jerry would arrive at the Gates of Hell together. Then they'd be able to serve their eternal damnation side by side. It was too perfect.

He leaned back in his chair, a genuine smile plastered on his face as he stretched his weary body. His next assignment would be finished by sunrise. In the meantime, he had another duty to fulfill just by being "Mr. Nice Guy."

"Which I am," he said to the empty room, "I just happen to be a super nice guy."

*   *   *   *

Jake's police cruiser slowly made its way down Route 7. It had been a slow day—a couple of traffic violations and an old lady locked out of her car just about summed up his morning activities. King paced in the back seat, occasionally stopping when something caught his attention. His mind was cluttered lately with the impending detective exam, crowing rooster ghosts, and the Captain's party on the horizon.

Spotting Hank's cruiser parked in an empty lot next to a busy gas station, Jake swerved in to unload some emotional baggage. If nothing else, a conversation with Hank always put things into perspective. He had proven to be an astute listener in the past. Rolling to a stop, Jake noticed that Hank had his head down, writing on a pad of paper that he quickly tossed to the side when he noticed he had a visitor.

"Hey, kid. What's up? King need to take a walk, or did he already leave you a gift on the back seat?"

"Just seeing what kind of trouble you're causing," Jake replied, ignoring Hank's comment about his dog. One little incident a long time ago and the dog was branded for life.

"Nothing much going on today, partner. It's been kinda slow, so I just thought I'd catch up on some paper work." Hank paused, taking a sip of coffee. "Speaking of paper work, how's the studying going for that test of yours?"

"I'm slowly plowing through it. There's a lot of shit to know. By the time I'm done, I can be a friggin' lawyer. Of course, if I don't pass, I might have to quit my job and become a professional pool player." Jake gave Hank a sly wink, referring to the week before when he had thoroughly embarrassed the old man by beating him five games straight.

"Yeah, well don't quit your day job, sonny-boy. You haven't seen the last of me," Hank rebutted.

"Hey—whenever you find yourself with a little too much cash on you, you know where to find me," Jake replied chidingly. He then paused for a moment, letting the question form in his mind before unleashing it upon Hank. He had never before discussed the subliminal crowing that plagued his mind from time to time, and he wasn't certain he should ever discuss it. After all, it was all so crazy. Still, if there were anyone to whom he could talk about this, it was Hank.

"Let me ask you something, old man," Jake began.

"Shoot."

"Have you ever had a gut feeling, a tiny little voice inside your head, telling you something just wasn't right?"

"You mean like intuition? Sure, all good cops have it."

"No, no," Jake said, looking away, "That's not exactly what I meant…" Jake faded away, unsure whether to come right out and say it. *Am I the only one who hears it?* he wondered. He was about to dismiss the subject when a 1145 call came over his radio to proceed to Bank Street for a domestic disturbance. "Hey, never mind," he said to Hank, flipping on his lights, "Gotta run!"

And with that, Jake sped out of the lot, leaving Hank with a perplexed look on his face.

* * * *

Maggie hid behind the counter, watching the clock slowly inch its way toward three o'clock. It had been a very difficult morning, and she couldn't wait for help to arrive. She had been left to face a barrage of angry customers all day long, and she was looking forward to redirecting some of their anger to someone else for a while. The only thing she took solace in was that they weren't angry with her or her establishment.

Mitchell's Menagerie opened several months ago in a nearby town. They were a husband and wife team who seemed more intent on driving Maggie out of business than caring for their own. Hank had informed her a while back that Mitchell's Menagerie was suspected of being a front for Chapman's import business. Drugs were smuggled in with shipments of live animals from various parts of Mexico and South America. Chapman had envisioned Critters as a part of this scheme as well, but someone got to him before he had the chance to complete that plan. It was Hank's theory that the rival pet store's main objective was to squeeze Maggie out of business.

Maggie knew immediately that the Mitchells knew virtually nothing about animals. Irate customers flocked to Critters with strange questions and tales of their experiences with the Mitchells. The Mitchells seemed more than just ignorant. At times, they seemed downright insidious, giving customers bad advice just to make a quick buck. This type of practice went totally against everything upon which Maggie had built her reputation. The Mitchells shared blatant disregard for their animal's welfare, and Maggie became increasingly enraged with each horrendous tale brought into her store.

"Think of it this way," Frank offered upon arriving. "The Mitchells are doing us a favor by turning off so many people. Customers aren't stupid, you know. If they get bad service or bad advice somewhere, they always go somewhere else. And after visiting the Menagerie, we certainly look pretty good in comparison."

"You always have a way of putting things in perspective," Maggie said with a smile. "Thanks."

She flashed him another smile and headed to the back room. He watched intently as she disappeared down the aisle. Once she was out of sight, he withdrew a flask from the inner pocket of his jacket and took a healthy swig.

* * * *

Dear Dad:

Well, another busy day. Busy with problems, not busy taking money. We end up okay, though. A whole lot of water testing (we should really charge for those, you know). A lot of dead or dying pets I can't seem to do anything about...the damage already done and out of my control. I've told you before about the unscrupulous behavior of the Menagerie, but they seem to be getting worse every day with their flippant attitudes. Not caring in the least what they tell people about buying anything from them. Half the time I think they enjoy sending the little creatures out to face certain death. Customers being fed so much misinformation it'll take months to straighten them out.

It's not the competition I hate, Dad, it's the bad name they give us all in the profession that's so hard to deal with. I mean, who can these people trust when the advice and opinions vary so much? You told me a long time ago not to try and fix the whole universe with all the problems out there. Just try to fix my little corner. I'm trying, but it sure gets frustrating. I know I'm going on and on. The Mitchells have certainly filled their share of pages in here.

I know it's crazy, Dad, but I can't help but think they were responsible for Rocky's death. I really feel they somehow poisoned him, to scare me into selling out. I know they used to come in to the store and spy around—or send others to do the spying. I just have no proof. On that note, I think I ought to get out of here before Jake drives by again and thinks I really don't have a life outside of this store. Jake and Frank are a whole other mess...so tell Mom I'll be writing to her later!

Love, Maggie

* * * *

He patiently sat in his parked car and waited for his appointment with the Devil himself. It hadn't been hard convincing the moron to meet with him so late at night. After all the planning he was a little disappointed that the man had taken the bait so easily. Part of the fun would have been hooking him and savoring the struggle on the other end of the line before reeling him in.

Submit this as yet another example that people were indeed ready and willing targets, just begging to be taken advantage of. The plan this time was simple. He placed a phone call saying he was the embittered ex-boyfriend of the little tramp at the pet store, and he'd like nothing better than to see her crumble. He had a secret, he told him—a well-buried, well-kept secret that would surely destroy her reputation and, in the process, her business. Of course, he couldn't tell him over the phone. Which is why he was waiting for him there in his parked car, with a half-emptied thermos of Southern Comfort in the passenger seat.

He poured a shot into his mug and quickly swilled it down. The sucker would be here any minute, right on schedule, he imagined. It would be only hospitable to offer him a drink. He opened his hand and regarded the capsules held there. How many should he use? Should the man go quickly or very, very slowly?

Checking his watch, he noticed his victim was late. So much for the decision-making. He would have to go quickly. He broke open four capsules and poured each one into the thermos. He slowly stirred the white powder until the scent of almonds reached his nose.

Headlights approached and were quickly doused as the victim finally pulled into the vacant lot. The fool eagerly hopped into the passenger seat, and after an initial decline, was finally persuaded to share a drink. It was over much too soon. The bastard deserved to suffer a little more. There were just a few convulsions, his face turned blue as he gasped for air, and he had a stupid, confused look in his eyes as the killer calmly sipped from his mug.

The man was a little heavier than he had imagined. He struggled with the dead man's limp body as he lifted it from his car, placing it behind the wheel of his own car. He reached out to close the man's eyes, wondering if their expression would give away his demise. He gave him a light pat on the head.

"So long, Jerry. See you in Hell."

He actually found he had worked up a sweat as he erased any heel marks left on the surface of tar between the two vehicles. Removing his surgical gloves, he fiddled with the radio until he found a station that played an "oldie but a goodie." The digital clock on his dashboard showed only a half hour had passed. The night was still young enough to pass by her house. There was always a chance he could be rewarded with another sight of her framed by her picture window. First, he needed a drink. Unfortunately, the damn thermos was now contaminated. Maybe he'd see her tomorrow and go home for a quick one, instead.

* * * *

The songs of crickets and bullfrogs filled his idle car. The usual static from the radio could barely be heard below the cadence of the tiny creatures inhabiting the field in the back of the deserted lot. In the distance, barely audible at first, another resonant voice joined in the symphony. With each refrain of the wild chorus it seemed to grow closer. It slowly overpowered the other noises surrounding him until it became the only sound he heard.

Jake swiveled his head in all directions in search of the source of this noise, but there was nothing in sight. The reverberating din filled both ears and rattled inside his head. He brought his hands up to muffle the sound penetrating his eardrums, but the noise continued louder than ever. He recognized this sound, although it had never before been so clear and persistent. It was the sound of a rooster crowing, followed by the calling of his name.

The crowing gradually dissolved with each shake of his head, but the calling still came until he realized it was coming from the radio. Shaken, Jake tried to regain his composure as he responded to the dispatcher. He managed to control whatever demon had possessed him by the time he reached the scene. But the demon reappeared when he saw a very dead Jerry Mitchell sitting sedately behind the wheel of his car.

CHAPTER 17

Frank woke to a strange sound coming from the next room. In fact, the bed seemed strange to him, also, as well as the bedroom he found himself scanning through cloudy eyes. He vaguely remembered the room from the night before, although he could not remember exactly how he got there. He tried to raise his head from the pillow, but rose too quickly and the room began to spin. He summoned familiar willpower to avoid vomiting, raising his hands to his temples.

As he attempted to piece together the previous night's events, he lifted the sheets over him to verify that he was indeed naked. Further investigation of the room confirmed that a rollicking good time must have occurred, as clothes were strewn about the room.

"I'm never drinking again," he murmured through a chalky mouth. He always hated these times, not knowing whom the mystery woman in the other room was. He could hear her gleefully singing in the shower. There were no pictures on the wall, no photos on the table or dresser.

The sound of the shower stopped, as did the singing. The time had come to reveal the mystery woman. Hopefully, she would give him enough time to escape out the front door, or even the window—something he had done in the past. Every time he attempted to lift his head, however, that nauseous feeling came over him, dragging his tired body back into bed. He brought the sheet over his head, unable to face the woman as she entered the room.

"What's the matter, sleepy head?" she asked, playfully. "Got a little hangover, or are you just tired from all the screwing around?" He could hear her chuckle, along with the opening and closing of dresser drawers. Through the sheet, he could faintly make out the outline of a body. She was slim, with short hair, and long legs. He slowly peeked over the sheet.

She turned her head slightly to look in the mirror, checking if he was still playing hide-and-seek or if he was watching the show. Finding she had his attention, her movements became slow and deliberate. Facing her reflection, she slid her hands erotically up her body and sensuously cupped her breasts.

Frank was so involved with appreciating the seductive dance of the woman, he hadn't bothered to look at her face. As she slowly turned to tempt him further, he finally recognized the woman. He even began to remember the evening of wild sex they shared the night before.

As she approached the end of the bed, she placed her thumbs inside the elastic of her panties, playfully teasing him by slowly drawing one side, then the other, a little lower each time. By this time, Frank was fully awake, watching her full breasts sway with the movement of her strip tease. Alert and aware now of who she was, he was tempted to get up and refuse to repeat the mistake he had obviously made the night before. His body, however, wouldn't allow him to escape.

Sleeping with the good widow Mitchell under the influence was one thing, but now it would be a conscious decision. As he looked into her eyes, he remembered the woman had her reasons that night, and so did he. It seemed reasonable for a man to console a woman after suffering such a loss. Besides, she didn't seem to miss him that much.

* * * *

The Captain's retirement party loomed on the horizon like a dark, ominous cloud. It wasn't that Jake feared an evening with Maggie and Hank and his friends at the precinct. Instead, the fear that welled within him originated from his fear of crowds. It was this fear that crept over him when he was a timid, fragile boy, nervously reciting essays in front of a snickering classroom. He would listen to his own voice quiver and crack, and cold beads of sweat would drip down his sides from under his arms. He could hear the whispering and when he would occasionally pry his eyes from the shaking paper in front of him, he would see the contorted faces of his classmates attempting unsuccessfully to contain their laughter.

Jake thought his experiences in the army would extinguish those fears forever. The heightened self-confidence he gained from that experience did help, but the persistent feeling he felt as a child would often return, often without cause or warning. In uniform, Jake was able to confront any number of people without fear. The uniform gave him uncontested respect. But out of uniform, the fear would return. As Jake sat in his parked car outside of the flower shop, he contemplated feigning illness to avoid the situation entirely. The fear would never leave him, however, unless he continued to confront it. He opened his door and entered the small shop.

Carrying his orchid purchase out to his car, he noticed Beannie's empty cruiser parked on the opposite side of the Green. Seeing the opportunity to kill a little more time before the party that night, Jake made his way up the sidewalk and past the bandstand, searching the storefronts for the man in uniform.

He stopped at the edge of the curb, waving past cars that slowed down to let him cross. Scanning the faces of people walking on the sidewalk across the street, Jake was surprised at how many he recognized. In the relatively short period he had been back in the small town, he had connected with many people's lives in one way or another.

He spotted Bean near the drug store, engaging in an animated conversation with the manager of the town's only movie theater. A woman left the drug store at that moment and walked in front of the two men. Jake watched as she hesitated at the curb, then crossed over to her waiting car. She waited by the door, then turned to look slowly up the Green and back. She fumbled in her purse and emerged with a pair of sunglasses, which she wore as she unlocked her door.

As she backed out of her spot, a wave of recognition suddenly washed over Jake. He found himself staring at the woman almost involuntarily, as if his mind wouldn't allow his eyes to leave her until the evasive itch in the back of his memory had been satisfied. There was no way of knowing for certain, but the association he made was perfectly clear. He felt compelled to run after the blue rental car and yank the driver from the front seat, if only to confirm that she was not the person he thought she was. Just then, Beannie spotted Jake frozen to the curb and yelled out his name.

*   *   *   *

Maggie turned on the shower and flicked her wrist under the running water to gauge the temperature. Waiting for the water to heat before she threw her entire body under the spray, she impatiently moved her hand quicker and quicker under the stream. She became aware of what she was doing, and found it funny that somewhere in her cluttered mind she actually believed that moving her hand faster would speed the heating process of the water, and with this recognition she laughed out loud. She was in a good mood for a change. It had been a long time since she took time off from the pet store. She almost felt guilty leaving Stacey and Frank to handle the hassles of cranky customers and messy animals, but she got over it quickly. Tonight was her night.

Both Stacey and Frank seemed to have something on their minds, though they didn't seem to have any desire to discuss it with her. Frank simply dismissed any inquiries with false apathy. Stacey seemed to be on the verge of tears most of the afternoon, but was unwilling to discuss her problem. Whatever was bothering them, they did their best to cover their feelings so that Maggie could feel comfortable leaving them and enjoy her night.

As she stroked her soapy legs with a fresh razor, Maggie considered her apparel for the evening. She planned to wear her hair up in a tight French braid, since it seemed to go with the original dress she had picked out. But the skimpy red dress Stacey lent to her caused a drastic change of thought. Attending a formal function in such a daring dress may be appropriate for someone like Stacey, but Maggie felt the dress was a little too wild for her taste.

Stacey advised her to throw caution to the wind and seize the opportunity to make everyone's head turn—including Jake's. Frank simply nodded his approval when asked his opinion. As she stepped out of the shower, she determined that she would at least try on the dress before settling for the original.

She eyed the dress lying on her bed and tentatively walked toward it, letting her towel drop to the floor. Uncertain of what undergarments were needed, she pulled the dress over her damp head and rocked it over her shoulders and hips. She hesitantly raised her head and peered into the mirror. It didn't look so bad. She angled slightly to one side, and then the other, noticing how the dress hugged every curve on her body. The bodice was so tight it pushed her breasts up and over the top. But swaying just a little, she surmised that the movement of the skirt would divert the eyes to a lower location.

Although the dress was relatively new, it was fashioned after an older style. In fact, catching her full reflection, she seemed to be a different person. The dress, the face, the hair, all came together in such a familiar way that she found herself digging through some old picture albums. Cracking the yellowing pages, she came across the picture she had seen in her mind as she looked at herself. There they were, Mom and Dad, on their way to the senior prom. They were so young, yet so dignified and elegant. The dress was a little longer, and the style was slightly different, but for the most part she was the spitting image of the pretty young girl in the picture with the long, blonde hair and the red dress.

If she had any doubts about wearing the dress before, they vanished the moment she found the old picture tucked away in the family album. With her hair down and a little makeup she might almost be as beautiful as her mother, twenty-five years ago. The smile on her father's face showed how proud he was to have such a beautiful woman on his arm that night, and she hoped she'd see that same smile when Jake came to pick her up.

Jake pulled his freshly washed car into Maggie's driveway, checking himself once more in the mirror. He smiled when Worm wasn't looking back at him. He decided to confront the evening with a positive attitude, and so far he was succeeding. He walked to the front door, feeling strangely nervous, like a schoolboy picking up his first date. He rang the doorbell, and then stood frozen in his spot when Maggie answered. She was absolutely stunning, a bold contrast to the denim-and-t-shirt look to which he had grown accustomed. She wore a radiant smile on her face, and he found himself speechless as he handed her a corsage without saying a word. She invited him inside, and he finally found his voice.

"You are absolutely beautiful, Maggie," he said, unable to divert his gaze.

"Thank you," she said, blushing slightly. "You don't look so bad yourself." They shared an awkwardly quiet moment as they searched for something to say. Finally, Maggie asked if he was ready to go.

"By all means," Jake answered, offering his arm in an exaggerated pose.

* * * *

Stacey hung up the phone after the first ring. After the argument she had with her husband the night before, she promised herself that she wouldn't make the first move. It had been a quiet evening with very few customers browsing through the store, and the work had been done for the most part. She found herself pacing the aisles most of the evening, looking for dust or misplaced items on the shelves, trying to occupy her mind with something other than her marital problems.

Frank was unusually quiet, avoiding Stacey either out of respect for her privacy, or because of some personal problems of his own. After a full day of wrestling with the issue herself, she needed someone to debate the issue. She had been struggling with the possibility that her husband was having an affair, and she felt herself drowning in self-doubt, anger, and fear.

The phone rested in front of her and she willed it to ring. It would be Michael, denying her accusations and begging her to come home. Just then, the phone rang, and after tentatively picking it up, Stacey replied, "Six o'clock," and slammed the phone into the cradle.

* * * *

Frank knew it was a little early to be feeding the fish, usually the last chore of the day before the store closed. But he ran out of things to do hours ago, and he was driving himself mad thinking about Maggie's romantic evening with Jake Allen. There was still an hour to go before he could get the hell out of there and head to the nearest bar. He watched as a hungry Oscar devoured another goldfish, and he mentally morphed the helpless goldfish into tiny Jake Allens. The foreboding, fearsome Frank fish chased the scared little Jake fish into a corner and swallowed his prey. Frank let out a small belch and laughed to himself. He thought about heading to the front of the store to hang out with Stacey, but she didn't seem to be in a very good mood, either. Then again, he thought, misery does love company.

* * * *

The gala event to honor Captain Esposito for all his years of service to the community was touted in the local papers as the most festive event of the year. Hundreds of friends, fellow police officers, and assorted V.I.P.'s gathered together to bid the captain a fond farewell, to offer advice, and to roast him one last time.

Jake and Maggie appeared at the entrance and, wading through an ocean of whispers, stares, and smiles, approached the man of the hour. They waited patiently as the captain talked with his son, David, who happened to play for the band performing that night. Maggie whispered to Jake that she knew David as a kid, and was surprised to see he was doing so well considering how radical he had been as a youth. To David's right, Maggie continued, was the Captain's oldest son Mike, who was a star catcher in high school. He played a few years in the minor leagues, she whispered, grasping Jake's arm and leaning in so that Jake could smell her perfume. Jake paused, closing his eyes to capture the moment in his memory.

Captain Esposito shared some embarrassing stories with Jake about Maggie's childhood, and was rewarded with a rosy blush washing over her delicate face. The happy couple continued through the crowd, making rapid progress exchanging social pleasantries with one couple after another, until they came to the Mayor, Maurice Brandon, and his wife, Patricia, who were transplanted from Memphis years ago. Their slow southern drawl slowed the pace of the evening and allowed Jake and Maggie to relax. They stood hand in hand, enjoying the moment, proud to be in each other's company.

Maggie was the first to see Hank enter the room with a tall woman on his arm. As she and Jake shared their first dance of the night, she took her time in assessing Hank's date before she informed Jake of his friend's arrival. The woman appeared to be in her late forties, and seemed to carry herself quite well. Her dark hair was swept away from her face. Her elegant black dress complimented her large dark eyes. She seemed almost regal, and Maggie watched curiously as Hank introduced her around the room.

Hank surveyed the room before his eyes rested on the couple in the middle of the dance floor. Immediately, he was drawn into another time, to another place where he stood away from the crowd with feelings of anguish and regret washing over him, drowning out the music and the laughter. Though he had a date of his own, he felt all alone the night of his senior prom. He watched from the shadows as Sam and Allison danced together on their special night. He knew somewhere deep inside that it could just as easily be his big night instead. He felt nauseous, either from his prolonged struggle that night to contain his tears or from the liquor he had consumed that night to drown his sorrows. As he returned to the present, he realized that the need for a drink had returned.

He led his date to the bar and ordered a drink for each of them. On the dance floor, Jake lowered Maggie into a dramatic dip at the end of the song. As the next song began, Maggie led Jake off the dance floor and approached the small gathering around the bar. She released her hold on Jake long enough to tap Hank on the shoulder, then blindly reached back to Jake again. She needed Jake for moral support, in case Hank found her silly to be dressed the way she was. But her hand found nothing but air as she fumbled around to make contact. Turning her head, she saw Jake a few feet away, slouched with his head down and his eyes turned upward, looking like a little child.

Hank interrupted her with a kiss to her cheek, and told her how beautiful she looked. He proceeded to introduce her to his date, Ida Adams, but when Maggie turned to introduce her to Jake, he had disappeared.

* * * *

By the time Frank reached the front counter, he discovered Stacey was weeping behind the counter, next to the phone. Upon approaching her, Stacey threw her arms around him, burying her face in his shoulder. He wrapped his arms around her, checking the outside of the store for approaching customers. After slowly peeling herself from him, Stacey apologized for her behavior. She then proceeded to confide the details to Frank, from the beginning. She told him about the late nights her husband supposedly put in at work, how her phone calls went unanswered when she'd call the office, and how she found motel receipts in his jacket pocket. She explained how her husband had denied the entire episode, had accused her of mistrust, and had threatened to leave her.

"It's all my fault, Frank," she said, "I wasn't giving him what he needed, I guess. If only I were younger and more attractive. He doesn't want me anymore, Frank. He doesn't need me. Hell, my kids need me less and less every day. What am I going to do?" She raised her eyes to look at Frank, knowing he couldn't supply the answers, but was glad he was there just the same. "I'm sorry, Frank. I don't know why I'm burdening you with all of this."

"None of this is your fault, Stacey. If something's going on here, then your husband is absolutely crazy. Whether you want to admit it or not, you are a very attractive and desirable woman. Any man would be lucky to have you."

Stacey looked away, desperately trying to embrace her self-pity. Frank grabbed her shoulders and turned her to face him.

"You are a very special woman, Stacey. Don't let anyone tell you otherwise," he said. "And as far as you getting older, well...you don't look a day over fifty," he grinned.

Stacey smiled a bit, and he gave her a playful hug. Without a thought, he kissed her gently on the cheek. Instinctively, almost unconsciously, he moved to her lips. Soon they were locked in a deep, passionate embrace. He held her tightly until he felt her body relax against his own, her arms wrapping around his body as she returned his embrace. Oblivious to their surroundings, the potential danger of being seen through the darkness into the well-lit store, they explored each other with their hands and mouths until the ringing of the phone interrupted them.

Suddenly, they both became acutely aware of the situation. Guilt replaced passion as Stacey ran to the back room while Frank answered the phone. He was surprised to hear his father's voice. He listened as his father relayed the news of a story a friend had told him. The friend recently returned from the captain's retirement party, and told his father of the spectacle Maria Mitchell made of herself that night, at Maggie's expense. Knowing Frank's connection to Maggie, he decided to give his son a call to warn him that Maggie might need a friend that night.

Frank thanked his father, and then hung up the phone. He hadn't heard a word his father said, as his mind was cluttered with the task of sorting out exactly what had just occurred. There had been sexual tension between he and Stacey before, but he never imagined they would ever act upon it. He smiled, determining it hadn't been so bad after all, and was pleasantly surprised when he turned to see Stacey returning his smile. They both knew it wouldn't happen that night. Stacey slid by Frank at the front counter, looking like a naughty schoolgirl. She emptied the register and asked Frank to turn out the lights and lock the doors. They left separately, without saying a word, but their eyes told them their affair would continue at another time.

* * * *

Jake leaned against a large oak tree outside of the hall, another wave of vomit reaching his throat. He searched the dark woods through watery eyes, looking for a place to hide, to catch his breath in solitude. His mind reeled with swelling confusion. He contemplated whether to abandon the event entirely, to drive home and lock himself indoors, and to worry later about explaining his behavior to his date. If he had any doubts about the ghost he had seen earlier in the day, driving away in a blue rental car, they were washed away the moment he saw his mother standing arm-in-arm with Hank.

He had looked directly into those eyes and knew immediately who she was. A flood of memories washed over him the moment their eyes met. He remembered all those lonely nights waiting for her to come home after his father died. He remembered the way she looked that day when she dropped him off at Uncle Henry's. He remembered being angry with her for not looking more upset than she did that day. In fact, he remembered she looked almost relieved to be finally rid of her burden.

This time, however, he saw something very strange in her eyes. She did not look upset or mournful or sympathetic or even apathetic. She looked at him through the eyes of a stranger. He could see no flicker of recognition behind her eyes, indicating she hadn't the faintest idea who he was. She could not even recognize her own son.

The surprise assault took his breath away. Then came the pain in the pit of his stomach. The self-discipline he thought he had mastered became less effective as Worm began to force his way through his subconscious. It was only after he screamed out loud that he felt more in control.

The fear drained from his body, and was replaced with defiant anger. He decided to return to the party, to wear his best plastic smile, and to act as though his mother was as much a stranger to him as he was to her. She obviously had buried him years ago, and now it was his turn to bury her.

Maggie sensed something had changed in her date, although he denied there was anything wrong. He just needed a breath of fresh air, he explained. He shook his mother's hand and, through clenched teeth, spat, "It's a pleasure to meet you, Ida." If there was any hint of recognition behind those empty eyes, she hid it very well.

Jake continued his act of indifference toward the woman in the black dress, for the sake of his date, who appeared to be having a wonderful time until Maria Mitchell strolled through the doors accompanied by her lawyer. Maria may have had many reasons to attend the event, but it seemed she had only one thing on her mind. Without a glance toward her chaperone, Mr. Monsanto, Maria ignored the whispers and finger-pointing as she walked unsteadily toward Maggie, who stood alone as she waited for Jake to return with their drinks.

Maria Mitchell was blatantly drunk. Maggie could smell the booze on her breath as the woman faced her, swaying slightly as she attempted to right herself. An awkward silence fell over the room as Maria spoke.

"It's so good to see you, Maggie," she slurred, "especially in that gaudy dress, which exposes you as the whore you really are. I understand you're dating a cop. Is he a special client, or are your services free to all cops? By the way, Frank gives his regards. It seems you weren't woman enough to satisfy him, so he came to me."

Maggie attempted to walk away, but Maria grabbed her arm tightly and squeezed.

"I'm not finished, young lady!" she laughed, "Lady...what a joke! You're a farce! Your whole life is a farce," she spat, her words echoing through the hushed hall. "I always knew you gave many services in that business of yours, Ms. McCarthy, but I didn't know murder was one of them. I have to admit, it's a novel way to get rid of the competition. We should have thought of it ourselves. That bird thing was nothing compared to this."

By this time, her lawyer was holding her hands behind her back in an attempt to drag the woman from the place. Maria no sooner mentioned the bird than Maggie struck her with an open palm. The sound of her hand slapping against Maria's face was followed by a collective gasp from the assembled crowd. Jake grabbed Maggie from behind, while Hank jumped between the two women.

Maria looked horrified at first, but soon an evil grin appeared on her rosy face. She laughed an insidious cackle as her lawyer dragged her from the hall.

"You see?" she cried, "Did everyone see that? That bitch has a mean temper! Don't get in her way, or she might just kill you, too!" The door slammed and an eternity seemed to pass where all eyes converged on the wild-eyed look of the young woman being restrained in the center of the room. The band attempted to restore order by playing a soft tune, and soon people began to talk amongst themselves in hushed tones.

The ride home was quiet. Maggie turned her back to Jake, staring out the window in silence, while Jake pondered the strange events of the evening. What was supposed to be a wonderful evening filled with happiness and romance turned out to be an evening filled with confusion and pain. What was his mother doing in New Milford? Why had she returned? Was she planning on staying? If so, how could he avoid her? Or should he confront her and demand that she tell him why she left him so many years ago?

As for Maria Mitchell, it was apparent the woman was suffering a great deal from the loss of her husband. She had no right to say those cruel things to Maggie, especially in the company of so many people. Maggie, however, had no right to strike her, especially in the company of Maria's lawyer. Perhaps that was Maria's plan the whole time—to push Maggie so far that she would retaliate in front of hundreds of witnesses. She would slap her with a lawsuit, claim whiplash, and sue her for everything she owned—including, of course, Critters Pet Store.

The car coasted to a stop in front of Maggie's lawn. They sat in silence, each bearing the weight of the evening's events. Outside the car, the song of crickets could be heard, floating through the air on a warm summer breeze. Still facing the window, Maggie broke the silence.

"I'm sorry our night was ruined, Jake. I was hoping this night would be the start of something, but…" Her words drifted off as her voice cracked beneath the strain.

"Don't let her win, Maggie. She went there tonight to hurt you, and you're letting her do that," he said, hoping to appeal to Maggie's stubborn Irish ego. "Is there anything I can do to help?" he asked.

"No," she replied, still facing the window.

"Anything at all? I could make you a nice hot chocolate to help you sleep. Or a nice massage to relieve some of that tension. How about boxing lessons? After seeing that left hook, I'd say you have a future. Or maybe you can have me kill someone else for you. I mean, why stop at poor Mr. Mitchell?"

He could see her shoulders begin to shake, and he knew he had gotten to her. He could hear her trying desperately to contain her snickering, but after delivering a few tickling fingers to her side, the laughter erupted.

"Stop it!" she squealed. "Don't ruin my bad mood!" She looked at him through glassy eyes and kissed him lightly on the lips. She gave him a deep hug, crushing her red dress. "Thank you," she whispered, and kissed him again. She smiled through dancing blue eyes, a dimple forming on her left cheek. "I'll see you tomorrow?" He nodded, returning her smile, and she bound out the door, fumbling in her purse for her keys. He watched as she opened the door to her house. She turned once more and waved, hesitating for a moment on the front steps. She was a vision of beauty, bathed in moonlight, her red dress accenting each soft curve of her body. She bit her bottom lip, waved once more, and disappeared through the door.

* * * *

Maria Mitchell had signed her own death warrant, a little earlier than planned. The original plan was to make her wait; to make her suffer; to watch her fear for her life. The bitch wasn't conforming to the plan, so her period of grace was over. Her death row march had begun, and no reprieve from a higher authority would save her now.

He'd wait all night if he had to. She had to come home sooner or later. He sat on an old bar stool near the back of her darkened garage, gently tipping a bottle of clear liquid in one hand and squeezing a roll of cloth in the other. At the sound of an approaching car, headlights shining through the paneled windows, he slowly stood up and vanished into the darkness beside an old upright freezer. The motor controlling the automatic door whirred into motion, lifting the heavy door, and the front of her car rolled inside. He waited for the sound of an opening door. Seconds passed, and he heard nothing.

He peered slowly around the corner of the freezer. Through the darkness of the garage, he could see the interior of the car back lit by the street lamp from the end of the driveway. There was a shadow of a woman hunched over the steering wheel.

He slowly emerged from his hiding place and approached the car. The woman's head was now tilted back against the headrest, mouth gaping open, and he could see it was his victim. He briefly pondered how she had managed to find her way home without wrapping herself around a telephone pole, then considered himself lucky that she hadn't. He had been looking forward to taking care of this one personally. Recent events only added fuel to that fire.

He paused to examine the woman's sleeping face. A faint snoring noise emanated from her nostrils. She was deep asleep under a booze-induced anesthesia.

He recognized it all too well. There would be no need for the chloroform, he determined. It was best to leave as little evidence as possible, anyway. Reaching past her with gloved fingers, he started the engine. On the way out the door, he pushed the button lowering the garage door. As the door closed, he peered through the dirty windows lining the top of the door. He smiled and waved as exhaust filled the room.

Poor woman. So distraught by the death of her husband, so irrational under the influence of alcohol, she sat in her parked car in an enclosed garage and committed suicide. Or maybe she was just so plastered that she forgot to turn off the engine. Either way, it was certainly a shame.

* * * *

The next morning found each of the players in life's roulette game waking up separately, but sharing feelings of unrest. Thoughts invaded their sleep throughout the night with each tick of the clock.

Jake was afraid to sleep, fearing that if he let his subconscious take over, Worm would take over his mind completely. He tried to convince himself that one woman could not undo all the progress he had made through the years. One woman could not tear down everything he had built—not when he was so close to accomplishing all the goals on his life's to-do list.

She had created him, and now she appeared to be on the verge of destroying him. He tried to focus, instead, on Maggie, and the good time they were having last night before the intrusion of that ghost from his past. He thought of how beautiful Maggie looked. Then he thought of the tall woman that left him at the door of the Cape Cod. He thought of the confrontation between Maggie and Maria. He thought of the confrontation between Worm and himself. He could feel Worm getting stronger by the day, and he could feel himself growing weaker. Maybe he would see Maggie today. But what would happen if he saw the other woman in his life as well?

* * * *

Maggie awoke without the alarm. She lay in bed thinking she hadn't slept a wink all night, yet she didn't have the energy to get up. The night had been everything she had wished for until that drunken Maria woman showed up. Maggie could not figure out what she ever did to that woman to deserve such vehemence and hatred. The things she said were so cruel, she could not imagine ever saying such things to anyone, no matter how awful she felt or how many drinks she had.

She decided to confront Frank, to find out what he knew about this woman. What was his connection to her, and how did Maggie get involved? Though she believed Frank was a good man deep down inside, she wasn't entirely sure she could trust him. He had been acting very strangely of late, and he had some explaining to do.

* * * *

Hank tossed and turned all night as well, berating himself for not sticking up for Maggie sooner. He had just stood there, dumbfounded by the spectacle of the drunken widow Mitchell, just like everyone else in the place. If he had it to do over again, he would have stepped between the two women and slapped Maria Mitchell across the face himself.

Aside from that ugly scene, his date with Ida went well. He hadn't heard from her in years, and was pleasantly surprised when he received her phone call a few days earlier, asking if she could meet with him. It had been so long since their brief fling that he had almost forgotten all about her. She looked good for a woman her age, and he regretted not inviting her back to his place after the event. His mind just wasn't on romance at the time.

* * * *

Frank slowly opened his eyes, afraid that he might not be waking up in his own bed. Breathing a sigh of relief at the familiar surroundings, he recalled his encounter with Stacey last night. He had no regrets, and wondered if Stacey felt the same as she woke up in her own bed. He wondered whether it would be wise to pursue that relationship any further, or whether he should just pretend nothing had happened. Stacey was a grown woman. She knew what she was doing. And if she wanted to use Frank to get back at her husband, that was just fine with Frank.

He debated whether or not to call her, but decided that it would be best to wait it out. Better to let her come to him. He'd be happy to follow her lead, whichever road she chose to take. Either way, he was just killing time waiting for Maggie to realize what she could have with him if only she'd stop wasting time with that loser, Jake.

* * * *

Stacey woke up next to her husband, just as she had done each and every morning for the past fifteen years. The only difference this morning is that she did not roll over and give her husband a "good morning" kiss. Instead, she rolled over to the edge of the bed, facing away from him, as far away as she could. She was upset at her husband and confused about what had happened with Frank the night before. She remembered feeling a spark that she hadn't felt in years when their lips met.

She told herself not to think about it, but she couldn't help it. She imagined what it would be like making love to a man other than her husband. Frank was right. She deserved better. She deserved to live, to feel that rush of excitement and adrenaline of new love once again. If nothing else, her husband deserved to feel the same mental torture she had been living with since his affair. At the moment, she didn't care whether it was right or wrong. The opportunity to replace some of the hurt she'd been feeling with some genuine pleasure and excitement was too delicious to resist. If Frank would have her, she would have him as well.

Chapter 18

Jake stood beside Hank in the small apartment watching the forensic team dust for prints. A medical examiner knelt beside the body lying on the bloodstained carpet while two paramedics stood patiently by the door waiting to haul the corpse away. From an adjoining bedroom, the sobbing of a woman could be heard as two officers questioned her. She was a neighbor who had discovered the body of Mr. Abraham Giddings after finding his door slightly ajar.

Jake calmly examined the surroundings, attempting to piece together the circumstances that led to this strange scene. He already determined there were no signs of forced entry. Mr. Giddings must have let the killer in on his own accord for whatever reason. There was no evidence of a struggle, and there was no sign of theft immediately visible. His wallet was resting in his back pocket, and there were no signs of freshly removed objects in the dust-filled apartment.

The most puzzling feature of the apartment was a spare bedroom in which several empty birdcages were piled in the corner. In the opposite corner there was a cage containing a beautiful, yet disheveled, white umbrella cockatoo. White feathers and seed were strewn in every direction from the base of its wrought iron stand. The bird had not made a sound throughout the entire investigation, but merely lifted its head menacingly whenever it was approached, spreading its wings and hissing. The delicate animal looked to be malnourished, and it was blatantly apparent that the cage had not been cleaned in quite some time. There was a small scar on its bare neck with black strands of stitching protruding from the skin. Jake assumed the parrot had recently had its voice box surgically removed. As it raised its wings, bare spots were exposed under the wings and on its chest where it had apparently plucked its feathers. Officer Bean joked that the thing looked like a plucked chicken.

"This thing would even pass Frank Perdue's strict tests, I bet," he snickered, but was met with a harsh glare from Jake.

The woman in the other room explained that the man loved birds. He always fed the wild ones outside his window and tried desperately to find a domestic bird that would be compatible with his lifestyle. He was a writer, she explained, and he demanded silence.

Hank pulled Jake aside, offering him some advice on the matter. "Don't you think it's kinda coincidental the way this guy died?"

Jake nodded his head, agreeing upon the similarities between this murder and the murder of Dennis Chapman.

"No apparent motive," Hank continued. "No witnesses. Same professional-looking slash across the throat, so the victims couldn't scream while they bled to death. In each case, the left arm was found resting across the lower back with bruises around the wrists. I think there might be a connection here, Jake."

Jake listened, yet a nagging voice inside his head kept interrupting. The voice told him the similarities didn't end there. As he arrived at the apartment building, he realized that he had been in that building before, just months ago, investigating the murder of Simon Haggerty, who had been found face-first in a murky pond back in April.

There was another theory itching the outer edges of Jake's conscience that became louder and louder with each bizarre murder scene he visited. It was a theory so ludicrous he feared he was growing insane. The image of the frightened, abused cockatoo in the next room kept flashing before him. Soon, the rooster could be heard crowing in the distance.

Jake excused himself. He needed to take a walk, to collect his thoughts. All those long hours of working and studying were taking its toll. He needed some time to rearrange his thoughts in some logical manner. He stepped into the hallway and walked past several curious onlookers barricaded by yellow tape. Just then, he heard a familiar voice.

"Yo, Supercop!" Frank yelled from down the hall. "What's happening? Another one of my neighbors go for a swim?"

As Jake walked toward him, he carefully inspected his face and body language for any clues to Frank's state of mind. "Funny thing you should say that, Frank. People seem to be dropping like flies around here. Any reason for that, you think?"

Frank studied Jake's face as well, knowing his every move was probably being scrutinized. "None that I can think of," he said sullenly. "How did it happen?"

"How well did you know Mr. Giddings," Jake asked, ignoring the question.

"Not too well. The old man was pretty quiet, kept to himself. Every once in a while you'd hear his bird screaming, but I've gotten pretty used to that noise."

"You know if he bought that bird at Maggie's pet store?"

"Yeah, he did. I remember he even paid cash for it. He must've had some money."

"Did you hear any kind of ruckus up there last night? Any shouting?"

"I wasn't even here last night. I was out, and didn't get home until past midnight."

Jake mentally recorded Frank's answers to each of his questions. With each question, he carefully examined Frank's body language. Believing Frank was telling the truth, Jake began to thank him for his time. Spotting Hank walking down the hall toward the two men, Frank waved him over.

"Hey, Sgt. Hank. Your order's in down at the store. A lot of lumber you got there. Must be some project."

"Just a little home improvement," Hank replied. "Ready, Jake?"

The two men walked out the door to their waiting cars, agreeing to meet later in the day. Jake immersed himself in paperwork upon arriving at the station, writing his notes while they were fresh in his mind. As he hovered over the empty pages in his notebook, he found ideas were coming to him much too slowly. With all the events of the past few weeks, his mind had become a muddled mess. He needed some time off, away from his worries. But he knew no matter where he went, he would carry with him the excess luggage of the heavy case load at his desk, his stalled relationship with Maggie, the little boy inside his head who wouldn't let go, and the ghostly rooster that always chose the most opportune times to crow. Not to mention the fact that Ida Adams, his mother, was wandering the streets of New Milford at that very moment.

He looked at his watch, then at the empty pages before him. He put in enough overtime today, he surmised. Besides, he was supposed to meet Hank for a beer pretty soon, and a nice cold one seemed to be just what the doctor ordered. He dropped his pen and headed for the locker room.

* * * *

Hank and Jake sat in a corner booth of the dimly lit tavern, alternating between idle conversation and eyeing the television propped up high on the wall.

"I've been going through this thing over and over so many times it's driving me crazy," Jake said between sips.

"Sometimes, it's best just to relax, step back, and get a little perspective," Hank offered in his usual fatherly tone. Sensing the need to change the subject, Hank asked about Maggie.

"I haven't seen her lately. Haven't really had the time. I've been so involved in my work and..." Jake paused, catching himself before mentioning his mother. The timing was right to investigate the subject. "How about you? Have you seen Ida lately?" he asked poker-faced.

"She left town shortly after the party. She said she had some sort of business to attend."

Jake had questioned Hank earlier to find out why his mother had returned to New Milford, but Hank offered few answers. "You know, you never told me how you two met," Jake inquired, trying desperately not to appear anxious.

"Ah, it was nothing, really. I went out one night and there she was. We saw each other for a while, then she broke it off. Got married. End of story." Hank stared at the ballgame on the television, swallowing the last drop from his frosty mug and pouring himself another from the pitcher in the middle of the table. "Speaking of dates, I think you and Maggie looked great together the other night."

Frustrated with the shadowboxing around the subject of his mother, Jake snapped, "Why are you so determined to play this Chuck Woolery role? We've had a couple dates and you're ready to march us down the aisle. I don't get it. What's in it for you?"

Hank stared at him stone-faced, a scowl forming on his brow. "I'll tell you what's in it for me. A while back, I promised my best friend I'd take care of his little girl. I made that promise as he died in my arms. As you know, we're not in the safest line of work, Jake. If something happens to me I want to be damn sure someone's there to take care of my girl. Now, maybe I'm an ignorant old fool, but for some reason I trust you. So just humor me and tell me you'll be there as my backup. Just in case."

Jake was surprised by the unexpected reaction he received. He felt guilty for lashing out at his friend so impatiently. "Of course I'll be there for her, pal. But I don't think you'll have to worry about going anywhere any time soon. Only the good die young, you know." Jake smirked, raising the glass to his mouth.

Hank returned his smirk with a hardy belly laugh. "Top of the ninth," he said, gesturing toward the game. "Looks like it's all over for your Yanks."

* * * *

It was a bright, beautiful day, but much of the heat from the sun was swept away by the cold autumn winds fiercely blowing the brittle leaves from their homes high above Jake's backyard. Jake swept the leaves into chaotic piles while King rested with his large head protruding from his kennel.

Suddenly, the beast awoke, raising its ears to some distant intruder. His barking alerted his owner, who was busy daydreaming through the mindless task of raking. Jake eyed his canine friend curiously, then followed the dog's movements to the front of the fence bordering the backyard. Rake in hand, Jake slipped through the gate, patting King on the head, and walked to the front yard.

His stride was broken as he looked in disbelief at the figure standing at the entrance to his driveway. It was Ida Adams. She was standing beside her blue rental car, wearing a red dress with an overcoat and sunglasses that hid her emotions as she examined the Cape Cod in front of her.

For years, Jake wondered about the whereabouts of his mother. He questioned her reasoning for abandoning him so many years ago. He wondered what her life was like after that day, and if she had any regrets for leaving him. For many years, he thought of searching for her, but the feeling would soon pass. He finally accepted the fact that he would probably never see her again, and that it would probably be best for both of them to put the past behind them and go on with their lives. When he saw her that day at the captain's party, standing with his good friend Hank, all the pent-up feelings he had been carrying around with him came rushing back. Not knowing how to react, he chose just to ignore her. Hank told him she left town, and as far as he knew she wasn't coming back. And that would be just fine with him. But now she stood there, in the very place where she left him fifteen years ago. And he was forced to make a decision.

"Can I help you?" he called out, walking slowly toward her.

She removed her glasses, placing a hand to her forehead while squinting at the young man with the rake. "Lovely place you have here," she said. "You know, I used to know the people who built this place. He was my uncle."

Jake approached her, attempting to contain the feelings within him. When Uncle Henry died, he remembered thinking that his mother might return to New Milford to attend the funeral. But she never came. He wondered why she had chosen this moment to return. He looked for some flicker of recognition in her face, but was shocked to discover there was none. She still had no idea who he was. Rather than unleash this news at that moment, he chose to keep it a secret for just a bit longer.

"Thank you. I just moved in about a year ago."

"Hank told me Henry was your uncle."

"Actually, he was my father's uncle," Jake replied without hesitation, though he had just made up that lie on the spot. He wondered how far he would continue this charade, but his curiosity over his mother's true motives outweighed his feelings of remorse for lying to her at the moment.

"So…your father must be my cousin Robert."

"Must be," Jake replied with a smile, though even he was beginning to get confused over his tangled web of lies. After an awkward moment of silence, Jake asked, "Would you like to come in for some coffee or something? I'd love to hear more about this place." He realized he would never rid himself of her ghost if he didn't confront her. The opportunity had presented itself for whatever reason on this day, and he was willing to take advantage of it.

She thanked him for his hospitality, and the two walked through the doors of the old house. Ida roamed from room to room, telling stories and sharing nostalgia about each room. She complimented Jake for the work he had done restoring the place.

"I don't suppose you could tell me what happened to the boy that used to live here with Henry and Vera?" she asked casually.

"You mean John? No, I haven't seen him since he sold me the house."

He excused himself, leaving Ida in the living room while he poured coffee in the kitchen. When he returned to the living room, he was startled to see his mother facing the fireplace with a lonely tear streaking down her face.

"This mantle used to be filled with trophies and pictures," she said without turning to face him. "Henry used to build fires and tell us stories of knights and princesses. They were such simple times. Such good times."

She turned to face him, wiping the tear from her cheek. "I'm sorry," she said. "I don't mean to carry on like I do. You're very kind to allow me in your home, and to bore you with my stories. It's just that this place is very special to me." She took the mug of coffee in her palms and sipped, the steam rising from the mug creating a veil over her face.

"I understand," Jake said, "and I don't find your stories boring at all. I'm sorry this house may not look the same to you now that I'm here." He paused for a moment, then asked, "Hank said you've been gone for a long time. What made you come back to New Milford, if you don't mind me asking?"

Ida returned her gaze to the mantle, then sipped again from her mug as she collected her thoughts. "I never really planned on returning once I left. I've spent my whole life running from some bad memories. But today I found myself drawn back to this old house. Part of me wanted to see if I had been successful in putting certain things to rest. Due to recent events, I find myself wanting to tie up some loose ends from the past, to right some wrongs, to make things better."

"Hank mentioned that you had some business out of town. I hope everything went well." Jake found himself clinging to the edge of his seat, hanging on every word from the woman's lips. There were so many questions he needed answered. So many empty spaces he needed to be filled.

"Well, actually, things did not go well," Ida answered. "You see, my business out of town was actually a visit to my doctor to get the results of some tests, and they didn't go so good." Her bottom lip began to quiver as she attempted to contain herself. "They told me I have inoperable cancer of the liver. They've given me three months. So, basically, I have three months with which to do everything I had planned to do over an entire lifetime."

Jake felt a numb emptiness inside him as she conveyed this news. He found himself feeling pity for the woman after so many years of feeling nothing but scorn. He searched for some little voice to tell him what to do, whether or not to expose his identity to the frail woman across the room. Before the voice came to him, however, she spoke again.

"Actually, Jake, I came here to ask you a favor," she said softly. She paused as if she were considering whether to divulge the information she had bottled up for so long. Jake anxiously awaited her next words.

"I need your opinion. I have some news I'd like to get to Hank before...well, I need to talk with someone close to Hank, and I hear you're pretty much the closest. Years ago, just before my marriage to my first husband, Hank and I had a brief affair. During that affair, we produced a child. He doesn't know this. No one knows. Except me, and now you. As a friend of Hank's, I need some advice. I need to know whether you think I should tell him about this. I'm not sure how he would handle it."

Jake's mind reeled with this news. He called upon every ounce of self-control within himself to keep from displaying all the horrific emotions welling inside him at that moment. He pondered the possibilities of the situation. Was Hank his real father? Was he the product of some illicit affair so many years ago?

He composed himself long enough to utter, "Maybe you ought to take some time and think this one through..." He caught himself before referring to the woman as "Mom."

"I shouldn't have come here," she said apologetically. "You've been more than kind for listening to me ramble all this time, and for allowing me in your home. I apologize for taking so much of your time." She rose from her chair, and gathered her purse. Jake rose also, and helped her to the door. He wanted to tell her about her son. He wanted to tell her all was forgiven. He wanted to console her in some way, to tell her that he had turned out okay. But instead, he simply stood in silence as she bid him good-bye. He watched from the window as she entered her car and drove away.

* * * *

Maggie stepped right over the letter on her way through the door, her mind occupied with the impending chores of another business day. Returning to the back room of the store, she noticed it sitting face-up on the concrete floor, the familiar typewritten words, "MAGGIE MCCARTHY" scrawled across the front.

It had been several weeks since she last heard from her secret admirer. In fact, she had almost forgotten about him. She began to shove the unopened letter in her pocket, intending to deposit it in her glove compartment with the rest of the letters. Somewhere in the back of her mind, she worried that if her secret admirer were to harm her in some way, the letters in the glove box would provide insurance for her as evidence for the authorities. After a lengthy internal debate, she had decided to tell Hank about the letters. He thanked her for bringing it to his attention, and assured her that there was little to go on. The anonymous writer seemed harmless enough, he said, aside from that one strange letter that didn't seem to fit with the rest. He told her he'd follow up on it, and see what he could do, but he couldn't make any promises.

Her iniquitous curiosity overcame her rationality, and she decided to open the letter. It had been a while since she had heard from him, and in a strange way she missed him.

To My Soul Mate,

I hope today you are smiling. Each time that you smile, radiant beams of hope reach out to me across the miles that separate us. I catch each one and hold it close to my heart. And as my heart fills with hope, I know the day we will be together again is coming nearer.

I have done my best to see that you are safe and sheltered from the evils in the world. But as I regard the full spectrum of challenges to your well-being, I feel it is becoming more and more difficult to fulfill my duty. I fear the day will come when I can do no more, when the forces of evil will gradually overpower you until you plunge into the dungeon of despair.

I want to keep you smiling, my love, for I am on the verge of a plan to ensure your safekeeping. As you have created safe environments for your menagerie of pets, so shall I create a safe environment for you.

Do not lose faith in me. As you give me hope, I shall return it doubly.

With Eternal Devotion

Maggie reread the letter several times before returning it to its envelope. She looked quizzically toward the front of the store, watching the traffic from the busy road. She wondered whether her devoted author was in one of those cars. Maybe he was on his way to the store, preparing to walk through those doors disguised as a customer. Or maybe he had been a customer before. Surely, he had been watching her. He frequently mentioned her appearance, stating even the subtlest changes in her hairstyle or clothing, which could only be noticed by someone who saw her on a regular basis. It was quite possible he was one of the store's many devoted customers that dropped by on a weekly basis. She knew several of them by name.

I am on the verge of a plan to ensure your safekeeping.

What did that mean? A cold chill crept up her spine, causing her to shiver at the thought. There was something about the latest letter that bothered her deeply. Her secret admirer had seemed quite sane and intelligent in the preceding letters. Even in the sexually explicit letter that had offended her, the writer seemed to describe the acts rather poetically. In the latest letter, however, she saw a man who was slowly becoming insane.

The back door to the store swung open behind her, forcefully whipping against the building. Maggie's heart leapt into her throat as she spun around to face her maniacal stalker, her arms raised in defense.

Stacey wrestled with the heavy door, her arms loaded with supplies. "Some wind out there today," she said cheerfully, then looked curiously at the ashen face of her employer.

"What's wrong, Maggie?" she said. "You look like you've seen a ghost!"

CHAPTER 19

Jake sank into his chair and scanned the file on the murder of Elizabeth Lapinski. Reports from the officers at the scene were interspersed with his personal notes and joined by the forensic and autopsy findings. The file on Abraham Giddings remained closed, but near to his hand. He filtered out the noise of the busy office and concentrated on the cases before him. The encounter with his mother intruded into his thoughts at irregular intervals, causing his level of concentration to wane. He attempted to dismiss any intrusions into his mind, from questions about Hank and his mother, to the tiny voice of Worm, which had been growing louder and louder over the past few days. He managed to steer clear of Hank after the encounter with his mother. He wasn't certain how to act when he faced him, and for the moment he was content just to block it all out and immerse himself in his work.

In the center of the scattered pages and files, the photo of Lapinski's pallid body seemed to scream out at him. Jake reached for the Giddings file and exhumed the photo of Giddings, placing it aside the Lapinski photo. There were striking similarities between the two murders.

Both bodies were drained of blood. The same incision with a sharp blade was neatly drawn through each of their necks. Small tufts of their own hair were found near both bodies. Both victims fell into the same death pose: left arm behind the back, bruises around the wrists. Jake re-enacted the murder in his mind, imagining himself the killer.

He is invited into Lapinski's home, and two weeks later Giddings also invites him into his apartment. There is no forced entry. The sole intent of the visits is murder, as there is no struggle, and nothing is taken. With comfortable ease, he performs a common restraining maneuver he himself learned as a cop, and earlier in the army. Grabbing the left arm, he imagines forcing it up against the back, held firm and high, rendering the victim powerless. A fist full of hair yanks back the head, exposing the jugular. Then one quick, well-executed slice of the blade with the free hand and it was all over. A quiet, efficient method of murder.

Satisfied that he had successfully determined how the murders had been committed, he then focused on the question of "why." In both scenarios, nothing had been taken from either their homes or their persons. Rings were still secured onto stiffened fingers, wallets still resting in pockets, jewelry still safely tucked away in its place.

There was something else the two had in common. It was something that seemed completely unrelated, yet something that inspired a cold shiver to work its way up Jake's spine. Both victims lived alone, and both owned pets. Giddings apparently owned several birds, though they found just one frightened, abused cockatoo in his apartment. Lapinski owned a dog. A very malnourished, tremulous animal they found tied to a tree in the backyard. Similar to Gidding's parrot, the dog had also recently had its voice box removed, causing the animal to emit a peculiar, low-pitched howling noise when it was approached.

Also, in the back of his mind, Jake knew there was something else the two murder scenes had in common. In both cases, he heard the resilient crowing of the rooster in his mind. His eyes flitted from page to page, searching for some unknown connection. The two files rapidly began merging together as strewn paper covered his desk. The crowing linked more than just these two homicides together. The boasting cry was the common denominator to other hapless victims as well. But before the seed could germinate and blossom into revelation, Jake found his attention diverted by a thumping on his back. He looked up to see Bean's stoic face.

"Thought you might want in on this. We just got a call on a domestic disturbance. 92 Applewood Drive. Your old pal Roy Davis is at it again."

Jake regarded his fellow officer, looked back at the strewn papers on his desk, then pushed his chair back and grabbed his coat.

Roy Davis had become an irritating thorn in his side. He was an ex-con with a mean temper and a tendency to beat his wife. A garbage collector by day, he became a raging drunk by night. The wife always called for help in a panic, then backed down once help arrived, refusing to press charges. Neighbors filed complaints about disruptions and loud arguments being carried out in public. Most of them called out of deep concern for the woman's safety. Roy Davis involved the whole neighborhood with his drunken antics, and that neighborhood included Maggie McCarthy.

As Jake pulled into the driveway behind Bean and his partner, he noticed Hank's cruiser parked in front of the house. He briefly paused before opening the door, debating whether his psyche was ready for an encounter with the man who may be his father. By the time Jake reached the front door, he heard a woman's scream, followed by Hank's booming voice ordering "Stop! Police!", then a shattering of glass coming from the rear of the house.

Running toward the sound, Jake turned the corner in time to see Davis stumbling across the backyard and into the neighbor's lawn. Jake sprinted after him and tackled him to the ground, forcing the man's face into the dirt. Hank appeared instantly and helped Jake raise the perpetrator from the ground after Jake cuffed him.

"Nice tackle there, Supercop. I remember I used to move that fast, too, at one time," Hank joked.

"Really? You can remember that far back? Good for you. Good for you," Jake replied half-heartedly, unable to look Hank in the eyes.

Jake led the man to the back door and stopped abruptly upon reaching the trashcans outside the house. Gripping the man's arm tightly, Jake motioned toward the can.

"What's this?" he asked.

"It's your momma's pussy," the inebriated slob snorted. A stream of blood ran down his nose and into his mouth. With his last word, he spit blood onto Jake's face.

Without thought of consequences, Jake slammed his fist into the man's gut, causing him to double over in pain. Shocked, Hank ordered the fellow officers to return to their squad cars. Hank looked around as if searching for witnesses, and not finding any, returned the look to his former partner's face. Jake had a wild look in his eyes that Hank hadn't seen before, and he wasn't sure what exactly brought on this outburst.

"Listen, you lowlife piece of shit. I'm going to ask you just one more time," Jake said slowly and deliberately, wiping the blood from his face with his shirt sleeve. "And I do mean just one more time. And if you don't answer me correctly those may be the last words you ever hear." Jake motioned once again to the trashcan outside the house, toward the mangled body of Maggie's cat, Apollo, resting on top of the plastic bag inside. "Where did you find this cat?"

"The goddamn thing was roaming around in my garbage. So I whacked him with a shovel. Got him good, didn't I?" the man boasted breathlessly.

Jake pushed the drunk over into Hank. "Get this piece of garbage out of here before I really get pissed." Hank led the man through the house and into the waiting squad car while Jake bagged the body into an empty trash bag nearby.

Back at the office, Jake placed a call to Critters Pet Store. Frank picked up on the other end.

"Frank, get Maggie on the phone," Jake said coolly.

"And whom shall I say is calling?" Frank answered sarcastically.

"Put Maggie on the phone right now, Frank. Police business."

Although it was, in fact, police business, it was also personal. Jake knew how Maggie loved her cat, and he imagined what his reaction would be if the same thing had happened to King. Seeing Maggie's dead cat brought back long-repressed memories of the brutal slayings of his old dog and pet rooster.

Maggie answered the phone with a cheerful, "Hello."

"Maggie, this is Jake," he said. "I'm afraid I have some terrible news."

CHAPTER 20

Jake sat on his back porch, overlooking the makeshift kennel, rubbing his dog on the head, and enjoying the cool evening breeze that ended a beautiful Indian summer day. He sat still as his mind reeled with confusing thoughts. The tiny seed that began to bloom had retracted to a small corner of his mind. Names marched through his head like a never-ending procession of soldiers, each with its own wounds, its own story to tell. Elizabeth Lapinski. Ida Adams. Abraham Giddings. Hank Beecher.

His mother had not been seen in some time. It was presumed she left town without saying a word to Hank or himself. He presumed it was just as well that she was gone. It was one less stress point he needed in his cluttered life. He managed to live without her for so long, he was not about to begin caring for her—especially when he would soon have to grieve for her. Perhaps it was better that she not know who he was. She had a reason for leaving him so long ago, and he was not sure it needed to be divulged. "Let sleeping dogs lie," Uncle Henry used to say. That was just fine with him.

Dealing with Hank was a little different, as he deeply cared for the old man. If he was, in fact, Hank's son, he supposed there could be worse scenarios. In a way, Jake thought of Hank as a father figure anyway, so he supposed the relationship wouldn't change much at all if it were true. Still, it was probably best to just leave it alone for the moment. He would eventually tell Hank what Ida had told him, when the time was right.

Since he heard the news, he often found himself searching Hank's face for any sign of resemblance. There was a familiar cleft in his chin that Jake recognized as his own, but for the most part he more resembled his mother. He found it amusing that his own mother still did not recognize him, despite the obvious resemblance. He had truly succeeded in becoming a whole new person. The Worm had become The Butterfly. He laughed at the analogy, and the dog looked at his owner quizzically as if he wanted in on the joke.

There was only one person left on the face of the earth who knew his true identity, and that person reaffirmed himself that morning. The dream was the same. Arctic ice. Freezing snow. Chilling wind. He was barefoot and wandering through the darkness until he hit the frozen wall. There through the frosted window was the same happy picnic, with the same happy couple. He heard his name being called.

Worm, Worm, Worm.

Knowing where the voice originated, he resisted every temptation to face it. He frantically scratched and clawed at the window, trying to open it, to escape from the freezing doldrums. Then, a bony hand clutched his shoulder and spun him around forcibly. There, the rotting corpse of Ida Adams stood, laughing and shouting his name.

Worm, Worm, Worm.

And that foolish rooster cackled maniacally. His mother motioned him into her arms, her toothless mouth dripping with rotted flesh and dirt. He awoke covered in sweat, shivering. And when he looked into the mirror, the laughing face of Worm looked back at him.

Jake sat in the chair, his hands gripping the cold steel as he remembered the dream. His mother's resurrection into his life had caused the dream to intensify. Perhaps when she died, she would take the dream with her. Perhaps it was only because of her that Worm lived on. When she was gone, maybe that chapter of his life would finally be buried. Then, and only then, would he be free.

Feeling deprived of attention, King plopped his bulky paw on Jake's lap, startling him back into reality. Two big, brown eyes stared at him from under hairy brows in a sympathetic gaze. Jake returned the gaze with a hearty pat to the dog's head and led him inside the house.

* * * *

Maggie stood at the front counter, waiting impatiently for Hank to arrive. She phoned him as soon as she discovered the latest note slipped under the door. The writer seemed to enjoy his new method of delivery. It was the third note that month. Each note grew more irrational and menacing, and it seemed as though he were planning on making some daring entry into Maggie's life. She wanted to be sure she wasn't alone when he got there.

Hank carefully scanned each letter, wearing a stoic cop expression as he read the words that sent chills through Maggie's body. For the longest time, he said not a word. It seemed as though he were ready to explode at any moment. He lowered the last letter from his eyes and, without a word, grabbed a brown paper bag with which to stuff the envelopes.

"I'm going to take these back to the office and submit a written complaint. I'll bring it by later for you to sign," he said, looking almost disappointed. "I'm afraid there's not really anything I can do for you, honey. Unfortunately, we don't know who this guy is, and there's really no way we can find out other than staking out the back of the store or the post office, and frankly I don't think the chief is going to allow that. We may be able to lift some prints from the envelopes, but I doubt this guy was stupid enough to leave them."

He found it difficult to look in her eyes as he spoke to her. "If you want some advice, I think you should get some protection. Some mace or…" He didn't complete the sentence, but Maggie was fully aware of his implication. She was also fully aware that Hank knew better than to suggest such a thing. A bullet from a gun took her father away from her, and she would rather die than hold a gun in her hands. And he knew it.

He kissed her on the cheek and gave her a hug. "I gotta get back to work," he said. "If you see anything suspicious or you feel you're in any danger whatsoever, you know who to call."

Maggie watched him leave out the front door, the cowbell above the door signaling his departure. An uneasy feeling came over her. In all the years she knew him, Hank was always a rock. He was always there with soothing words and comforting advice, and he always left her feeling protected. This time, she felt as though the situation was beyond even his control, and she sensed a feeling of helplessness in him, which scared the hell out of her.

* * * *

"You don't know me," the voice on the end of the line echoed, "but you know my daughter…that is, you *knew* my daughter." The voice began to quiver, and Frank listened curiously, wondering whether the woman had the right number.

"My daughter's name was Kathleen Stephnowski. She died about a week ago." Frank could hear the broken woman bravely attempt to contain herself. The name did not sound familiar to him at all, and he wondered once again whether the caller had found the right "Frank Wilson."

"I'm very sorry for your loss, Mrs....She was a fine woman," he said.

"The name is Stephnowski," the woman said, sounding suddenly perturbed. "The only reason I'm telling you this is because she died of the AIDS virus, and before she died she made a list of former lovers to notify...so that they would get themselves checked out, and so they wouldn't spread the disease. Your name was on that list, Mr. Wilson. I hope you get yourself checked." With those words still echoing in his ears, the woman abruptly hung up.

Frank stared wildly through the door of his garage, the phone still dangling in his hand. Sawdust was strewn across the floor and down the front of his shirt. Who the hell was Kathleen Stephnowski? He tried adamantly to piece the face together with the name, but the image did not come to him. Then, suddenly, the image of the girl's face came to him from the depths of his memory. It was a hazy image, as all images were from his college days. A girl named "Kat" with a tattoo of a butterfly on the small of her back. They met at a party. She was smoking hot. He was shooting heroin on the back porch and she asked to join him. One thing led to another. They hung out together for a few weeks, but when he left school, he never heard from her again. Nor did he ever want to hear from her again. She was part of a lifestyle from which he was trying desperately to escape. He had succeeded in doing so. Until now.

He looked down at his watch and realized he had gotten so caught up in his remodeling that he had lost track of the time. The pet store was about to close, and he hadn't even bothered to call. Perhaps Maggie had called him and he couldn't hear the phone because of all the noise. The last thing he needed was to be on Maggie's shit list. He hurriedly changed clothes and hopped into his car. As he drove to the store, his mind raced. Could he be possibly be infected with HIV? Given his history of anonymous sex and careless drug use, it was certainly possible. But he felt completely healthy. His thoughts turned to Stacey. If he were indeed infected with the virus, perhaps he should warn her, too.

* * * *

Jake arrived at the pet store just before closing. He hoped Maggie would join him for dinner. He badly needed a pleasant distraction from all the day's frustrations, and he missed her company. He stood at the front counter and saw Maggie near the back, holding a ten-gallon tank and helping a young girl select gravel. He expected to see Frank floating around, but spotted Stacey instead, retrieving fish from a high tank for a kid and his dad. A couple stood watching some parakeets flutter around from perch to perch while another couple waited near the guinea pigs. Jake recognized the couple and walked over to greet them. Maggie soon appeared and offered her assistance, though without her usual exuberance and characteristic friendliness. Jake knew she was upset about Apollo's death, and thought that a night out might just be what she needed.

The couple watching the birds left hand-in-hand, and Stacey blew a sigh of relief and sat down hard on the stool nearby. She complained to Jake about how busy it had been all day, how Frank was missing in action, leaving the two of them to run the place on the busiest night of the week. She complained, but Jake saw the smile hidden behind her eyes, understanding that she'd rather be there than back home with her husband. Maggie had told him all the details one night over dinner and made him promise never to tell.

Stacey excused herself to the back room, and Maggie appeared with a cardboard box, the furry nose of a guinea pig protruding through tiny holes. He began to detail the events of his day when a loud crash rang from the back room. Running toward the back of the store, Jake and Maggie found Stacey kneeling on the floor surrounded by shattered glass. Her hands were badly cut, and blood mixed with the shards of glass from the broken tank on the floor. Maggie stepped gingerly over the glass to attend to her friend while Jake attempted to pick up some of the bigger pieces on the floor.

Frank opened the back door to see Jake on his hands and knees, and Maggie and Stacey at the sink with their backs to him. Thinking Maggie had been hurt, he rushed past Jake to the two women. The sink was filled with bloody water, but with four hands under the stream from the faucet he couldn't tell who was doing the bleeding. Seeing Frank standing there with the dumb look on his face, Maggie instantly laced into him for not being there. If he had shown up to work this would never had happened.

Frank's attention was drawn to the cut on Stacey's hand, and the fact that Maggie was making contact with what could be infected blood. He grabbed Maggie's arm and flung her hand away from Stacey's hand so hard that she lost her balance, slipping on the wet floor and falling hard onto the cold concrete next to Jake. A wild look of fear, mixed with livid anger, reflected in Frank's face, both confusing and frightening the crowd in the back room.

Jake leapt to his feet and grabbed Frank's arm, spinning him around. Frank faced him angrily. If he did have the disease, then there was no way he'd ever have Maggie, and if he couldn't have her no one would. Frank exploded with a fist to Jake's chin, knocking him to the floor. Before Jake had time to react, Frank was on top of him, pounding him with blow after blow as Maggie screamed for him to knock it off. Though Jake had been trained in hand-to-hand combat, both in the army and at the academy, and had taken down assailants twice the size of Frank in the past, he found himself helplessly frozen as long-repressed memories of his assault on the high school football field so many years ago invaded his senses.

The pounding continued until Frank abruptly stopped. He paused for a moment, looked strangely at Jake, then turned his head to the side, and his eyes filled with a tiny flicker of recognition. Suddenly, Frank burst out into mad laughter. Stacey and Maggie just sat idly watching the display, unable to fathom what brought on the sudden attack by Frank or the insane laughter.

Frank sat on top of his opponent, still laughing at some joke that only he found funny. Maggie cast a curious look at Jake, who lay on the floor bleeding from the nose. Stacey held a moist towel to her hands and attempted to determine the severity of her wounds.

Maggie finally leapt to her feet and confronted the madman. "What the hell is wrong with you, Frank?!? What the hell are you thinking?!?"

Frank continued his mad laughter, wiping tears from his eyes. "I can't believe it!" he said. "I can't believe I didn't figure it out sooner! All this time…if only I had known sooner…oh man!"

Maggie felt anger replace the fear inside her as she pushed Frank off of Jake. "Are you okay?" she asked of Jake, helping him up.

"You know what it was?" Frank continued. "The eyes! The freakin' eyes! What is it they say? 'The eyes are the windows to the soul?' You know who this is, Maggie? You know who this little geek is that you've been dating? My god, man, I can't believe none of us saw this! This is too great!" He paused for dramatic effect, then said slowly and proudly, "Maggie McCarthy, I'd like you to meet Worm. Mister Worm Adams. Alias: Supercop." He then broke out into more insane laughter, doubling over and slapping his knees.

Jake felt like a little boy again, wanting to roll himself up into a little ball and disappear—or split himself in two, like all good worms do. He couldn't bring himself to face anyone in the room, but quickly walked out of the back room toward the front of the store. Maggie flashed Frank a harsh look and called after Jake, which only made him walk faster. She caught up with him, pulling him inside.

"Wait a minute. Please stay," she pleaded. "Frank is an asshole. I don't know what his problem is lately, and I don't know what got into him just now. Needless to say, he won't be working here any longer. I don't care how much he knows about fish." She desperately tried to make eye contact with him, but he stared through the floor like a boy who had just been caught doing something wrong.

"I gotta go, Maggie," he muttered, without raising his eyes.

"Just stay, Jake. I want to talk to you."

"There's nothing to talk about. It's over. It's all in the past. I'm fine with it, really. I just want to go home and be alone for a while. I'm sorry."

Jake removed Maggie's hand from his arm and left out the front door, leaving Maggie staring out the foggy glass door, shaking her head.

CHAPTER 21

Jake was in the middle of his morning routine when he heard a knock at the front door. He opened the door to find Maggie standing on his front porch wearing an uneasy smile.

"May I come in?" she asked, timidly.

Jake hesitated for a moment, trying to conjure up an excuse, but reluctantly opened the door when none came to him quickly enough. He realized that eventually he would have to face Maggie and talk about what had happened. He had spent the better part of the morning—not to mention the night before—obsessing over it, replaying the events of the previous day over and over again. He was embarrassed to have his secret revealed in such a humiliating way. He was embarrassed to have appeared so weak and powerless in front of Maggie. He was embarrassed for letting Frank get away with it all.

He replayed the event over and over the night before, thinking of all the things he should have said or done. He had planned to tell Maggie about his past, eventually. By this point in his life, he had developed enough confidence in himself, and in Maggie, to realize that she wouldn't reject him if she knew the truth. He had been waiting for the right moment to tell her. Unfortunately, that moment never seemed to come.

"Coffee?" he asked, motioning for her to sit at the kitchen table.

"Yes, thanks," she replied, searching for some hint as to his frame of mind. "I tried calling you several times last night."

"Phone was off the hook," he replied tersely, setting a steaming mug in front of her.

Jake sat down at the opposite end of the table, and there was a brief moment of silent tension before they both said, "I think we should talk" simultaneously. The tension eased with light smiles, Jake motioned toward Maggie. "Ladies first."

"Well, first…are you okay?"

"Aside from a bruised ego, yes, I'm fine," Jake replied.

"Listen, I want to apologize for Frank's behavior," Maggie said, fidgeting uncomfortably in her seat. "I don't know what got into him. What he did was inexcusable."

"Don't worry about it. Frank and I have never exactly been pals," Jake stated matter-of-factly.

"About what he said…"

"I've been meaning to tell you for a while now, Maggie. Needless to say, I didn't expect you'd find out like this."

"Why keep it a secret? So you were a little shy as a kid. That's nothing to be ashamed of, Jake."

"There's a little more to it than that, Maggie."

For the next forty-five minutes, Jake laid it all out on the table. He told her about his tortured childhood; of the abuse he suffered at the hands of his father and Aunt Vera. He told her how his mother had abandoned him. He told her how his mother, Ida Adams, had recently reappeared, complicating his life even further. He told her of his mother's terminal illness. He did not mention, however, his newly-discovered relationship to Hank. Nor did he mention how Worm was still a part of his life, making occasional appearances in his mirror and in his dreams. Some secrets are better kept to oneself, he thought.

All the while, Maggie quietly listened, hanging on each and every word. Her eyes welled up at the beginning of his monologue, and by the end, he noticed she was crying uncontrollably. His childhood had been so unlike her own. She imagined him as a little boy; so unhappy, so lonely, so devoid of a loving, caring relationship. She shared his grief over losing his mother. She was proud of him for overcoming such a tortured past to become the man he was. She felt relieved that he had opened up, and honored that he had chosen her to share his story.

Feeling a strong urge to comfort him, hold him, and pull him closer to her heart, she rose from her chair and made her way across the table. He met her with a warm embrace. His expression betrayed his feeling of relief. He smiled back at her and lightly touched her cheek. He couldn't help but notice how beautiful she looked in the morning light. He pulled her toward him, softly kissing her lips. She returned his kiss, as her hands explored his shoulders and back.

A ringing noise interrupted their embrace, and Jake reluctantly reached over and grabbed the phone hanging on the wall. He glanced at the caller ID panel, grimaced, then answered with a curt, "Yeah."

"I'll be right there," he said, his voice filled with reluctance.

"I should get going, too," Maggie said. "Maybe we can pick this up again some time?"

"It's a date," Jake said with a smile.

CHAPTER 22

There was a bitter chill in the air. The sky was cloudless and gray, and the ground was frozen solid under their footsteps. But the falling temperature was the least of their problems, for it was also getting dark, and time was running out for the search team to find the missing four-year-old boy.

Jake remained at his desk studying the files from the unsolved murders that plagued most of his waking thoughts. He monitored the progress of the lost boy by the crackling of the scanner on the edge of his desk. He knew that with each hour that passed, the chances were lessened that the boy would be found in time. He had considered becoming involved in the search himself, but the case was in good hands, and the files on his desk called out to him more loudly.

He felt close to finding the missing piece in the puzzle. That piece was right in front of him, and he knew if he just looked long enough he would find it. Three files were arranged in a triangle on his desk. The two on the left had much in common with each other. The third file on his right was a newly assembled case submitted just the day before. That case was presumed to be open and shut, but for some reason Jake knew it wasn't that simple. In the center of his desk was a small yellow post-it, a misplaced and forgotten memo he had made to himself that suddenly resurfaced.

Jake tapped the memo in the center with his middle finger. He glanced around the empty desks, thinking he should have put it all together by now. But with all the turmoil in his personal life, police business reluctantly was placed on the back burner. He focused on the cryptic note, the words leaping off the page and into his mind's eye:

ROOSTER
PETS
ANIMALS
THEORY OF REVOLT

Jake had learned to accept the rooster as some sort of internal alarm that signaled a murder had occurred. He wasn't sure why the mysterious bird haunted his mind, but he believed it was an internal defense mechanism of some kind. He was never one to believe in the supernatural, but if the rooster could help him solve the case, then he would welcome him with open arms.

Pets were a common factor in at least two of the cases. The file to the right contained no mention of pets of any kind. He found it preposterous that there could be some deranged serial killer of abusive pet owners, but nevertheless let his mind wander in that direction.

The words "THEORY OF REVOLT" uncovered a memory of what Bean had said so many months back, at the murder scene of Fred Wilkins. Mr. Wilkins had a heart attack, bringing down several tanks of rats in his fall, and the rats proceeded to feast on his lifeless body. Bean commented how ironic it was that all those caged rats, which were to become food themselves, used Mr. Wilkins for that purpose. He then remembered the woman that was bitten by the rabid squirrel, and searched through his files to find that case. Sheila Bennett was her name. Now there were four cases of "animal revolt" in the last year. Suddenly, his theory became more plausible. Or was it all just a coincidence? After all, Ms. Bennett never did any harm to anyone, did she? He made a note to pull the Bennett file, on the outside chance that there was a connection.

This is absolutely crazy, he thought to himself. *Either you're nuts, or there's some whacko out there killing people because they abuse their animals.* Just then, Hank's voice came over the radio with an update on the search. The boy still had not been found, although one of his mittens was discovered snagged on a tree about a half-mile away from his house.

Jake took a deep breath and slid his chair away from the desk. Hearing Hank's voice broke his concentration, and he decided it was just as well since the job at hand seemed to be going in a bizarre direction, and he wasn't sure he wanted to know the destination. He ran his fingers through his hair and glanced out the window. If he wasn't going to make any more progress on his cases, the least he could do was join the search.

He summoned King over to his desk and attached his leash. King had an acute nose for drugs, but he had never sniffed out a kid before. It was worth a try, though. He grabbed his coat and a flashlight and descended down the stairs to his waiting vehicle.

Cars were strewn haphazardly along the dirt road leading to the Patterson's house. Several police cruisers and an ambulance were parked in a cluster near the garage doors. Jake pulled behind Hank's cruiser as Mrs. Patterson emerged from the back door with a tray full of steaming mugs. Hank and Bean walked toward him as he opened the back door for King.

Jake was briefed on the situation, and was told what areas had been searched. Mrs. Patterson softly thanked him for coming, and handed him several articles of clothing. Hank gave Jake the solitary mitten, and Jake proceeded to place the various items under the dog's nose. King sniffed the items, but seemed disinterested. Jake patiently placed each item under the dog's nose once more, giving the search command. King's ears suddenly perked, and he strained against his leash. Jake followed the dog as he pulled him into the woods.

Through brush and brambles, over fallen limbs and under brushes, the three men and the dog sliced through the cold, dark night. Across a gentle flowing stream and deeper into the woods, King would charge and then slow down as if the scent was irregular and changed with the breeze. They scaled a short pile of rocks, causing smaller stones to cascade down to the mossy floor.

Jake made the decision to free King from his leash, allowing him to travel faster toward the lost child. King quickly disappeared into the darkness as the three men raced to keep pace. Intermittently, one of the men would call out the boy's name. Jake stopped abruptly, listening to the sounds around him. He yelled to the men behind him to stop, also. He listened to the quiet stillness around him while looking toward the last spot where he had seen his dog running in the moonlight. For a few moments, each man stood rooted to his spot, waiting for King's familiar bark indicating his mission was successful.

Several yards in front of the men, King gave them a sign that he had found something. Jake led the pack to the slight incline, cursing under his breath as briers from a large blackberry bush seemed to grab hold of him and detain him with its sharp tentacles. He reached the top of the precipice and spotted King regally standing guard over little Tommy Patterson.

Tommy was alive and unharmed, with the exception of a few minor bruises and scratches. He was cold and afraid, but amused by the furry beast that had found him. Jake wrapped his jacket around the boy and carried him back through the woods. Upon reaching his home, the glassy-eyed parents descended upon the trio, taking the boy in their arms. Friends and neighbors gathered around the family, reveling in the happy ending. Flashbulbs lit up the darkness as reporters swarmed the three heroes. Hank gave a brief synopsis of the rescue, then informed the reporters that it was time to get back to work.

The photo of Jake, Hank, Bean, and the dog made the front page of the local paper, and the story was spread through the AP wire, receiving national attention as a human interest story. In her hotel room, Ida Adams stared intently at the photo of the two men in front of her, her mouth agape.

CHAPTER 23

Jake went to bed early and enjoyed a good, solid night's sleep for the first time in a long time. His recurring nightmare, starring Worm and the rotting corpse of Ida Adams, had taken the night off. He sat on the edge of his bed, with King resting peacefully at his feet, and ever so gradually, the tangled web of thoughts and ideas that clouded his everyday existence began trickling into his consciousness.

There were simply too many issues to tackle, too many problems to solve. He had barely had time to come to grips with his mother's reappearance into his life when he received the shocking news about his real father. The emotional one-two punch had sent him reeling, and he hadn't had time to fully digest it all. Knowing the truth was one thing; knowing what to do with that knowledge was another.

As soon as he rose from bed, King galloped toward the door. Jake opened the door a crack and the burly beast sprinted out into the cold. Jake worked his way back to the kitchen and activated the coffee maker. He sat at the kitchen table with his head buried in his hands.

All these years, he had been working side-by-side with his father without knowing it. Thinking back, he could recollect a couple of times when he actually wondered whether Hank could be his father. But this was nothing unusual. Nearly every man he passed on the street that was roughly of the right age group was subjected to the same scrutiny. His mother never talked about his real father, though he was sure he must have asked her about him. Perhaps she did tell him about Hank when he was a young boy, but the memory of her doing so had been repressed along with all the other memories from his childhood.

His one source of true happiness was that his relationship with Maggie was finally going somewhere. He made it a point to stop by the pet store on a daily basis, if for no other reason than to steal another kiss. They had grown very close over the past two weeks, though finding time to be together for an extended period of time had been a challenge. His job had simply taken over his life, and he found little time for anything else. If only he could make as much progress on his cases as he had made with Maggie, he'd be sitting pretty.

The barking at the back door signaled that it was time to begin another day's work.

* * * *

Maggie affixed a look of consternation on her face, trying to stay focused on one of her customer's latest problems. Her mind kept wandering, however, to images of Stacey and Frank. She learned a while ago about the illicit affair the two had shared together. While she understood Stacey's problems at home, and showed sympathy toward her face-to-face, she found the whole situation nauseating. Stacey was a married woman and had an obligation to try to work it out with her husband as long as the two were still married—especially when there were innocent children involved. Two wrongs simply don't make a right. As for Frank, the loathing she felt toward him when she first learned of the affair was slowly being replaced with pity.

Frank once had it all in the palm of his hand. He could have achieved so much in life, but a freak accident took it all away from him. He had his good qualities, to be sure. Beyond the facade of bravado there was a good man with a good heart. He was also extremely helpful around the store, and his knowledge and love of tropical fish was matched only by her father's. She knew it would only be a matter of time before the intricate filtration system her father installed would spring a leak, and she would be left with several hundreds of gallons of water all over her store. She felt safe having Frank around, both because of the knowledge he carried with him, and because she knew he would never let any harm come to her.

What he did to Jake, however, was inexcusable, and she let him know that when he came back to the store a couple of weeks after the incident, begging for forgiveness. After giving him a lengthy lecture, she reluctantly allowed him to come back to work with the promise that he would apologize to Jake, and that he would never mention the name "Worm" again.

She noticed a strangeness in Frank's demeanor when he visited her that day. The usual bravado and sense of humor had disappeared behind a veil of depression. He looked at her as if he were seeing her for the last time. She allowed that his behavior was partly due to his embarrassment about the whole incident with Jake. But there was something else, something hidden that he was trying to keep from her. There was a certain sadness behind his eyes.

The cowbell rang, and Stacey emerged from the front of the store. Standing with a customer in the rear of the store, Maggie thought it was strange for her to use the front entrance, and even stranger that Stacey was standing by the front counter, still wearing her jacket, and looking very upset. Neither Stacey nor Frank was due to report to work for another hour.

Maggie excused herself from the customer and hurriedly walked to her friend. Tears sending rivers of black mascara down her cheeks, Stacey wrapped her arms around her friend and sobbed into her shoulder. Spying the perplexed looks from the customers in the store, Maggie whispered to her, "Come on, let's go to the back room," and led her toward the rear of the store, explaining to the customers, "I'll be right back—don't go anywhere."

Stacey sat down on the empty stool near the sink, her hair falling over her face. "Frank is HIV-positive," she blurted. "He just learned it this morning."

Maggie felt a cold sensation down the length of her spine, and her knees almost buckled under her, causing her to sit on the cold, gray floor. Stacey continued her crying, and as Maggie began to pick herself up from the floor to hold her friend, Stacey suddenly became violent.

"What the hell was I thinking!?! How could I be so stupid?!?" Stacey shouted, well within range of the confused customers in the store. "I can't believe this is happening to me, Maggie. I could die from this shit!"

"Okay, calm down. You might not be infected, Stacey. Have you been tested?" Maggie asked gently.

"No I haven't been tested. Not yet. But you know it'll be positive," Stacey spat. "You know, I make one small mistake. One stupid mistake and now I'm going to die now because of it."

"I'm so sorry, Stacey. Is there anything I can do for you?"

"No one can help me now," Stacey muttered in self-pity.

"What about Frank? How is he feeling?"

"Who cares how Frank feels!" Stacey screamed, grabbing the nearest object and heaving it against the wall. The container of bleach used to sanitize the filter pads crashed against the wall, forcing the top of the container to pop off, sending several gallons of the toxic liquid into the main holding tank of the filtration system.

Maggie scrambled to catch the container before all the contents were spilled, but the damage had been done. A sizable amount of the liquid had mixed with the water in the holding tank. The bleach would rapidly drain into the tanks lined against the other side of the wall, and within minutes there would be hundreds of dead fish floating on top of the water.

Maggie tried desperately to find a way to stop the flow of the water into the tanks, but could not find the valve that controlled the flow. After several minutes, she discovered the valve and was finally able to turn her attention back to Stacey. But by that time, she had disappeared.

Maggie felt her blood begin to boil as she frantically dialed Frank's number. All she received was his answering machine. She apologized to her customers, explaining that they could not buy any fish that day because the water had been contaminated. For the remainder of the day, she sectioned off the rear of the store, explaining time after time to the customers the situation at hand. In between waves of customers, she desperately tried to replace the contaminated water in the holding tank. She netted hundreds of dead fish in the wake of the accident. Several hundred dollars down the drain, so to speak.

Throughout the day, her thoughts turned to both Stacey and Frank. She tried to imagine the emotional anguish each of them must be going through, and she wished there were something she could do. She placed another call to Frank and hung up when she heard his answering machine once again. She thought about calling Stacey, but surmised that she would need to spend the evening with her husband, uninterrupted, in order to explain what had happened. She could not imagine what it must be like for her to have that conversation.

At the end of a very unprofitable business day, Maggie attempted to vent all of her frustrations to her father in her journal, but it wasn't in its place. Searching further, she found it had been pushed to the back of her drawer. She never put it away like that, and she wondered whether some nosy customer or friend had been snooping in her things recently. It was no secret that she had the journal, but it made her uncomfortable thinking that someone would actually go through it. The thought occurred to her that the book might have been shoved to the back of the drawer during the fracas the other night. It had been a very stressful day, and she was afraid it was getting to her. She needed a friend in whom to confide the day's stressful events.

Dear Dad,

I love Stacey like a sister, I really do. And I'm very concerned about her health and her family. But it seems that now even she is becoming a major source of stress in my life...

A half hour later, Maggie went home.

An hour after that, the back door was opened with a key. Fingers punched code numbers on the wall, deactivating the security system. A shadow lurked through the darkened room, fumbling with the top drawer of the desk. Flashlight in hand, he thumbed through the pages to find her latest entry and his next mission. When he read the victim's name, he slammed the journal shut and quietly muttered, "Damn."

CHAPTER 24

Jake pulled into the motel parking lot, searching each brightly colored door for Ida Adams' room. Finding the room, he allowed the truck to idle, deciding how to approach her. He noticed the curtain in the front window being pulled to the side. The curtain closed, and his mother appeared at the front door, motioning for Jake to come in. She waited for him as he slowly walked toward her. She took him by the arm and led her into her room.

The room was like any other hotel room in any other part of the world. There was a double bed, a plain dresser, two straight-back chairs, a small maple table between them, and a television that was switched off as he entered the room. He noticed there were few personal items in sight and wondered where all the woman's belongings were stored. Knowing her tendency for a nomadic existence, he bitterly surmised that she probably had no need for sentimental belongings to conjure up old memories.

He sat in the chair closest to the door as she searched through one of the drawers, producing a large manila envelope. She placed it on the table next to him and sat in the remaining chair. She had been quite successful in her plan to have Jake meet her there. She had called him to inform him that she was on her way to tell Hank about his son. Jake insisted that she meet with him first.

"Go ahead. Open it up," she said, motioning toward the envelope.

"No thanks," he said. "Not interested." She was playing some kind of game with him, and he wasn't about to play along. He had seen hundreds of witnesses take the silent approach to questioning, refusing to utter a sound until their lawyers were present. He wasn't about to flinch until she laid all her cards out on the table.

Jake considered leaving. Initially, he was concerned about how Ida would break this shocking news to Hank. But now that he was sitting across from her once again, staring into her dying eyes, it just didn't seem as important anymore. If she wanted to tell Hank about his son, it was fine with him. He would never suspect the boy would be in his own backyard, never mind right under his nose. Jake stared at the woman and began to rise from his chair.

"Sit down, Jake," she said. "Please. I have a story to tell, and you may want to hear it."

There was nothing she could say to erase all the hurt she had caused over the years, he determined. He had been successful in ridding himself of her over the years, and he wished she had never come back to haunt him. The sullen look in her eyes, though, forced him back into his seat. As much as Jake wanted to leave, Worm needed to hear what his mother had to say. For Worm's sake, he stayed.

"Let me tell you a story, Jake," she said, rising from her chair and pacing slowly around the room. "Once upon a time there was a princess who lived in a castle with her royal parents, an evil king and his bride. The queen was treated like a servant by the domineering king, and the king frequently abused and raped the princess until the day he died. The same tragic accident also took the queen. The princess was forced to live with her peasant relatives after the death of her mother, as no princess could ever claim the throne.

"Life was hard. The peasant couple had an only son, who was their pride and joy. The princess, meanwhile, was treated like a servant. The princess accepted her role until the day the blessed son tragically died. The tortured parents vented their pain and grief upon the poor princess. She would have run away if only she had a place to run.

"One day, a stranger came into town and swept the princess off her feet, promising to take her away from all the cruelties she had become so used to. But his heart belonged to another, and he refused to leave his betrothed for the princess, forcing the princess to bear his child alone. Her guardians were not pleased with her and her bastard son. They locked her away in her tower and refused to let her leave. Until one day a man came and took her away. She was a dutiful, grateful wife, but the man abused her and her son until she could stand it no longer. When the hand of fate offered an escape, she could not take her son with her, as she wasn't sure where she was going. She left her son with her peasant relatives, knowing that they were responsible people and would take care of her son. Through the years, the princess prayed that she had made the right decision. She made several efforts to contact him, but he was nowhere to be found."

She paused to look in the distance, perhaps at some faraway magical castle in her mind's eye. Jake listened to the story, and understood the implied meaning, but was unimpressed with the explanation.

"You have about thirty seconds to get to the point," he snarled.

The old woman looked sadly at him from across the table. She knew too much time had passed to heal all the emotional wounds she had caused, and she knew it wouldn't be easy to get through to him. The picture in the paper sparked something within her that she suspected all along, but which she was afraid to confront. The similarities between Jake and Hank were undeniable. Seeing the two standing together, their arms around each other, looking so proud, there was no doubt in her mind that Jake was her son. Now that she had another chance to see him in person, to look into those dark eyes, she found it hard to believe that she didn't see it sooner. A feeling of guilt washed over her the moment she recognized him. All this time her son had been right in front of her, and she didn't even recognize him. She knew she had not been a very good mother, but she hoped she had better maternal instincts than that.

"It's all right in front of you, Jake. Do with it what you like; it's up to you. It's all up to you. You decide whether or not to tell Hank about his son. You decide whether or not you want a mother." She slid the envelope across the table to him. He carefully scrutinized the envelope, then took it in his hands and slid the contents from inside. A portfolio lay on top of the stack of papers inside. There were many assets, several properties and IRA's, a long list of financial rewards. The next stapled section was a will—the last will and testament of Ida May Adams. He flipped through the pages and came to a photo of him and Hank together after finding the missing Patterson boy.

He looked up at the woman across the table and noticed a tear rolling down her cheek. She lightly shook her head at his perplexed expression.

"I must call and thank the family of that boy," she said. "If it weren't for him, I never would have pieced the whole thing together. Seeing you two side by side, it finally struck me how much you two look alike. It isn't something readily noticeable, but to a mother…" She drifted off, smiling.

"I have accepted who I am, Jake, and what I've done. I have accepted the fact that I'm dying. I can even accept the fact that you may not want me as part of your life. But please don't reject what I have to leave you. Help me make something right with my life. You'll note the name of the benefactor on my will is 'Jake Allen.' Your secret will die with me, John Adams."

Jake suddenly felt as though someone had punched him in the gut. He stood on wobbly legs and peered down at the taunting picture of himself and his smiling father, then at the ghostly figure of his mother. The voice inside his head screamed out to him in agony.

Worm. Worm. Worm.

Scenes from the reoccurring nightmare cut through his mind's eye like a searing jolt of lightning through thick winter air. He felt his feet leave the ground, lifted and shoved by mighty arctic winds, and he sprinted over a sheet of ice to his waiting truck. He threw it into drive, and screeched out of the lot, becoming a distant pair of red lights on a lonely road. About a mile down the road, he skid to a stop, and on the side of the road he lowered his head and wept like a lonesome, terrified little child.

CHAPTER 25

"We need to have ourselves a little chat," Hank said to Jake, as he stood at his desk at the station. Hank felt sorry for the boy. He could tell the investigation was taking an emotional toll on him, and he thought Jake could use a friendly ear. "Let's grab a conference room."

The two walked toward a darkened conference room, with Hank leading the way. He flipped on the light switch, motioned for Jake to take a seat, then shut the door behind him.

"What've ya got, Jake?" Hank questioned, leaning back in his chair.

Jake gave a little laugh, shook his head, and said, "You wouldn't believe me if I told you."

"Try me," Hank challenged.

Taking a deep breath, Jake proceeded to lay it all out on the table. He explained that he had discovered a connection between nine murders that had all occurred within the past two years. He explained that each victim had been abusive to animals in some way. He even explained—after much hesitation—about his experience with the rooster's crow, joking that he was probably just going insane.

Throughout the entire monologue, Hank sat calmly and listened without judgment, wearing his best poker face. Every once in a while, he slowly nodded his head as if he totally understood. At the end of Jake's soliloquy, Hank stood very slowly and ran his fingers through his graying hair. He knew Jake was waiting to hear something profound and supportive, but he had trouble thinking of something to say that wouldn't sound condescending.

Hank cleared his voice, and Jake held his breath. "I have to admit," Hank said. "This whole thing does sound a bit...well...crazy, Jake." Jake's face dropped instantly.

"I do believe strongly, though," Hank continued, "in going with your gut. Why or how it happens, I'll never figure it out. But I am familiar with that particular sensation, and it has served me well over the years. This whole thing might sound crazy to me, but that doesn't make you crazy to believe it. If you believe in it, run with it. Maybe give things a rest for a little while. Step back and view it from a distance. See if it still makes sense to you."

They would have continued debating the issue had it not been for Bean's interruption, informing Hank that he had an important phone call.

"We'll talk later," was the last thing Jake heard. He realized that the entire conversation hadn't helped him much at all.

* * * *

He ambled into the bedroom carrying a fifth of bourbon in one hand and a fresh pack of Marlboros in the other. One was a dear, reliable, old crutch he had grown to love as a valued friend. The other was an old acquaintance he had discarded years ago. Tonight, he felt he needed them both, considering it was such an uncomfortable occasion. He placed them both gently on the nightstand and fluffed up a couple of pillows leaning against the headboard. He threw himself down on the bed, fully clothed, and lit his first cigarette. A healthy swig from the amber bottle followed, and he closed his eyes to enjoy their familiar impact. He wished that perhaps when the two containers were empty, he'd be able to get some rest, and erase the image of the dead body on the floor.

It was, by far, the most difficult of any mission he had directed upon himself. It wasn't easy being detached and dispassionate when the victim was a personal friend. But an order was an order, never to be questioned or debated. He learned that the hard way many, many years before. He consoled himself in the fact that the victim didn't seem to suffer.

She came to him easily, as a trusted friend in need of help. They held a very casual, very friendly conversation together in the moments before she died. He wanted nothing more than to grant her a peaceful death. She struggled a bit when he held her down, the full weight of his body pressed against her as he inserted the hypodermic needle into her neck. He tried to calm her, telling her the heroin would work quickly and would soon make her feel at peace with herself.

He explained to her, as best he could, why this had to be done. He explained how she had brought much pain and stress into the life of his loved one. The girl merely looked at him with a confused look on her face, as if she had no idea about whom he was talking. She deserved to die. She deserved to be poisoned, just as she had poisoned the fish in the pet store.

As promised, the lethal injection was quick and painless. He held her hand as she took her last labored breath. He thought she actually smiled up at him, but he could have been mistaken. He would spend the rest of the night trying to erase that image from his mind. He tilted the bottle once more and noticed that the last drop had been taken. The bottle slipped silently to the carpeted floor and a tear rolled down his cheek. He had done everything possible to ensure the past would not repeat itself, but the situation was growing out of control. Something had to be done soon. The room became blurry as his eyes rolled back into his head. His head crashed down into the pillow and he bit his tongue on impact. But he didn't feel the pain.

CHAPTER 26

Maggie was delirious, huddled in the arms of Hank as the uniformed men searched her store with gloved hands. The limp body of her best friend was zipped into a body bag, and she watched two men in white lift the body from its spot on the floor, leaving nothing but a chalk outline. An empty syringe was deposited with gloved fingers into a plastic bag and marked, "EVIDENCE."

Hank wrapped his fatherly arms around her and whispered words of comfort in her ears as he stroked her hair. Maggie blamed herself for not noticing how distraught her friend had been. All the signs were there: the trouble at home, the affair with Frank, and the threat of a terminal disease. It was too much for anyone to bear.

"She was screaming for help," Maggie said through watery eyes, "and all I did was scream about a bunch of dead fish. How could I have been so selfish?"

Jake watched the two huddled figures in the front of the store, and determined that Maggie was in good hands. He was absorbed in his own mental chaos, having heard the ghostly rooster crow once again. The immediate conclusion at the scene was that Stacey's death had been a suicide. There was no evidence or motive to suggest otherwise. He knew better, for he had his own evidence that suggested quite the opposite. The rooster was never wrong.

He was so absorbed in his investigative work, he barely said a word to Maggie. The image of the chalk outline was burned into his brain. There was the outline, lying next to the vat of water Stacey had contaminated just days before. The words flashed before him like some bizarre subliminal message: THEORY OF REVOLT.

The low laugh he had heard in his dreams filled his brain. It was all too much of a coincidence to ignore any longer. The little voice inside his head was impossible to ignore as well, as was the crowing of the rooster and the haunting laughter. His mind swelled with the blending of sounds and disturbing thoughts. Suddenly, he felt his body taking control of his mind, as he dashed across the store, stepping over investigators and under yellow police tape to his waiting vehicle. He felt a penetrating pain in his skull, as if Worm were boring himself a hole and letting himself out. He grabbed the steering wheel and glanced into the rearview mirror and there he was, staring back at him with an evil grin on his face as if to say, *"Move over Jake! Worm's taking the wheel!"*

* * * *

The files were still scattered over his desk like some giant jigsaw puzzle waiting to be pieced together. The corner pieces had been found, but there was still a lot to fill in the middle. Jake rifled through his desk drawers, searching for the elusive note that possessed him to leave the crime scene and return to the jumbled mess on his desk.

Why don't you look in your front pocket? Worm said sardonically. Jake reached into his front pocket and produced several folded pieces of paper, one of which was his tattered old list of things to do, another was the missing list he had been searching for.

Thanks, buddy, Jake replied, and studied the list. It was a list he had composed several months earlier, and with each crow of the mysterious rooster, he would write down the time and the date of the occurrence. He added the previous night's entry to the list and folded the note to return it to his front pocket.

NO! the voice of Worm echoed. He unfolded the list and scanned over the dates. He then looked down to the two files scattered over his desk and noted that the dates of the murders coincided with the dates on his list. He rushed to the file cabinets on the other side of the office and pulled the files of all the murders occurring on the remaining dates on his list, and one by one he surveyed the contents.

January 29th: Fred Wilkins. Suffered a heart attack in his basement.

His body was unrecognizable…eaten by his own rats…rats that were to be food themselves had they not escaped their prisons, the voice reminded him.

March 4th: Simon Haggerty. Found floating in Conn's Pond. Apparently slipped on the wet rocks at the edge of the pond. Hit his head and drowned.

Simon Haggerty...didn't he drown some of his unwanted kittens a short while before he died?

May 12th: Tucker Quinn. Teenage boy found in bathtub. Electrocuted.

Didn't Maggie mention something about the boy doing the same thing to his sister's guinea pigs? the voice inside his head said sarcastically, almost laughing.

July 4th: Dennis Chapman. Murdered gangland style—his throat slit from ear to ear.

"No connection to the animal revolt," Jake muttered to himself.

Yet the rooster still crowed, the voice reminded him.

August 30th: Jerry Mitchell. Found in his own vehicle in a remote parking lot. Poisoned. Ruled a suicide.

Jerry certainly inflicted his fair share of damage to all things small and furry, didn't he, Jake?

September 25th: Maria Mitchell. Found in her vehicle in her enclosed garage with the motor running. Suicide.

The Mrs. was no saint, either.

October 12th: Abraham Giddings. Throat slashed gangland style. Possible connection to the Chapman case.

Remember that sickly cockatoo in his apartment? Remember its laughing eyes?

October 19th: Elizabeth Lapinski. Throat slashed. Same m.o. as the Giddings and Chapman cases. A possible victim of a random serial killer.

Find any connection yet, Detective? the voice mocked, its laugh filling Jake's cluttered mind.

Jake's rational mind fought the temptation to believe the voice inside his head, the insane laughter that seemed to mock its logical counterpart. Even if he did believe the killings were connected in some way, how would he explain this connection to anyone else? There were only two scenarios in his theory: either animals were revolting against their abusive owners and killing them in the same fashion in which they were abused, or there was a lunatic animal lover on the loose who committed the vengeful murders himself.

"So tell me, Detective, how did you ever put this connection together?" Jake muttered to himself in his best Captain's voice.

"Well, sir. It's like this. See, there's this rooster in my head that crows every time..." Jake's eyes suddenly lifted from the files on his desk as he became aware of his surroundings. He found a pair of extremely confused eyes staring back at him from across the room. He gave a shrug of his shoulders and smiled, then turned back to his work, red-faced.

Jake thought about the rooster. The mystical bird seemed to be a messenger sent from his subconscious. He tried to remember when he had first heard the mysterious crowing. There were times, before his list had begun, when he had heard it. It wasn't until later that he actually started writing down the exact times and dates of the intrusions. He remembered the time he read the article in the morning paper about Dick Williams, the horse farm owner who hung himself. The rooster's crow seemed so real that morning he wondered whether there was actually a real rooster perched outside his window.

He also remembered being called to the accident scene of Sheila Bennett, who had driven her car off of an embankment over a year ago. He couldn't forget the sight of that crazy squirrel bouncing around the inside of that car. He also couldn't forget how victorious the rooster sounded that day. It was the most victorious crow he had heard since...

His mind seized as he remembered an event from his childhood, when he looked upon the white-blanketed body of his Aunt Vera after she had set herself and her home on fire while smoking in bed. He wrestled with his mind in an effort to remember a time further back than that day, when he had heard the rooster for the very first time. But the memory wouldn't come. The further he reached back into the life of Worm, the grayer his memories became. There were certain memories better left undisturbed from their graves.

CHAPTER 27

Maggie stood among mournful friends and family, feeling as though all eyes were fixated on her. She had killed her best friend. She killed her because she ignored her cries for help. She may have even antagonized her friend further by getting so upset with her for poisoning the fish.

Stacey's husband and two small children stood nearby. Her husband, Michael, bravely attempted to console the loved ones around him while his two children appeared confused by all the sad faces. Maggie imagined the feelings of guilt that must have been swirling around in Michael's head. His infidelity led to the unhappiness that caused Stacey to take her own life. She noticed that Frank was conspicuously absent from the ceremony, and she imagined the guilt that must be filling his mind as well.

Jake and Hank stood on either side of Maggie, paying their silent respects. Jake's mind was cluttered with problems of his own. As much as he wanted to begin his life with Maggie, there were giant roadblocks that stood in his path, and they needed to be removed before any life with Maggie could be possible. He mentally perused the list of connected victims in his mind several times over, searching for a more plausible explanation for their connection other than the crowing rooster. He contemplated talking with Hank once again about the murders before going public with his theory that they were somehow all connected. He trusted Hank's opinion, and thought the time was right to invite the old man out to the bar for a few cold ones and some casual conversation about baseball, hypothetical rooster ghosts, and possible blood relations. It was all so ludicrous.

The three friends joined the procession, which snaked its way past the open casket of the devoted wife and mother, and ended with the grieving widower and his two children. They paid their respects to the family and slowly headed toward their cars. Jake and Maggie walked hand-in-hand while Hank walked several paces behind them. Jake walked Maggie to her SUV, and gave her a light kiss before making his way to his own vehicle.

Later that night, Maggie disappeared without a word.

CHAPTER 28

Jake found himself in a familiar position: in front of his desk, hunched over the files of seemingly unrelated murders. He had become a permanent fixture in that chair, and popular opinion around the precinct was that the rookie detective was in over his head, wasting time doing paperwork when he should be out in the streets trying to find that serial killer. It would only be a matter of moments before word of the connection between the three killings leaked out to the press. Then panic would surely wash over the quiet little town.

It had been a few days since Maggie left town, and Jake found her image intruding upon his thoughts more and more often as the days went by, adding to the already crowded ghosts of Worm, his mother, his father, and the faces of the eleven victims of the ghostly rooster. Hank informed him that Maggie mentioned to him that she needed some time away. It had been almost three years since her last vacation, and she felt as though she were being suffocated in the little town of New Milford. It seemed odd that Maggie would have left without saying good-bye to Jake, but he understood how distraught she must be over the death of her friend.

Some concerned customers phoned Hank after encountering the locked doors of the pet store, and a visit to Maggie's house found a note tacked to her front door, explaining that she would be visiting her aunt and uncle for a while. In the letter, she directed the reader to call Frank to take care of the store in her absence. It was unusual for Maggie to take such a cavalier attitude with her animals, but Jake concluded that the stress of Stacey's death must have overshadowed the obligation she felt toward her business at that point.

Shaking his head vigorously in order to force his train of thought back to the cases at hand, he stared at the photos on his desk and flipped through his personal notes on each murder. He scanned the list he made of the rooster's crows and wished he had made more detailed entries of the events. Once again, his thoughts turned to Maggie, who had once suggested to him that he write a journal of his own. Putting your thoughts on paper is very therapeutic, she had said.

He arranged the pictures on top of his desk side by side, each corpse striking its own death pose. Each helpless victim had its own story to tell. Each victim was connected with pets in some way. And every one of them died in much the same manner as they had mistreated their own pets. All except Dennis Chapman. He searched his notes on the Chapman case once again. He had visited the murder scene that day, and once before, and neither time had he seen a pet of any kind. He scanned his list of rooster crows once again, and found that the Chapman murder did indeed coincide with the rooster's crow. He logged on to the office computer and entered the date once again into the search queue. Again, only one murder case appeared. New Milford had never been a very plentiful source of murder cases in all the years he had lived there. Perhaps it was mere coincidence that he heard the rooster crow on the same dates as eleven of the fourteen deaths that occurred over the past year. But the cold shiver up his spine and the laughing voice of Worm told him otherwise.

Dennis Chapman was a sleaze ball who probably deserved the fate he earned. But there was no apparent connection to the other names on the list, other than the fact that he had indirectly affected pets in his treatment of a pet shop owner. Suddenly, a cold chill ran up Jake's spine, and he heard the maniacal laughter of Worm echoing through his mind.

There was a connection between all of these victims, and that connection may be Maggie. He surveyed the list once again. Some of the victim's names jumped off the page as obvious connections to Maggie McCarthy's life. Others were more obscure. The victims were all pet owners, but there was no proof that they had purchased those pets at Maggie's store, or that they had affected her life in any way. There was only one way to find out. He had to see the diary.

He inserted the key and yanked open the back door to the pet store. He couldn't remember the last time he had to use it, but he remembered Maggie handing it to him "in case of emergency." Entering the dark room, he swiftly punched out the security code on the pad, deactivating the alarm. It surprised him that, despite all of the things that haunted his mind, he was able to remember the code Maggie had contrived when he helped install the system almost three years ago.

He felt like a spy, or in the least an unwanted intruder. The birds and animals became suddenly quiet as he fumbled for the light switch. He contemplated the legality of his actions, but surmised that since Maggie had given him the key out of trust and friendship, that he was entitled to enter the store without her knowledge. The morality of flipping through her private journal bothered him greater, although he felt the end justified the means.

He searched the contents of each drawer, encountering loose makeup, scattered pictures, receipts, and assorted order forms. Finally, his fingertips reached the object of his destination. He gently placed the heavy volume flat on the desk and paused to consider his actions. Either the journal held nothing of great significance, or it was the key to solving the murder cases that filled his mind on a daily basis.

He extracted the folded list of rooster's crows from his front pocket and searched for the matching dates in the journal. Upon passing certain entries, he couldn't avoid the iniquitous urge to browse certain entries. He came upon the June 15th entry and read about the death of the store mascot, Rocky. He read about how Maggie felt before and after the death of her beloved pet, in her own handwriting, and he understood exactly how she felt because he had been there with her. He found nothing particularly unusual on the dates that coincided with his list. There were just the usual complaints and concerns, which she had often related to him in the past.

He began thumbing through each page, searching for a key name or phrase to jump off of the pages. He stopped upon encountering the name of Dick Williams. "The man abused defenseless horses," Maggie had written to her father. She continued on a tirade about Mr. Williams for two full pages, and ended with the suggestion that the man should be hung.

In the back of Jake's mind, he pictured a scenario where a crazed Maggie McCarthy went on nightly rampages, butchering all those who crossed her path. But the scenario was just so ludicrous, he ceased the thought almost immediately. Maggie could be a very stubborn, very temperamental person, but if there was one thing he knew about Maggie McCarthy, it was that she was also very kind. She would never harm any living creature no matter what cruelties that creature may have inflicted.

He continued thumbing through the entries, reaching August 12th.

Dear Dad,

Remember that Sheila Bennett woman I told you about a while ago? Well, I read in an article today that her dogs attacked some poor little boy. Turns out the dogs had rabies, and now that boy is suffering for her stupidity. I tried to warn her, Dad, but she just wouldn't listen. That woman deserves to be locked up forever—preferably in a cage full of rabid squirrels.

Jake's hands grew cold and numb as he read the horrific passages that gave credence to his theory. A nauseous feeling welled deep in his gut, but he pressed forward to find more evidence. By the time he came to November's entries, he found himself pleading with Maggie not to mention Stacey's accident with the fish. He closed his eyes and slammed the book shut after discovering the dreaded entry.

He opened his coat and began to place the book into his front pocket. He reconsidered after debating the legality of his method of search and seizure. Later, after he had compiled enough evidence to pinpoint the killer, a warrant would have to be obtained in order to retrieve the book. Warrants were the last of his worries, however.

In retrospect, his theory of animal revolt had not been so off-base. The common denominator was not the pets themselves, however. It was Maggie. Anyone that knew Maggie knew that she was not capable of the kind of inhumane carnage the killer had wrought. And the notion that Maggie hired a hit man to eliminate those people was also absolutely absurd. Only one possibility remained: someone was using Maggie's diary as a blueprint for murder.

He paced about the length of the store. He passed by rows of placid aquariums; past captivated reptiles, past vigilant rodents and hushed birds, toward the front window where he stood with all eyes upon him. Somewhere out there was a serial killer with a deep obsession for Maggie McCarthy. Someone wanted to protect her from all the evils of the world. Someone who would kill for her. Someone who had access to her diary.

This last thought sent a cold chill up his spine. There could only be a handful of people in the world who knew about Maggie's diary, and the ones that did were all of her closest friends. Someone close to Maggie was using the journal to ensure that she was safe and protected. The killer was following a simple directive: hurt those who hurt the girl. Serve and protect.

It was all hitting too close to home. Lesson One in the detective's handbook was to never get personally involved with a case. But this case had become uncontrollably personal. He found he was not only able to read the mind of the criminal, but he also found himself feeling sympathetic to his cause. Maggie had been through a lot in her young life—more than the average person could tolerate. The killer was simply taking the law into his own hands and eliminating some human garbage that probably deserved what they got.

The pain in his head swelled as he brought his hands to his head. He waited for the voice inside his head to begin its evil laughter. He waited for the howling wail of Worm and the mocking crow of the rooster. There was silence. He released the pressure from his ears and listened again for the laughter, but it never came.

What if the rooster had been trying to tell him something other than the fact that a person had died? What if he himself had the key to some knowledge that had been simply forgotten or purposefully locked away? What if he was not in control, and had never really been in control? What if Worm had controlled him all along, and he was just a puppet in some child's game?

He felt light-headed and breathless as he stared through a dark tunnel to the door at the end of the pet store. He propelled his body toward the pinhole of light through the swirling blackness. Fumbling for the knob, he managed to turn it enough to pop the door open slightly. He felt the coolness of the night air wash over his numbed face before his entire world turned to black.

When he awoke, he wasn't certain where he was, or what time it was. He only knew that Hank was kneeling beside him with a concerned look upon his face, cradling his head in his arms.

"Jesus, Jake, what the hell happened?" Hank asked frantically. "Are you okay?"

Jake took a moment to consider, then replied, "I guess so…I'm not really sure what happened. I guess I just passed out."

"You're lucky I came by here or the wolves might've gotten to you before I did," Hank said with a smirk. "Hop in the car. I'll give you a ride to the hospital."

The memories of the hours past rushed back into his mind as he attempted to prop himself up on his elbows. There was a lot of work to be done. As intricate as his theory was, it was still far-fetched to the average person who didn't hear the rooster's crow. To divulge the entire theory at this point, with only an imaginary rooster and a diary full of complaints as evidence, would be detrimental to both the case and his reputation. Once the entire plot was revealed clearly and definitively, the world would hear the whole story. But for now, there was much more work to be done.

"No thanks," Jake said, returning to his feet. "I'm fine, Hank. Really. I think I've just been working too hard. Too much stress."

Hank shook his head. "Well, whatever it is, do me a favor. Go home and rest a while. And if you still feel like shit, see a doctor! That's an order, soldier!"

"Thanks, Sergeant," Jake replied. "But really, I'm okay. I just haven't eaten in a while. I'm going to go home, get some food in me, let my dog out, and crash on the sofa for a day or two."

Back home, Jake did let the dog out the back door, but he knew he couldn't rest until he had put some more of the puzzle together. He poured himself a cup of coffee and stared at the files on his kitchen table. He awoke the next morning to the sound of King's barking. There was a truck parked in his driveway, and a delivery person was stepping toward his front door. Jake reached for the door just as the man prepared to knock. He signed for the package and examined the large manila envelope with no return address. Bending back the clasp, he pulled out several files. Ida Adam's portfolio spilled out onto the maple three-legged table and the memory of that day suddenly reawakened within him.

He had no recollection of his visit with his mother until the package arrived. As soon as he viewed the familiar contents, the memories returned quickly and painfully. His mother had recognized him, and Hank was indeed his father. Somehow, he had suppressed that whole incident as if it had never occurred. He stared at the contents of the envelope and noticed an unfamiliar pink envelope with the hand-written message on the front stating, "Please Open."

Jake gathered the papers together and stuffed them back into the envelope. He regarded the pink folder on the floor, then stepped over it to walk back into the kitchen, leaving it and the portfolio behind. He managed to suppress the memory once before; perhaps he could will himself to do it again. There were too many things going on in his life. The last thing he needed was another ghost haunting him. His mind was crowded enough without Ida Adams forcing her way into his thoughts, too.

CHAPTER 29

Maggie slowly paced about her room. It had all the comforts of home: a four poster bed with two plump pillows, a vanity stocked with her favorite cosmetics and perfume, a bureau in the corner filled with lacy undergarments and silky gowns, an open-shelved closet containing neatly folded jeans and a wide selection of sweaters and shirts, a small table and chair tastefully tucked into one corner, and a delicate arrangement of artificial flowers placed on top of a frilly doily as a center piece. The room was small, but seemed larger by the way it was designed. It was vaulted, with a large skylight high overhead showing the lapsing of the day. French doors to the right led to a private bath. Two rooms thoughtfully constructed with her in mind, and both immaculately prepared for her arrival.

She clicked on the television and began flipping through the channels. A solitary tear streaked down her swollen face. "No, not again," she scolded herself out loud. "You have to get a hold of yourself. Everything will be okay. Just give it time and we'll figure something out."

She stared across the room to the thick door on the other side, half expecting him to enter. It was difficult to predict when he would make his next appearance. She had yet to figure out his schedule, though she doubted that even he knew what his timetable was. The hourly newsbreak told her it was noon, and he would most likely appear soon with her lunch. At times he would deliver the food himself, other times he would slip it through the window in the door without uttering a word. She imagined it depended on his mood, and how receptive she was to his intrusion.

She had not been the most gracious guest, and she detected a noted disappointment in her captor when he informed her of his plan. Apparently, she was not as receptive to the idea as he had imagined. In retrospect, she probably should have acted a little more civilized. Perhaps then he would allow her to leave her confines for a short period of time. Then, when he wasn't looking, she could run for it or hit him with something and escape from her prison. But instead, she made the situation even worse with her outbursts. She got on his bad side, and she imagined that was not the best place to be in her situation.

She was a prisoner held against her will for an offense unknown to her. Bringing her knees to her chest and wrapping her arms around them, she cautioned herself to remain calm. She knew it was impossible to think clearly once she lost her temper. He would soon arrive, and once he did she would need something from him. There were a lot of things she needed to know, but most of all she just wanted to know why. She felt she needed a good icebreaker, a minor request that would seem innocent enough on the surface that he just might produce a firm answer. He was a tough man to fool, and even tougher to manipulate. She picked up a book he had left for her and pretended to read, just in case he happened to walk in, but her mind was flooded with questions for him. She would ask him about the weather, about the pet store and, if he seemed to be in a good mood, why the hell she couldn't go home. And how long did he intend for her to be his guest—or was she his permanent captive?

She turned slightly and offered a big smile as he opened the door and entered with a tray of triangular sandwiches and a heaping bowl of green grapes. He smiled back, a suspicious look behind his eyes. She watched him without losing her happy expression, but noticed he had forgotten to close the door behind him. She debated whether he left enough room for her to run for it, but decided he could easily grab her. There would be other, better, opportunities, she concluded. It was better not to forfeit any future opportunities for escape by being carelessly impatient.

She invited him to join her for lunch and after an initial look of shock he declined. He had to get back to work, he told her. Perhaps he would stay for dinner. She watched him leave out the door, her plastic smile still molded to her lips. The smile vanished as she listened to the key locking the door from the other side. It had been nearly two weeks. Thirteen days to be exact. It was all so unbelievable. She had wasted too much time pouting and fighting and feeling sorry for herself. If she thought about it every waking moment, perhaps she could concoct a plan masterful enough to get her out of her prison. No one else would help her—at least, not for a while. The note he forced her to write back at the store would ensure that no one would be looking for her for quite some time.

Chapter 30

Jake slouched behind the wheel of the unmarked police van, with Bean at his side. Despite his protests, the captain had given him a mandatory hiatus from his work on the apparent serial killings of Chapman, Giddings, and Lapinski.

"You need some time away from it, Jake," the Captain said. "I can see the stress is getting to you. You look like shit. I'm giving you another assignment for a couple weeks. I think once you take a step back, you'll be able to get a little perspective."

His new assignment consisted of sitting in a musty old van, eating out of cardboard boxes, and listening to the mindless banter of an overzealous Bean experiencing his first stakeout. Lately, however, Beannie was unusually quiet. Whatever was bothering him, it seemed he had no urge to discuss it. So the two men sat in the rusty van waiting for help to arrive, each alone with his thoughts.

Jake drummed out a tune on the dashboard and stared at the building across the street. For days, he tried to block out any thoughts about the serial killer or his personal problems. The Captain was right. He needed a little time to step back and gain some perspective. Most of all he needed to talk to someone to get his mind off his problems. He looked over to the passenger seat and spied Bean with his head tilted back, his eyes wide open.

"Earth to Beannie," said Jake with a crooked grin. Bean slowly turned his eyes toward him and forced a smile in return. "What's eating at you, anyway? You've been out in left field for about an hour now."

Bean returned his intense stare to the ceiling, then turned toward the passenger side window. "Nothing," he said. "Nothing. I just can't help thinking I have better things to do than sitting here letting my ass go numb."

"Well, well…didn't take you long to lose that enthusiasm I saw when this assignment began." Bean simply nodded, continued to gaze out his window, and tightly gripped the handle of the door. Jake could see his reflection staring back and wondered whether Bean was actually looking at him instead.

"Is there something bothering you, Bean? Something other than the fact that you'd like to be someplace else right now?"

Bean relaxed his grip on the door handle and began to cross his legs. He stopped in mid-motion and drew one leg up to his chest instead, resting his foot on the seat. Although he moved with great deliberate motions, Jake noted that his far hand came to rest on the top of his gun. Bean managed an uneasy smile and turned toward Jake.

"Have you heard the scuttlebutt around the office lately?" he inquired shyly.

Jake returned a confused shake of his head, uncertain whether he wanted to discuss the latest office gossip for the next hour.

A look of surprise crossed Bean's face, and he asked, "Are you sure you haven't heard? About a certain cop down at the station who may be a little mentally unbalanced, if you know what I mean?"

Jake played along, responding, "I don't usually go for idle locker room chat, but go ahead. I give up. What the hell are you talking about, Beannie boy?"

Bean seemed to be nervous. He shifted his position once again, and he continued to play with his gun barrel, although Jake supposed he wasn't supposed to see that as Bean tapped on the back of his seat to divert Jake's attention.

"It's just the two of us here, you know, Jake. If there's anything you want to tell me, it doesn't have to go any further. I hope you know that. We are friends, right?"

Jake's frustration at the seemingly incoherent banter grew steadily. He let out an exasperated breath and said, "Let me ask you something. Am I supposed to know what the hell you're talking about? Jesus…I know I've been a little out of it for a while, but what did I miss?"

Bean shook his head slightly and slowly turned toward the front window, flashing a glimpse toward the building. Either the man was a very good actor, he thought, or he really didn't know what was going down.

"C'mon, Bean. Spit it out. Like you said, it's just the two of us, so what've you got?"

Bean released his grip on his gun and began rubbing his hands over his pant legs. "We are friends, so I guess I could be the one to tell you. I haven't decided if I really believe it or not. Maybe you can tell me something to set things straight." He took a deep breath, then spoke. "The rumor has it that you've gone off the deep end, Jake. Actually, no one could blame you, what with the creepy nature of the cases you're working on and all the pressure the Captain's put on you to find the killer and all. There's talk of you hearing little voices inside your head...something about a rooster...and that you've got all sorts of bizarre theories about the serial murders. And there's something else, too, but I don't know if it's my place to tell you. You've helped me out a lot and I owe you for all the times you've saving my ass both on duty and with the sergeant."

Jake was stunned. How could Bean know about the rooster? How did the whole department seem to know about it as well? He shook his head in disbelief, but before he could ponder the possibilities, Bean cleared his throat and spoke again.

"You gotta admit, you've been acting a little weird lately. I guess that's why a lot of the guys think the rumors are true. The hardest thing to believe is what happened a couple days ago." Bean paused to consider whether to reveal his next bit of news. But the damage had already been done. "The other day we got an anonymous tip that you were seen leaving Giddings' apartment shortly before the neighbor found his body. What's more, the caller implied there was a witness, afraid to come forward, that puts you in the home of Elizabeth Lapinski the morning before her body was found. The caller wouldn't tell us anything more, and he refused to come down to the station, so it's really just his word. This guy could be anybody, Jake. Think of all the guys you've locked up over the years. That's why a lot of us aren't taking it too seriously. Unfortunately, Internal Affairs is looking into it anyway. My guess is, as soon as we get finished up here, you'll be getting a visit. They'll ask you a few questions, but really, Jake, I don't think they have much to go on. It's just procedural, you understand."

Jake began to mouth the words, but stopped himself when the voice he heard was that of Worm. Inside his head, he heard the strange, taunting laughter he heard before. He could almost picture Worm sitting next to King George; the two of them reveling in the fact that Jake's cover had been blown. The whole world knew about them, it seemed, and the boy's victorious laughter filled his head as a startled expression fell over Bean's face. Bean appeared to say something, but his words were drowned out by the deafening laughter. Jake sat motionless as he watched Bean leap frantically from the car and run across the street.

Suddenly, Jake was snapped back into reality. He regained control over his body and discovered that he was alone in the car. He watched as Bean entered the building, and he immediately sprinted after him. Nikki Starr, the young hooker who agreed to participate in the sting operation in exchange for leniency, had been at her window when she saw the sleek black caddie pull up in front of her building. She nervously poured two glasses of Chianti in anticipation of her company. The plan called for her to act as though she were upset with him for having her wait so long. He liked it when she played the angry bitch. The act would also buy her some time until the two dopes across the street came to her rescue.

Alberto Ruiz managed to dodge the police for months, and he climbed all the way up into the top five most wanted men in the county. He was easy prey, though, with his pants around his ankles and his face buried in Ms. Starr's bosom when Bean arrived. Bean tackled Ruiz to the floor and cuffed him. Jake entered the room soon after, and cuffed the woman as well, in order to protect her status as police informant. The two officers escorted their prisoners down the hallway of the apartment building as nosy tenants peered through cracked doors.

When they returned to the station, Jake noticed for the first time the looks in the eyes of his fellow officers, and understood what Bean had told him earlier. Their eyes followed him as he walked to his desk. The stares were quickly averted, however, when he attempted to make eye contact with any of them. He sunk into his chair and retrieved some paperwork from his desk drawer. The conversation with Bean replayed itself over and over again in his head. Admittedly, his behavior had been somewhat bizarre lately to the average bystander. He spent a great deal of time pouring over the same files on his desk, staring at the same pictures, and blocking out the outside world. Perhaps he had been a little too distant, both with his co-workers and his friends. Maybe he had allowed his personal problems to dominate his professional life. What bothered him the most was how anyone could have learned of the rooster.

He suddenly noticed his body was rocking back and forth in the chair, the squeaking from its springs reverberating off the walls. He watched his hands playing with themselves on top of his desk and realized he was making himself a nervous wreck. His desk was a mess, full of assorted notes, pictures, crumbs, and coffee rings. He reached into his back pocket and produced a handkerchief. Moistening the corner with a little saliva, he began to erase the coffee rings from the plastic cover over his desk calendar. He gathered the crumbs into a small pile and began to wipe them off the edge of his desk, but the blotter stood in his path. He moved the blotter and several sheets of folded paper moved with it, causing them to fall to the floor and into his lap. Unfolding the papers, he noticed that they were pages from his personal notebook. Pages had been torn from his records and entries detailing the rooster's crowing and his theory of animal revolt. There were even recent notations detailing his theory about a maniacal vigilante with insider motives.

Jake quickly looked around and noticed the staring eyes had found other things with which to occupy themselves. He gathered up the loose papers and stuffed them into his coat pocket. He reached into his memory to recall a reason why he would rip the pages from his notebooks and surmised that someone must have stumbled across them. This, he thought, would explain how they knew about the rooster. It would explain all the ugly rumors about his apparent insanity, yet it did not explain the gossip about the anonymous phone tip that led to an investigation by Internal Affairs.

Too many thoughts swirled around in his mind; too many questions with too few answers. He needed some rest. He needed to sprawl out on his couch in his bare feet, watching television, with a cold beer in his hand and a warm dog at his feet. He turned off his desk lamp and began to walk away when he stepped backward and scrawled a note on a piece of notepaper:

To Whom It May Concern:
DON'T YOU HAVE ANYTHING BETTER TO DO?!?

He shoved the paper under the blotter and stood to survey the desktop. Everything appeared to be in order, just as he had left it before. For most of the ride home, he blasted the radio. He drummed his fingers on the steering wheel and sang as many words to the song that he could remember, humming the rest. Each time an unpleasant thought crept into his mind, he turned the volume up a notch.

From the way King acted, it seemed as though he had been alone for weeks. The furry dog bounded out of his pen upon being released and Jake gave him a big hug as the dog wrapped his paws around Jake's head and licked his face. As Jake walked to the back door, he hummed along to a familiar tune in his head. He couldn't remember the lyrics, but it was a haunting melody just the same. With each step he took toward the door, the words of the song began to form. He soon realized that he had stopped humming, yet the song continued. He fumbled for the keys, dropping them several times in his rush to escape the music. He finally managed to open the door, and following King inside, slammed it shut. He remained with his head pressed to the cold window of the door as the music seemed to follow him through the wood of the door and into his head once again.

The worm goes in...the worm goes out...into your stomach and out of your mouth...He'll eat your eyes...he'll eat your toes...even the boogers out of your nose...

A loud bark from King and the sound of metal hitting the floor like a pair of cymbals being smashed together at the end of the stanza, caused Jake to whirl around. King cocked his head back at the empty stare from his owner, and flipped his water dish once again with his paw, sending it tumbling across the floor.

"Sorry, buddy. I've had a rough day," Jake said, filling the dog's dish with tap water.

Just before climbing into bed, Jake popped four sleeping pills into his mouth. He placed the small bottle on the nightstand near his bed, within reach in case four weren't enough. Maybe he should take the whole bottle, he thought. That would surely make that damn song go away.

If you see a hearse go by
You will be the next to die.
They'll cover you up with a bloody sheet
And lower you down to about six feet.
If all goes well in about a week
Your coffin will suddenly spring a leak.
Then close your eyes, bite your lip.
The worm will start to feed and nip.
The worm goes in, the worm goes out.
Into your stomach and out your mouth.
He'll eat your eyes, he'll eat your toes.
He'll eat all the boogers in your nose.
So if you see a hearse go by
You will be the next to die.

CHAPTER 31

The following morning, Jake woke up to King's sloppy wet kisses. He went through his morning ritual, letting King out before starting the coffee maker and jumping into the shower. Standing under the hot stream, he tried to remember the events of the preceding day. Yet beyond the arrest of Ruiz and the order to appear for a meeting, the rest of the day's and night's activities were lost in a hazy mental fog—much like the bathroom, which had become thick with steam.

He couldn't shake the feeling that he was forgetting something important. The impending meeting most likely involved the IA investigation, and he was not looking forward to walking into that bee's nest. By the time he finished his shower, he felt foolish to be nervous about anything. He certainly had nothing to hide, and thereby had nothing to fear. He assured himself that the IA investigators were merely doing their duty to ensure there wasn't a mentally unstable cop on the payroll.

He had decided to move all of his notes from the office to his home, and at that moment, the photos and post-it notes on the wall downstairs beckoned him. He knew he was very close to cracking the case. If there really were a link between Maggie's pet store and these killings, it would be in the best interests of Maggie's safety to solve this puzzle as quickly as possible.

As he pulled on his socks, a thought occurred to him, and he sprinted downstairs to the wall in the kitchen. He stood before the wall, scanning the photos of the victims, newly arranged from left to right by time of death. Below each photo was a post-it note summarizing the details of each death: how each person had died, and his or her connection to the pet store.

He sat at the table, his eyes affixed to the wall, as he knotted the laces of his shoes. He leaned back in his chair, mulling over his latest idea. We weighed its merit against its feasibility. He had a gut feeling that Maggie had all the answers whether she knew it or not. Of course, she didn't know it. She had no idea she was the motivation for a string of bizarre serial murders. If she knew, it would devastate her.

He checked the time and realized he was late for work. He jotted down a brief note to remind himself where he had left off in his thought process, grabbed his coat and headed for the door. On the way out, he passed by the manila folder lying on the side table, and then spotted the pink envelope on the floor. The image of Ida Adams flashed into his mind. It happened so quickly, he couldn't stop the flow of his personal problems from interrupting his train of thought on the case at hand. All the way into work, his thoughts revolved around his dying mother, and not the unsolved serial murders, nor his impending meeting with Internal Affairs.

* * * *

Maggie awoke deciding today was the day. She was going to confront her captor or die trying. She was going to get some answers, and she was going to demand to be released. She had rights, and he had no right to keep her as his personal property, like some pet in her store. She needed freedom and fresh air. She needed contact with the outside world. She needed a plan.

She thought about the possible reasons behind her imprisonment. She immediately ruled out kidnapping. As she had no family and no assets other than the store, kidnapping her would not be a very profitable venture. She also doubted that she was being held as some sort of fantasy sex slave, as her captor had yet to make any advances toward her. She seemed to have only one thing in common with the typical hostage in that she was given absolutely no information. Any question or reference to her situation was met with complete indifference and blank stares as if he failed to hear her. He either smiled and told her not to worry or he turned and stomped out the door. She found that if she pressed him too hard, he would disappear for a couple of days, sending food and supplies through the narrow window in the door. She upset him the night before, and she wasn't sure how long it would be until she saw him again. She began to formulate two specific plans of attack. Today, she would try the first plan, and hope that he would give her enough motive not to use the second one.

* * * *

Roll call was unusually subdued, void of the usual interruptions and joking. The joking stopped the moment Jake walked into the room. All talking ceased and all eyes shifted to the desks in front of them. All except for Bean, who flashed Jake a Mona Lisa smile and a quick nod of the head before he, too, put his pencil to blank paper.

Jake was prepared when the Captain pulled him aside after the meeting ended. He had prepared a statement and felt he was ready for any questions Internal Affairs may have for him. If worse came to worst, he would tell them the whole story, including the rooster's crowing that led him to believe that thirteen murders were committed by the same perpetrator in the last year and a half. All he needed to do was remain calm and composed, and they would see that he was mentally competent and able to fulfill his duties. As for the alleged phone tip, the caller had very little credibility since he failed to give his name, nor any details about the incidents he claimed to have witnessed.

The meeting took all of fifteen minutes. Jake didn't have to say a word. In fact, the only person to speak in the room was the Captain. He felt a little nervous when he walked into the room and saw the two men from Internal Affairs standing near the Captain's desk, but aside from a polite introduction, they never spoke. The Captain gave Jake a new assignment that was to take priority over the slasher cases. It was an unpleasant assignment, but a necessary one. Under any other circumstance, Jake would have objected to the assignment, but he felt he was in no position to argue at that point. The most amazing aspect of the entire meeting was that there was no mention of the rumors surrounding Jake's mental health, nor the anonymous caller. As he reached his desk, walking past hushed whispers and cold stares, he realized his days as the hotshot young detective-on-the-rise were over. He was no longer the golden boy of the precinct, and he feared that status had been lost forever. And if his fellow officers were shunning him now, just wait until he took down one of the family.

The new assignment dropped on Jake's lap that morning consisted of finding a sizable amount of heroin that had been confiscated from the evidence room—a very important piece of evidence crucial to the Ruiz case. Jake tried to be inconspicuous as he studied the faces of the men and women that passed by his desk. It occurred to him that he need not consider each one of them a suspect, as only certain individuals had access to the evidence room. The evidence room was only legally accessible to the rank of sergeant and up. Of course, illegally, he imagined almost anyone could have taken the dope if he were clever enough. Unfortunately, he'd have no supernatural help on this case.

Ain't that just like them, Jake thought. *Never a damn rooster around when you need one.*

* * * *

Maggie sat on the edge of her bed, knees together, swaying rhythmically as she waited for him to come to the door. He was late. By the volume of her stomach's growling, she estimated that he should have arrived over two hours ago. She didn't believe he'd let her starve to death. He hadn't gone to all this trouble for that. He was probably just trying to make a point about who was in charge and exactly who had control. It certainly went against her grain, after all the hard work she had done to become an independent person, to have to surrender to someone else's rules of behavior. He wanted her to be totally submissive, completely obedient. He didn't come out and say it directly, but it was implied. She felt as though she were being trained like some dancing poodle: good behavior rewarded, bad behavior punished. Last night, she provoked him. He took the tray with him when he left, uttering the threat, "Don't bite the hand that feeds you." But she was prepared to pick up where she left off if and when he showed up.

She paused to consider the ramifications if he never returned. If something happened to him, no one would know where she was. He may not be the ideal companion, but he was all that she had. She wondered whether anyone had missed her or suspected foul play. She shivered and clenched her fists, shaking the upsetting thought from her mind.

She began to plot her next move. The first phase of "Plan A" began the night before. She coaxed her captor into believing that she desperately needed to make a trip to the pet store. It seemed like a reasonable request, especially after the added suggestion that they go in the wee hours of the morning, when no one would be around to see them. He knew of her commitment to her animals, and it only followed that she would be concerned about their welfare. The pitiful look she gave him had been so successful in the past for her, and she was sure that she struck a chord with him somewhere deep inside him. Behind those vacuous eyes, she could almost see the familiar friendly person she once knew. She anticipated his reaction, but she figured he had an entire night to think about it and he would eventually come around to see things her way. As insurance, she developed one more reason to justify her need to visit the store, and she was ready for him—whenever he would arrive.

* * * *

By late afternoon, Jake was exhausted after a full day of wrestling with his conscience. The harder he fought to concentrate on the new case at hand, thoughts about the serial killer intruded more often. The possibility that Maggie was somehow connected to the killings made the thoughts even more difficult to erase. He was glad she was away from New Milford, safe and sheltered by her loved ones. It was a little odd, however, that she was able to pick up and leave so easily, especially considering her store hadn't been open in quite some time. It had been several weeks since he heard from her, and it disturbed him that she would leave for so long without calling him. He felt they had made some advancement toward growing closer in their relationship, but his obsession with the serial killings and with his mother detoured that growth.

He shook his head vigorously, trying to shake the thought away. He looked at his watch, then returned to the case at hand. Any one of the officers could have lifted the heroin from the evidence room. Unfortunately, the room was not as secure as it could be. He supposed it was because New Milford rarely produced the type of evidence worth stealing.

As for motive, Jake reasoned that the cop might have needed the drugs for his own use, or for a personal friend. The cop also may have taken a bribe from Ruiz himself to discard of the incriminating evidence. He cursed the Captain for handing him an assignment that was clearly an Internal Affairs problem. They needed somebody to be the undercover guy on this assignment, though, and knowing they had Jake in a compromising position, their decision was easy.

It would be a very difficult, very time-consuming task, and he wasn't sure he had the time for it. His thoughts reverted back to the thought he had earlier about the possible identity of the serial killer. He already knew the killer's motives revolved somewhere around Maggie. He also knew that it was Maggie's words that propelled him into action. He wished that Maggie were around to set a decoy for him with another entry in her journal. He found it hard to believe that the store's doors were locked during the busiest time of the year. It wasn't like Maggie to pass up lucrative Christmas sales. He made a note to himself to phone Hank and ask if he had heard from her. It had been a while since he had seen his old friend, anyway. Other than a passing greeting, their schedules seemed to conflict.

Jake discovered he lost contact with a number of people, including his mother, who had not made one of her infamous intrusions into his life in quite some time. He also had not heard from Worm lately. That familiar insane laughter and the tiny voice that frequently controlled his thoughts had been relatively quiet lately. He grew to regard Worm as the little boy inside who refused to grow up. It was as though the boy were fighting him, contemptuously despising him for having buried him so long ago to assume a new identity. Was it possible that the boy had been buried alive in his brain tissue, and was clawing his way back into existence through memories and dreams? The thought was ludicrous, but disturbing. He looked again at his watch. It was fruitless to sit at his lonely desk any longer. It was apparent no work would get done until he could resolve the conflicts inside of him.

* * * *

Maggie's stomach was growling so loudly she doubted she could fall asleep through all the noise. He had to know she was starving. Didn't he have any compassion for his private pet? He must know that she hadn't had a thing to eat since early yesterday afternoon. It was bad enough being there in the first place, but the least he could do was take care of her and make sure she was as comfortable as possible. The animals in her pet store received better treatment than the kind she was getting.

"God, Maggie. You're starting to lose it," she told herself.

She rolled over on the bed and flipped through the channels once again. She watched the news to see if there had been any breaking news about a kidnapping, but again there was not a word. Apparently, no one was worried about her. That damn note she left certainly didn't help her cause, but it was amazing what a person will do with the cold steel of a pistol pressed to her head. At the time, she was relieved that was all he wanted.

He would show up eventually, and she would use the opportunity to hit him with her best guilt trip. Then he would concede to her a little trip to the pet store. It was that thought that carried her through the day. The opportunity for some fresh air. The opportunity to see her pets again. The opportunity to escape.

Chapter 32

Jake awoke with a stiff neck and assorted cramps in his arms and legs. He remembered falling asleep on the couch, but as his eyes slowly adjusted to the brightness of the morning sun filtering through the room, he discovered he had moved to the leather recliner at some point during the night. King stretched his legs as well, and ambled over to his master to lick his face and give him the signals to let him out.

He watched the dog bound toward the back door as he began to lift himself off the couch, and he wished he had King's energy. He could feel every muscle in his body ache as he walked into the kitchen and opened the door. He poured some coffee grinds into a filter and pushed a few buttons, then sat on the wooden chair next to the table and waited for the magical waking serum to brew.

He wondered whether the coffee would be enough to stir him from his condition, and thought a bucket of ice water thrown over his head might be a better solution. The reference stirred his memory to a time when his father did just that, laughing all the while as he shivered in the wet sheets.

Why did that memory just flash into his head? He shook off the shiver that suddenly jolted his mind into full alert. He refused to allow the memory to dominate his thoughts, for the mission of the day had been determined the night before. He would find proof that Maggie's poison pen pal and the serial killer were one in the same. Maggie mentioned to him shortly before she left that she had been receiving anonymous love notes for a few months. He even thought she might have been telling him just to see his reaction, as if he were the culprit. Once she determined that he was not, she informed him that the letters had been getting a little stranger, and that she was a little worried by them. She told him she would show him some of them, but the store was packed and she didn't have the time. The letters were forgotten during the time he was investigating the serial murders, but resurfaced last night as he lay on the couch.

Maggie said that the writer wanted to protect her, and she was pretty sure that he was a little unbalanced mentally. Jake rose from the table and poured himself a cup of coffee. He peered out the window to check on King, and watched the dog stand in the middle of the yard as if he were a sentry, staring off into the horizon. He returned to the table and his thoughts returned to the journal. How many people had access to it? For that matter, how many knew of its existence? It wasn't a secretive journal. There could conceivably be dozens who knew of its existence, yet few who had access to it.

He stared at the collage of pictures decorating the table he had used as his personal headquarters since he was removed from the serial killer case. His stare found the photocopied pictures of Giddings and Haggerty, then panned down to the picture of Stacey. His thoughts immediately fell upon Frank's connection to the three people and his access to Maggie's diary.

Jake rose once again from the table and stepped back. Coincidence or not, Frank's connection in this scenario could not be overlooked. Frank lived in the same building as both Giddings and Haggerty, and his affection for Maggie was not a secret. He certainly had displayed a tendency toward violence in his lifetime as well. Jake imagined it was conceivable that Frank would forcibly eliminate any and all competition for Maggie's hand. He had threatened Jake many times for getting "too close." Perhaps the only reason Jake was still alive was because of the badge. Even the most disturbed of psychopaths would think twice before killing a cop. Would it be beyond Frank, however, to place an anonymous phone call to get a cop out of the way?

He pondered this last thought while cautiously sipping his coffee. After discovering his life-threatening disease, would Frank even risk the chance of infecting Maggie? He glanced at the photo of Stacey sprawled on the concrete floor of the pet store and received an answer to his question. He had not considered Stacey's well-being, after all. After giving her the disease, she ended up full of heroin. Wasn't that the drug they found on her? The same drug missing from the evidence room? The coffee mug suddenly slipped through Jake's fingers, crashing to the floor.

He shook his head and bent down to pick up the broken pieces. There was no concrete justification to suspect Frank was the author of Maggie's anonymous notes, nor the anonymous caller, nor the murderer for that matter. His investigative instinct, however, wouldn't let the feeling pass without pursuing it further.

He thought about Hank, and wondered whether the old man might have an opinion to share with his boy. A little fatherly advice, one might say. He thought about letting his dog back in the house, but a look outside at the slumbering beast told him that King would be all right for a little while. He wouldn't be long. He just needed a little advice from a good friend.

*　　*　　*　　*

Maggie discovered the sandwich on the shelf outside of the narrow window and wondered how long it had been there. She didn't hear him come home last night, and she hadn't slept very well. She was mad at herself for letting the opportunity pass her by, but the sandwich erased her anger quickly. She wondered what his new game plan was. He seemed to want her to slowly go insane with boredom and a minimum of food. She almost liked it better when he paid attention to her. Maybe that was his plan.

There had to be a way to get to him. She used to have the power. She wasn't sure where or when she lost it, but it shouldn't be too difficult to find it again. She stared up at the skylight overhead. She imagined it was very cold outside, and the gray sky probably meant snow was near. Perhaps there would be a white Christmas. A tear streaked down her face and she forcibly brushed it away. She wouldn't give him the pleasure of seeing her cry.

*　　*　　*　　*

Jake inserted his key into the lock and punched out the security code once inside. He would visit with Hank soon, but first there was more investigating to be done. A pungent stench fought through the cold draft from the outdoors and found Jake's nose. He walked toward the front of the store in the direction of the smell and noticed the familiar whirring of the filtration system was conspicuously absent. The water level on the tanks was a few inches lower than usual, and the water itself was stagnant and green. Decaying pale bodies floated on top of the water, surrounded by muck and slime.

He also noticed little noise coming from the front of the store. Most of the putrid smell came from the small animal section. The cages looked as though they hadn't been cleaned in weeks. Tanks and wire cages were thick with urine-soaked cedar and piles of feces. He did not notice any dead bodies, but was amazed that the food bowls and water bottles were filled. The bird section fared a little better, although most of the cages were empty, as were the reptile tanks.

He scolded himself for being so self-absorbed. Maggie had been away for weeks, but he was so involved with his own problems that he hadn't even checked on her store. He should have known that Frank wasn't responsible enough to take care of such an important task.

He strode quickly to the back room, pulling the neck of his shirt over his face. He searched through each drawer of the desk, but found no notes. He hoped to find some clue about the author from their content. If his theory were correct, the author of those notes and the serial killer were one in the same. And to this point, those notes were the only clues the killer had left.

As he drove toward Hank's house, the idea struck him to visit Maggie's place. Perhaps she had returned without telling anybody, he thought. Upon reaching the house, he discovered that her SUV was still parked in its spot on the road in front of her house, the shades were still drawn, and the house was still locked. He walked back toward his car, and he thought how strange it was that Maggie had left her car behind. Knowing how frugal she could be, however, it was actually pretty typical that she would rather take a taxi to the airport than pay the parking fee for a few weeks. He smiled at the thought, and felt an emptiness without her. He opened the car door and peered over at the parked SUV. It was strange for Maggie to park on the road when she knew she'd be gone for so long. If it had snowed, she would have been towed away.

He suddenly closed the door and walked toward the SUV. He peered through the window and was stunned to see the keys lying on the floor of the vehicle. He was even more stunned when he tested the door and found it to be unlocked. He walked around the SUV and hopped behind the wheel, intending to move it into the driveway. A curious feeling came over him, and he began looking around the car in search of some unknown clues. He opened the glove compartment and dozens of letters spilled out into his waiting hands.

He observed that there was no return address on the envelopes, and he began to tear one open when a car passed slowly by, the driver eyeing Jake suspiciously. He returned the driver's curious look and stuffed the envelopes into his jacket. Perhaps it wasn't the time or the place to examine these new clues. He parked the SUV alongside his car and stuffed the keys into his pocket. He would scold Maggie later for carelessly leaving them in an unlocked car. It was a good thing she lived in a decent neighborhood.

He pulled into Hank's driveway and knew immediately he wasn't home, but as he began to back out, he was pleasantly surprised to see Frank pull in behind him.

"Frank...fancy meeting you here," he said as he approached the car. Frank stepped out of the car and faced Jake. He was wearing a baseball cap and some raggedy sweats, but that wasn't the reason he looked so terrible. He looked as though he had lost twenty pounds since the last time Jake saw him.

"Just dropping off some supplies from the store for Hank. How've you been, Jake?" He seemed to be more pleasant than usual, especially toward Jake, but Jake found it hard to get a read on his emotions, as he wore dark sunglasses over his eyes.

"Jesus, Frank...are you okay? You don't look so hot," Jake said, then bit his tongue.

Frank laughed uncomfortably, then said, "Yeah, well. That's what happens when the virus becomes a disease."

The two stood awkwardly for a moment, each wondering what their next question would be. Jake spoke first. "Have you heard from Maggie?"

"No...haven't seen her, haven't heard from her...of course, I've been a little busy. She might have called, who knows? How is she?"

Jake shifted his weight as he formulated some tactful questions in his mind. "I haven't heard from her, to tell the truth. She just left without saying a word to anybody. I was hoping Hank would have some news, but he's not home." He paused for a moment, then said, "I sure hope nothing's happened to her. She's a strong girl, but sometimes she needs a little protection, know what I mean?"

He looked for some signs of emotion, but Frank merely stared at him—almost seemed to stare through him. "Yeah," he said, "she's something else. I'm sure she's all right, though. She's a big girl."

"Stacey was a big girl, too, Frank," Jake blurted.

Frank seemed to become irritated with the line of questioning. "Yeah, well, Stacey had a lot of problems. She wasn't as strong as you think. That's probably why she killed herself, huh? Listen, I gotta run. Nice talking to you." Before Jake could say a word, he hopped back into his car and sped down the road.

Jake arrived at his house to the joyous welcome of King's barking. He strolled into the kitchen and opened the door for the shivering beast outside. In typical New England fashion, the temperature had fallen ten degrees in the last hour. Jake began removing his jacket when he noticed the manila envelope still resting in the place where he had left it days before. He stood for a moment at the closet door, wondering how long he could ignore it. He reached for the thick pamphlet first, but his hand continued deeper into the envelope, producing the pink envelope instead. He timidly turned it over and ran his thumbnail across the seal. A handful of pictures were placed inside, along with a hand-scrawled note on matching pink stationary.

> *Jake—*
>
> *Thought you might want these. It may show you that I do have a heart after all. And maybe you'll see that there was a time when I was a good mother.*

Jake examined one picture at a time, unsure whether he even wanted to see them at all. The voice of Worm grew stronger than his own, however, and Worm wanted to look at each picture and reminisce about the way it used to be. There was a photo of a rosy-cheeked young Worm and his loving mother, standing with their arms around each other and smiling in front of a Christmas tree. Another picture showed the same smiling couple in front of the old Cape Cod. Uncle Henry could be seen in the background, looking proudly at the two of them.

There was another, more compelling, picture of Worm and his mother at the stables on their old farm. Two men stood in the background on each side of his old horse, Daisy. One scowling face he could never forget—that of his old father. The other man looked familiar, but he couldn't place his face. Worm's laughing voice grew louder with the next picture uncovered. It was a picture of Worm, about eight years old, a pout on his lips, his body covered in clothing from head to toe while his mother donned a bathing suit and was attempting to squirt him with a garden hose. An eerie sensation washed over him, and he felt as though the memory of that moment was dancing on the edge of his conscience. The insane laughter of Worm filled his head once again, echoing throughout the room as his mind fought another battle against itself. All of the pictures fell from his lap as he rose to his feet. One solitary photo remained in his hand, and he staggered toward the window to get a better look at it in the daylight.

He held the picture taken at the stables up to the light and examined once again the men in the background. A familiar young man with a cleft in his chin stood next to his baneful father, and he recognized the man as a younger version of Hank. He turned the photo over, hoping to reveal some clue as to why the insane laughter persisted in his head. He began flipping the other pictures over, each revealing only a date scrawled by his mother. All except one—the picture of the bundled-up Worm being squirted by his mother—which contained a note, as well. It was a comment about Worm needing to cool down after being so mad at his father.

Jake felt his strength return as the laughing suddenly waned, perhaps because he had the nerve to ask aloud, "Which father?" and also because he had finally recognized the laugh. It was the same contemptible, drunken, frightening laugh of John Adams, the boy's father. It was the same guffaw that accompanied the ice water that morning, and the same laughter heard each day as Worm found himself subjected to the torment and humiliation of the man who called himself his father. A sly grin formed on Jake's face and he pumped his fist through the air.

"I gotcha!" he shouted. "I got you—you son of a bitch! It was you. It was you all along."

The smile slowly disappeared, however, when he questioned why the man had intruded his existence into his mind at all. Perhaps he was working with Worm to drive him insane. It didn't make sense. Worm hated the man as much as he did, and perhaps more. He gathered the pictures from the floor and tossed them onto the sofa for future consideration. Though he had made great progress in solving his personal mysteries, there were other mysteries yet to be solved. Foremost on his list was the opening of those letters he found in Maggie's glove box.

Later that evening, Jake walked around his backyard. A light dusting of powdery snow had fallen over the land, giving a pure, clean look to the cluttered lot. The notes were of little help, revealing nothing other than the fact that the writer was clearly obsessed, and was likely in need of psychiatric help. There was no indication that Frank was the writer. In fact, the evidence seemed to point away from Frank, as the writer seemed far too articulate. Frank may have gone to the University of Miami for a few years, but it wasn't for the academic experience. He had reached an impasse on all three cases. He was no closer to solving any of them since he began working on them that morning. He had looked forward to his day off, to gain some perspective, but it had thus far proven to be a waste of time.

He felt a cold, slimy object touch his hand, and he jerked away, looking down into two warm, brown eyes. King leapt onto his hind legs and wrapped his front paws around his master's waist, licking his neck with giant, sloppy affection.

"Okay, okay," Jake said, examining his hand, then wiping it on his shirttail. "Well, I guess you're healthy," he said with a smile. "I guess you want to go lie on the couch for a while and watch some TV, huh? Sounds like a good idea. Then it's time for a nice, long nap."

* * * *

The nap was long, indeed, but it was anything but nicc as far as he was concerned. He was facing the icy wall again, peering through to the other side, watching the happy couple on the blanket, when she snuck up from behind him and laid a cold finger on his bare shoulder. The snowstorm was as blinding as ever, and though his steps were slow he knew the destination. He also knew that when he turned to face her, he would see the rotting flesh frozen to the bony frame of his mother. He was prepared to face it. It had become a familiar routine. Only this time when he turned, she had altered her appearance. Perhaps if she looked as she usually did, he wouldn't have been so frightened. But she was young and beautiful and wore a bright, wide smile on her face. He tried to speak, but she placed her index finger to her lips to quiet him. She motioned to him to follow her toward the laughter that grew louder in the background. Her dark locks of silky hair whipped about her smooth face as the wind gathered strength and threatened to carry them both away. He could see her lips moving, but he could not hear her words.

She pointed toward two figures in the distance coming toward them. It was difficult to tell how far away they were, as the snow obscured his depth perception. He could tell that one was taller than the other, but he could not make out their faces. He looked back toward the woman next to him to see that she had reverted back to the decomposed skeleton he had known before. She attempted to speak once again, but her frozen lips shattered and were swept away by the wind. She raised one thin, bony finger, and he thought she intended to impale him with it. Her finger continued past him and began scraping away the frost on the windowpane with elongated nails. He watched as she chiseled out four words:

I CAN HELP YOU

He looked back toward her face and discovered she was once again young and beautiful. A lonely teardrop froze to her cheek as she raised her hand to stroke his hair. He turned toward the approaching figures and saw that they were just yards away from him. The woman disappeared and he was left to confront the men on his own. He looked once again toward the window, to the carefree couple on the other side, and saw that they appeared to be looking back at him, anxiously awaiting his next move. He heard the crunching snow underneath their footsteps as they approached. The howling wind was mixed with the mad laughter of his stepfather, the crying of a child, a rooster's crowing, and off in the distance, the barking of a dog. He knew there wasn't much time before the figures would descend upon him. His body was frozen as he closed his eyes, awaiting his fate. He braced himself for the takeover and woke to the barking of King, who stood inches away from his head.

* * * *

Maggie was wrong. She had miscalculated and underestimated her captor. She thought it was a reasonable request to check on her store, so she saw no harm in asking him a second time. She was shocked to discover that he had a ready answer for her. She was even more shocked to feel the cold steel of a gun barrel on her temple again, as he forced her to sign a letter to her lawyer.

CHAPTER 33

The air was cold and raw, and the sky was dark with ominous snow clouds. It would be a terrible storm, to be certain. Jake guessed that was why the stores were so full of frantic customers piling their carriages with snow shovels, toilet paper, bottled water and canned goods. It always amazed him that there was so much rapid panic among people during the first storm of the year when most of them had lived in New England their whole lives. By their frenzied actions, one would think that they were being holed up in their houses for weeks instead of hours. He found the whole thing amusing as he strolled from aisle to aisle carrying only a basket to pick up a few essentials.

He stopped to chat with a few people he knew, glad that they seemed to treat him as they always had, and not as the freak he had become around the office. The chief had called him into his office earlier that morning and "suggested" that he take some time off. Jake knew by the look on the chief's face that it was an order. Just the same, he figured he could use the time off to collect his thoughts in an orderly manner.

Jake returned home, driving ahead of the approaching storm. He hooked the leash to King's collar before letting him out of the truck. He went in through the basement and locked the gate behind him. He peered through the darkness of the staircase and saw the sorrowful expression of King staring back. "Sorry," he said, "but I need to be alone."

He stared straight ahead as he passed through the kitchen, stopping only long enough to deposit the groceries on the table. He proceeded to the living room and pulled the drapes closed before he collapsed onto the couch. His fingers formed into fists as he prepared himself for what he was about to do. The evidence was laid out before him on the coffee table, summoning him to procrastinate no longer. He discovered the items the day before, quite by accident, when he went to the attic to store his mother's documents.

It was a long, hard day. Each time he tried to make some progress with one of the cases, he was interrupted by either the forces inside his head or by outside influences. Hank paid him a surprise visit. It had been a while since he had seen him, and they had a lot of catching up to do.

"Wish I knew when, or even if, Maggie figures on coming home," Hank said solemnly. "It would be nice if she would just call to let me know what's going on. The poor girl was so upset. I'm worried about her."

Jake watched the man slowly push his fingers through his graying hair. He couldn't believe Maggie would never return. She was merely taking some time off to regroup, much as he was doing. "What makes you think she might not come back?" Jake asked.

Jake heard Hank clear his throat and saw him slowly shake his head in disbelief. "Our Maggie is obviously going through a very painful experience, Jake. It seems like she wants no reminder of what happened here, or of this town, and she obviously wants nothing more to do with that store."

"What do you mean?" Jake asked.

Hank raised his head and took a deep breath. "She wants to sell the store, Jake. A friend of mine downtown says he received a letter from Maggie stating that she wants out. She instructed him to sell the store and any remaining supplies. She's through with the pet business, apparently."

Jake stared through him, his brow furled and his mouth opened slightly. Surely this must be a mistake, he thought. That store meant everything to Maggie. "Is she okay, Hank? I mean...is she mentally okay, do you think?"

"I just don't know, Jake. I really don't know. If I could just talk to her..." He paused, shaking his head once again. "You know Maggie, Jake. She's a stubborn Irish lass. If she doesn't like the way something's going, she does something about it. She's stubborn and she's impulsive and she's probably trying to get herself a fresh start somewhere. If that's the case, I wish her the best. You should do the same, too. I'll let you know if I hear from her, and you do the same for me. I'm sorry I can't stay a little longer, but I have some things to do. Take care, Jake."

He rose from his chair and shook Jake's hand for a prolonged moment. Jake thought he saw the old man's eyes get a little glassy, but before he could speak, Hank was out the door. After he left, Jake returned to his business, pouring over the contents of the manila folder. He calmly read through the will once again, then impartially browsed over the old pictures. He collected all the papers and pictures and pulled the metal chain in the ceiling that lowered a set of stairs into the attic.

He had not visited the attic in quite some time, as there had been no need to review any of the old remnants stored there, covered in cobwebs and dust. The room was neat and organized and filled with mementos and files and discarded furniture. There was an old wooden rocker, a few tables with missing legs, and a couple of musty old paintings—all left-over property of the old couple who used to live there. They didn't take up any needed space, and he didn't have the heart to throw them away. He walked straight past the stack of articles to the other side of the room, watching his head for both protruding rafters and intruding bats. On an antique maple table, he found Henry's old toolbox right where he'd left it years ago. He blew the top of the cover gently, sending a cloud of dust into the cold, crisp air. He remembered filling it with personal mementos the day Henry died. Only the most rare and valuable items earned a place in the exclusive memory chest. All the rest were set on fire in the backyard, or loaded into his truck on the way to the dump. He held the manila envelope in his hands as he contemplated whether to add the item to the collection inside. It seemed like the appropriate place to keep it, alongside his birth certificate, mortgage to the house, and other forms and documents he might find interesting some day. He noticed how quiet and peaceful it seemed in the attic, and he wondered whether the voices could penetrate the ceiling and find their way to him.

He unlocked the clasps of the toolbox and opened the lid. The manila folder dropped to the floor and he took a step away from the toolbox. He spun his head around as if he were being watched, as if the person who had planted the items in the box were crouched behind a cardboard box, laughing at the expression on his face. Inside the box, a ten-inch blade rested on a bloodstained handkerchief. A small vial of clear liquid lay next to it. A bottle marked "chloroform" stood on the end near the corner alongside a couple of letters addressed to Maggie. The voices found their way through the thick floor of the attic and crept into Jake's head, laughing and screaming. The toolbox seemed to dance in front of him in taunting defiance, and soon the entire room faded to black.

The next thing he remembered was sitting on the couch in his living room. He did not remember how he got there, nor did he care. That was yesterday afternoon. Today, he found himself sitting on that same couch, with exhibit "A" sitting before him. His mission for the day was to confront whatever ghosts were haunting him and solve the mystery once and for all, even if it killed him.

He opened the toolbox and deposited each item with a gloved hand onto the table. He doubted the killer would be stupid enough to leave his prints on the evidence, but it was worth a try. He extracted his kit from the floor beside the couch and applied the solution to the items on the table in front of him. He waited a moment, and then used a brush to expose any incriminating evidence.

He smiled victoriously as he exposed prints on the items. They were good prints, too. The killer had been very careless. His joyous feeling waned quickly, as he heard the voice inside his head exclaim, "Uh-uh-uh…not so fast, bub." He removed the latex glove from his hand and brought his own fingers to his eye. He slammed the glove to the floor in disgust, then dropkicked the next one, sending it hurtling across the living room. "SHIT!!" he screamed, drowning out the laughter in his head.

He tried to remember whether he had touched the items during his blackout the previous night, but could not recall. It didn't matter. It was clear someone was out to get him. He knew for certain that he didn't place the items there himself. He hadn't opened that toolbox in years. He had no reason to open it.

He knew exactly what the weapons were—there was no need for forensics. The knife was, of course, the one the slasher used to murder Giddings and Lapinski. The blood on the handkerchief most likely matched that of one of the two. The substance in the vial was heroin—most likely the heroin that was missing from the evidence room down at the station. The chloroform was a mystery, but it was most likely also used to kill one of the thirteen victims. The notes written to Maggie were the icing on the cake. These notes were more graphic than the ones he had read, but the intention was just the same.

The evidence was all there in front of him. Somehow, some way, it had found its way onto his coffee table. He could carry it all into the police station at that very moment and he'd be a hero. Until, that is, they asked him how he got it. And why his fingerprints were all over it. He could explain, of course, but given his status at the station, he didn't feel it was the wise choice. The answers were all there. There was only one way to get them—it was time to confront Worm head-on.

* * * *

Jake focused on the photo of the farm that taunted him from the table, and he sat mesmerized by its haunting power. He tried to relax his mind, to extend an open invitation for the boy inside of him to appear. He was determined to confront the boy on his terms for a change. He prepared himself for the rushing wave of memories that he allowed to be freed from their rusting shackles. In the end, he felt, he would either achieve complete liberation from knowing the truth, or ultimate destruction.

He worked most of the night on his latest theory, and now it was time to test it. He fixated on the photo, challenging the elusive imp to come out from hiding.

Olly olly oxen free. I can't see you, but you can see me.

He screamed out loud the child's name, hoping to scare him out of hiding. He felt the room darken and the picture began to sway, making it difficult to concentrate. He could feel his heart pounding, and he heard its loud beating in his head. The sound became so loud that it took him a moment to realize there was a second beat that accompanied his own. The boy had finally taken the bait.

"Come on out you little son-of-a-bitch," he whispered softly, as if he were afraid to scare the boy away. "Come on out."

The outer edges of his vision became blurred, and he could feel the picture begin to move toward him until he found himself completely inside. Two men and a woman were talking in front of the horse, Daisy, near the fence of the stable. Worm rigidly stood near the center, his fists clenched, his body quivering. The boy turned his sunken eyes in Jake's direction, wisps of wet hair fell down over his forehead and Jake realized that he was now standing in Henry's backyard.

Worm was wearing jeans and a long-sleeved black shirt. The sun beat down upon Jake's skin like a thick, suffocating blanket. Streams of sweat rolled down his face as he watched his mother soak the young boy with the garden hose. Worm just sat there, arms folded across him, shivering.

He heard the voice of Aunt Vera and turned to face her.

"Do as your mother says, John! Take that shirt off this instant!" Aunt Vera screamed. Uncle Henry merely stood in the distance, shaking his head. His mother spoke next.

"I'm sorry, John, but this is for your own good. You've been playing out here for hours—you'll get heat stroke."

There was a clicking sound behind him, and Jake turned to see his stepfather, laughing hilariously, a camera in one hand and a bottle of beer in the other. A cigarette dangled from the corner of his mouth. "Ain't that just the damnedest thing…a Worm crawling around in the mud!" He let out another guffaw, dropped the camera to the ground, and slapped his knee. Jake turned again to the small boy. His black, wet hair stuck to his shivering face and he couldn't tell whether the rivers that streamed down his cheeks were made of tears or water. Suddenly, he discovered the boy was lying in his bed.

"Time to get up, boy!" his father shouted, an empty metal bucket slung in his left arm. "Didn't you hear me calling you from outside? What's the matter with you? We got chores to do this morning. Now go grab a shovel and start cleaning Daisy's stall. Then, when you get done with that, I'll find something else for you to do. No free rent here, boy."

Jake could almost see the anger well up inside of the boy. His face became red and contorted, and he could not believe the word that escaped the boy's mouth at that moment. "NO!!" Worm shouted.

The old man appeared stunned at first, then angry. Then a crooked smile bent his lips. He laughed menacingly and unhooked his belt, drawing the belt from his ragged jeans. The petrified boy knew he had made a costly mistake. He pulled the blanket to his neck and jumped to the far side of the bed, tucking his feet under his body. The old man pounced on him and threw him across the bed, ripping his shorts off. He folded the belt into a loop, gripped the ends, and began administering the usual punishment.

The boy simply winced, but did not shed a tear. Jake imagined Worm did not want to give the man the satisfaction. The old man stopped his whipping for a moment when he noticed the peculiar silence. "Oh…I guess you're a tough guy now, huh?" he said with an amused laugh. "Well, we'll just see about that, I guess."

Jake watched in horror as the man removed his own pants. Suddenly, Jake felt the boy's searing pain. He felt the boy's terror, and he felt his humiliation. He looked into the boy's eyes and as Worm looked back at him, a tear rolled down his face.

The pain stopped, and Jake was again transported to the original scene in front of the barn. It was only a few hours after the incident, and his stepfather insisted on snapping a family portrait. Worm had been shoveling most of the afternoon when he spotted them coming toward the barn. His first instinct was to run, but when he saw his mother and the other two men with her, he figured he would be safe. After the picture was taken, however, the three of them left, leaving himself and his stepfather alone.

He could see the swagger in the man's step and knew he had been at the bottle again. "Goddammit, boy! You call this clean?!? Shit—my father woulda whooped me good if I did such a shitty job as this…maybe that's just what you need as well." He began removing his belt, and Jake could imagine a repeat performance of the day's earlier event. The boy watched the man intently, his grip on the shovel tightening with each step taken in his direction. Jake could feel his heart pounding faster and stronger, and he began to feel dizzy. Suddenly, everything faded to black and he found himself sprawled out on the couch, covered in cold sweat.

He remembered that day as the day his father died. The old workhorse, Daisy, had kicked him in the head. Jake closed his eyes and he felt himself being led down a dark tunnel. Worm was not finished with him yet. *You called* me, *remember?* the voice said angrily.

He suddenly found himself standing at the bedside of Vera at the old Cape Cod. She was complaining about the noise, and Worm explained to her that he was helping Uncle Henry move some things to the dump. "No need," she barked, taking a drag from her cigarette. "The whole backyard's a dump already. Might as well save yourself a trip." As Worm began to leave, Vera called to him, "Be home by five o'clock—I'm cooking you some chicken." Her words seemed to touch a nerve in the boy because he stopped in his tracks. He remembered the last chicken dinner she had cooked for him.

"Oh! Before you leave," she coughed, "get me some matches, will you, boy?"

He remembered running from the room, spitefully ignoring her request, then bringing a box out to the waiting Uncle Henry. He remembered driving home in the rickety old pickup and arriving to the smell of burning wood. He remembered the triumphant crowing he heard that day as they carried away Vera's body.

Jake threw himself back against the couch. Physically and emotionally drained, he pleaded with Worm to release his grip. He learned enough. He didn't need any more Scroogian trips down memory lane. He got the answers he'd been searching for, and he solved all the riddles. The man he'd been looking for all this time was the same man he saw when he looked in the mirror. He was the one responsible, even if it had been Worm all along. He closed his eyes and slowly drifted to sleep. It was over. It was finally over.

* * * *

Maggie stood at the door, a broken-off bed slat perched high over her head, waiting. She would have to hit him hard enough to knock him out for a while, and she wondered whether she had the strength. She certainly had the motive. She was tired of being his personal pet, and she was going crazy being all alone in that room for so long. She wondered what was taking him so long. She had heard the key in the lock five minutes before. Her arm was growing tired and numb. She pictured the surprised look on his face when he saw what she was up to. He probably didn't think she had it in her. But she had tried to reason with him.

She lowered the slat for a moment to allow the blood to flow back into her arms. She put her ear to the door and tested the handle to see whether he had left it unlocked by mistake. No such luck. Maybe he finally had the nervous breakdown she had predicted for him so long ago. He had changed so drastically, she hardly recognized him anymore. Behind those eyes she could see only a hint of the man she once knew. The longer she stayed with him, the more nonsensical his daily banter became. She often found herself just nodding her head politely when he would make one of his infrequent appearances in her room. She wondered whether her expressions looked sincere enough. She wondered whether he knew he was becoming unstable. He needed help and she felt sorry for him.

She heard some footsteps in the distance and she frantically argued with her conscience, deciding whether or not to go through with it. She stood motionless for what seemed like an eternity. She watched the doorknob intently, and thought for certain it would turn and he would see what she was doing. She kicked the slab under the bed just as the knob began to turn.

Chapter 34

Jake awoke relaxed and ready for the coming day. There were no nightmares that night. He begged Worm to take the night off, for he needed his rest. He prepared himself a feast at breakfast: pancakes, sausage, homemade biscuits, and home fries with grilled onions. Breakfast was always his favorite meal of the day. Apparently, it was King's favorite meal as well, as he seemed to inhale his portion, which Jake served on one of his best plates. He spent most of his morning hours cleaning the house and the kennel. A fresh bowl of water and a heaping bucket of dried food awaited his pet after he shared a playful moment with him in the backyard. He gave the beast a pat on the head and shouted, "*Sprung! Sprung!*" The animal responded by leaping into his master's arms, giving him a big bear hug and a lick to the face.

He closed the gate behind him, looking over his shoulder to see King lying in the sun underneath the oak tree. It was a beautiful day—one of those teasers Mother Nature hits New Englanders with before she unleashes her winter fury. He closed the door behind him and grabbed a cold beer from the refrigerator. It was a little early, but he figured he deserved it after a long day's work.

He sat down at the kitchen table and perused his latest list of things to do. The list was checked off in order, all except for the last item. He guzzled the remainder of the can and reached into the pocket of his jacket, which hung on the chair behind him. He placed his badge on the upper left corner of the kitchen table. An addressed letter to Maggie was already on the top right. He folded his hands and stared at the revolver in front of him.

He felt an ethereal calm come over him as not a shadow of doubt remained that he was doing the right thing. He glanced at the clock on the wall and waited to complete the last item on his list. Any minute, Hank would return his call. He thought of his old list, the ubiquitous folded piece of yellowed paper that called his front pocket its home for so many years. Gently unfolding it and smoothing out the wrinkles, he placed it next to the new list. He expected to feel regret that his nostalgic old list would never be completed. It surprised him to feel dispassionate. He guessed a little bit of Uncle Henry rubbed off on him—he never finished anything he started, either.

He looked again to the clock on the wall. Hank should be getting home any minute. His eyes were drawn down to the bulletin board on the wall, still containing the pictures and notes from his investigations. He thought of taking it down, but decided it did not matter. The truth would be known soon, anyway.

He toyed with the gun on the table, checking the chamber once again to ensure it was loaded. He picked up the letter and considered its contents. He debated whether he should have added a postscript to the letter explaining how she was the catalyst of the entire operation, but he determined it was better that she didn't know.

With all of his chores completed, Jake Allen felt at peace sitting in his chair in the kitchen of his comfortable Cape Cod. His mind devoid of emotion, his body relaxed, he simply accepted his fate and waited for the phone to ring. Once he had said good-bye to the only person left that mattered to him, he'd be free to finish the job. He figured he owed the old man at least a few words to let him know what a good friend he was. He debated whether to call him "Dad," then decided it was better to lose a friend than a son.

He was staring into the distance when the phone rang. He already rehearsed what he was going to say. It was going to be short and sweet; a simple good-bye. After the second ring, he picked up the receiver expecting to hear the gravely voice of Hank, but heard a woman's voice instead.

"Hello…is this Jake Allen?" the strange voice inquired.

There was silence for a moment, then Jake answered, "What can I do for you?"

"Mr. Allen, this is Betty Walsh. I'm Maggie McCarthy's aunt." She seemed to be a little upset. He could hear it in her voice.

"Mrs. Walsh, I'm so glad you called," he said. "How's Maggie?"

There was a long silence, and he thought for a moment that the line had been disconnected. "Well," she said, sounding a bit confused, "that's why I'm calling you, Jake. We haven't heard from her in ages. I've been trying to get in touch with her for weeks now, and she hasn't answered her phone. My husband and I wanted to tell her how sorry we were to hear about her friend. We didn't hear about it until a few weeks ago when a friend told us about it. That same friend gave us your name as someone who might know where she is. We were hoping to get together with her after the holidays."

Now it was Jake's turn to experience confusion and offer dead silence.

"Hello? Are you still there?"

"Yes...yes, I'm here...Mrs. Walsh, I don't know what to tell you. Maggie left a note when she left saying that she would be going away for a while. She said she would be visiting you in Mexico. We all assumed that's where she was. If you have any luck finding her, please give me a call." His words filtered into his brain, and after realizing what he had said, he added, "Better yet—give Hank Beecher a call. He'd probably be the best person to call right now."

"Okay. Thanks for your help. Sorry to bother you," she said and hung up the phone. Jake lingered over the conversation for a moment, then looked back toward the clock. He had waited long enough, and he was afraid if he waited any longer he might not go through with it. He grabbed one of the notebooks from his pile of notes and quickly scribbled his rehearsed message to Hank. He folded it once then placed it on top of the letter to Maggie.

He took the gun from the table and walked out of the room, looking over his shoulder to check on King one last time. The dog was still basking in the glow of the bright winter's day. He walked toward the living room couch and took one last look at the pictures still resting on the coffee table. He thought he should feel deep remorse, but felt relief instead. After months of investigation, he had found his man. It would be the last great solved mystery in the short career of an ace detective. He loved Maggie, and killed anyone who got in her way. He supposed it was Worm who loved her most, for it was he who did the killing. It was Worm who learned to kill by killing his own father and aunt. And it was Worm who used the rooster as his personal megaphone of victory.

Jake cocked the revolver and slowly raised it to his head. He closed his eyes as he inserted the barrel into his mouth. He wondered whether he would feel the pain. He wondered whether his life would pass before his eyes slowly enough for him to see all the details he had missed. He wondered whether there was anyone at the other end of the tunnel ready to greet him. And he wondered whether those people included Vera, his stepfather, and all the innocent people he killed. Would he spend eternity paying for his sins on earth? If so, he deserved it.

As his thumb began to press against the trigger, he heard a ringing in his ears. He opened his eyes to discover that someone was leaning on his doorbell. He took the gun from his mouth and placed it on the coffee table. He stomped across the room and threw the door open, slamming it into a picture on the wall.

Glass shattered around his feet as Ida Adams drifted past him into the living room.

Jake watched incredulously as his mother ambled into the room and sat down on the couch, in the place where he had been moments ago—the place where they would have found his bleeding body if she hadn't interrupted him.

"What the hell are you doing?!?" he shouted, his face reddened, his veins protruding from his forehead, and his hand still holding the door open.

"I've given it some thought," she said casually, "and I really don't care what you think. I'm dying. Therefore, I can do and say whatever I like. And right now I'd like to talk to you." She folded her hands over her crossed legs, and he knew she wasn't about to leave.

"Fine," he said, slamming the door shut. "Let's talk."

"You don't look so good, John. You should get some sleep."

Jake stood at the door with his arms crossed. "Yes, Ida, I do look like shit. Thanks for noticing. Listen, I'm sort of busy right now. Maybe you could drop by another time."

She looked to the coffee table and noticed the pictures she had given him, along with the folder containing her will, and the gun that rested beside it.

"Yes, I see..." She looked to him as if she knew what he was thinking, and it sent chills up his back. "You really shouldn't leave guns lying around the house like that, John. You could hurt yourself."

"The name's *Jake*, Ida. *Jake,*" he said defiantly.

"Oh, yes, I know," she said, waving her hand. "I am glad to see you had a chance to look over my package. That's one of the reasons why I'm here. I had the feeling you wouldn't open it. You were always so stubborn."

He couldn't shake the shiver that flowed through his body like a wave on the ocean. He looked back toward the door to see if he had not closed it completely. He could hear his teeth begin to chatter and his fingers became cold and numb. *It's all in your imagination*, he thought. *It's just Worm playing his insipid game again.* He looked at his mother sitting on the couch, holding one of the photos in her hand, and he could see her lips move, but the words failed to reach him over the howling winds that filled the room. *Cut the shit, Worm*, he thought.

"Cut the shit!!"

He felt a cold hand on his shoulder and he felt afraid—afraid to turn and face the old rotting corpse in his nightmare. "What's wrong, Jake?" his mother implored. "Come on...come to the sofa. You're shivering like crazy. Let me help you."

The familiar words echoed in his ears. *Let me help you.* He looked at his mother standing so peacefully in the middle of his living room, her hand outstretched. But all he could see in his mind's eye was a much younger version of the woman, waving to him as she drove away from that old Cape Cod so many years ago.

"I know I've let you down in the past," she said softly. "But I can help you now if you'd give me the chance. I'll listen to whatever you have to say, as soon as you're ready."

Ida waited patiently for her response. Jake remained motionless, his dark eyes focused on something so far in the distance, only he could see it.

"You want to help?" he said suddenly, his position unchanged. "After all these years you finally want to help me. Where were you when your old man was beating me?" He took pleasure in the look of guilt he now saw on her face.

"Where were you when he...*raped* me, Ida? Huh? What did you do for me after I bashed his head in with a shovel? 'It's okay,' you said. 'It's all over,' you said. Just forget about it, right? Well, I forgot all right, but a part of me didn't. A part of me has been carrying that baggage around for years."

He paused to consider the look of confusion on her face. Just another defense mechanism, he surmised. She was always big on denial. After her husband died, she acted as though it had never happened. She started going out for big nights on the town, leaving her son at home alone worrying about her. Then she left him on a doorstep as if he had never existed either.

"One question, Ida: is that the real reason why you left me? You didn't want a killer in the family? Thought old Aunt Vera would straighten me out, did you? Well you thought wrong, honey, because I knocked her off, too. Am I getting warm, though? Did you leave me on that doorstep so you could forget you ever had me?"

Jake's eyes darted back and forth, searching for an answer to appear on his mother's face. But all he saw was confusion. He expected her to grovel, to beg for forgiveness. He was surprised to hear a sharp-tongued retort instead.

"You're not being fair. In case you forgot, I wasn't exactly treated with kid gloves, either. In fact, I got more than my share of beatings and abuse from that bastard, too. I never would have married him in the first place if it weren't for you, John. I was a scared 17-year-old kid, and I did what I thought was best for you and for me.

"As for leaving you behind on that doorstep, you have no idea how much that hurt me, John. It was an act of selfless love for you. I was in no position to be a loving mother to you. I had a problem with alcohol, John. I was neglecting you as a parent, and I knew it. But I just couldn't stop doing what I was doing. In my heart, I honestly thought I was doing the right thing when I left you at this home with your aunt and uncle. I had no idea you would be in any sort of danger. Vera always doted on her son when he was alive, and I thought she'd treat you the same. I figured between the two of them, they'd give you a happier childhood than I ever could. I had no reason to believe differently."

Jake sat passively in his chair, listening with his head in his hands. Tears streamed beneath his fingers.

"I can't go back and fix what happened. I made a choice and we all have had to live with it. It's hard not knowing whether or not you made the right decision. I cried myself to sleep every night for years, John. I stayed in touch for a while. I sent you letters. I sent you gifts at Christmas time. And I'd send Uncle Henry some money every now and then to buy you something nice. But in the end, I knew you'd probably be better off without me until I was able to straighten myself out. Unfortunately, that took a lot longer than I had planned."

Jake continued to silently weep. All the pain he'd been feeling his entire life, all the painful memories he had tried so hard to repress, were raw and exposed in the open. He tried desperately to hold onto the hate. Hate was something he could control. Hate gave him the power. But his mother's words slowly ate away at the hate. Hate was gradually being replaced with sympathy and understanding.

Throughout his young life, Jake had assumed his mother left him because she didn't love him. And any child that is incapable of earning his own mother's love must be incapable of earning the love of anyone else. He recognized his life's pattern of pushing those he loved out of his life the moment they got too close. Every person he had ever loved had left him. Rather than suffer the pain of losing another loved one, he chose a life of loneliness instead. Perhaps his mother shared the same social disorder.

"I've said my peace, John. You can do with it what you'd like."

Jake rose from his chair, wiped his eyes, and walked over to the window. The wintry scene outside the window reminded him of his recurring nightmare. He realized that for the past several minutes, he hadn't thought once about Worm, the rooster, and all the murders he had committed. Those thoughts came flooding back into his conscience, reminding him of what he was about to do before he was interrupted.

Almost as if reading his mind, his mother stood up from the couch, walked over to him and put her hand on his shoulder.

"As for your stepfather, you didn't kill him, John. You probably wanted to, but you didn't. I don't know why or how you believe that you could have done such a thing, but it's not true."

Jake turned around and faced her, with a look of confusion in his eyes.

"We found you inside the stall, on the floor..." Her voice began to waver as she searched for the words. It had been so much easier to dismiss it—to tell the boy that Daisy had kicked the old man's head in.

"Your stepfather...had his pants down around his ankles when we walked in. I carried you to your room when Hank told me to leave. He said he wanted to have a little man-to-man chat with Big John. I checked you over from head to toe, and you seemed okay...at least on the outside. I ran back to the barn in time to see Hank standing over John's dead body with a shovel. That was when we came up with the story about Daisy. It was the best way to handle it with Hank being a cop and all. And after all that went on with his partner just a few weeks before...well, it was just best."

Jake shook his head in disbelief. At the same time, he felt an enormous weight lift from his shoulders. He was not a killer after all. Soon, great empty spaces in his memory were filled. He remembered the guilt he felt over Vera's death, yet it was guilt because he had wished her dead so many times, and not because he had done the deed himself. He remembered having the idea, the horrific idea, to burn his Aunt Vera with her own matches, just as she had done with King George. But there were no matches to be found. He would not have gone through with it if there were, but it was fun to fantasize once in a while. He remembered running from the house, victorious that he had disobeyed her command to fetch her matches, yet fearful of her wrath when they returned home from the dump. But his fear was groundless. She was dead by the time they returned. She had burned herself with her own matches, falling asleep while smoking in bed. She had done it hundreds of times before, only this time it proved fatal.

If the seeds of murder were not planted in his childhood, it was entirely possible that he did not commit those other murders, either. Perhaps there were some other reason for the existence of all that evidence he found in the attic. Perhaps there were some other explanation behind that rooster crow.

He felt the need to celebrate. Both he and Worm were innocent. He felt the edges of his mouth curl upward involuntarily. He looked into his mother's eyes, at the woman who had first given him life, then later saved it. She read his thoughts and returned his smile. He slowly realized his own need to forgive her. She tentatively held out her arms and he embraced her, burying his head in her soft shoulder. She stroked his hair lightly with long fingernails, tears welling in her eyes and cascading down her creased face into the corner of her mouth.

"Thank you," she whispered. "Thank you."

CHAPTER 35

The sun just peeked over the horizon, but Jake was already awake and ready to face the day. He had many things written on his new list of things to do, and number one was finding Maggie. The phone call from her aunt disturbed him greatly. The killer was still out there, and Jake feared that in order to find Maggie, he'd have to find the killer as well. A late evening phone call to Hank went unanswered. He figured the two of them together might be able to solve the mystery. He also wanted to talk to him about an incident long ago. Perhaps when it was all over the two of them would sit down over a beer and talk about it.

He quickly showered, then shaved off the thick beard he had grown. After breakfast, he took a little time to run around the backyard with King. It was an even prettier day than the day before, and he was grateful he was still around to experience it. He breathed in the crisp, cold air, and wrestled playfully with the big beast before returning to the house. He removed all of his visual aids from the bulletin board and shoved them into a box along with the evidence he found in the attic. By the time he finished, it was seven o'clock—a reasonable hour to begin knocking on doors. He pocketed his badge and placed his gun in its holster.

With King riding shotgun, he drove straight to Hank's house. Hank was emerging from his house just as Jake's truck pulled into his driveway. It looked like he was getting an early start also, as boxes were piled up near the garage, and he was juggling two more as he descended the front steps.

"Too cold for a tag sale," he yelled, stepping from the truck.

Hank did not appear to be in a very good mood. "My friggin' back is killing me," he snarled. "And it's colder than a witch's tit out here." Jake took one of the boxes from him after a brief tug-o-war.

"What are you up to, old man?" Jake asked.

Hank cocked his head slightly, then returned the question. Jake walked the box down the slight incline of his front yard, walking ahead of Hank and talking over his shoulder.

"It's kind of a long story," he said. "Have you heard from Maggie yet, by any chance?"

Jake dropped the box on top of the stack near the garage and turned to find Hank further behind than he had thought. His movements were slow, and by the expression on his face it appeared that his back was worse than Jake thought. He rushed over to him and took the box from his arms.

"Come on. Let's go inside for some coffee or something. You need a break." He put the box on the stack with the others, then followed Hank into the house. He sat at the kitchen table while Hank brewed a pot of coffee.

"I think Maggie may be in trouble, Hank."

"Why's that? Have you heard from her?" Hank said, his back still facing him.

"No. No one has. Not even her aunt and uncle from Mexico. That's the problem. I think she may be in danger, Hank. Have you been to her house lately?" Hank nodded his head, and he joined him at the table. A stern expression crossed his face.

"Then you've seen her truck outside. Why would she have left her truck at home? How did she get to the airport?"

Hank thought for a moment, then said, "I'd be willing to bet she had a friend drive her to the airport."

"Frank?"

"Frank. He's hasn't been around lately to ask or answer any questions. He was supposed to do some work for me over the winter. Last time I talked to him, he asked me if I had any odd jobs to do for him. I guess the landscaping business slows down a little when there's three feet of snow on the ground."

"When did you last see him?"

"Oh…about a month ago, I guess. Before Stacey died."

Jake hesitated for a moment, considering the possibilities. "I'm still not sure about this whole thing. Something's strange. Maggie wouldn't just take off like that without saying a word."

"She said a word to her lawyer, didn't she? I mean, she's trying to sell the store, Jake. It looks like she just wants to forget this little town and put it all behind her. I can't say I blame her."

Jake was silent for a moment, contemplating whether to divulge all he knew about the serial killer, about the connection to Maggie's secret pen pal, about the mysterious rooster and the appearance of the murder weapons in his attic. The question suddenly entered his mind: *If I didn't do it, then how did that stuff get there?* Someone either thought his attic was the perfect place to hide the evidence, or someone was trying to set him up.

"I don't mean to be rude, Jake, but I have a lot of work to do here. A neighbor of mine is coming down to pick all this stuff up and haul it off to the dump. I don't know what to tell you about Maggie. She's always been stubborn and independent. She's stronger than you think, and I don't think she's in any danger. Like I said, I'm sorry to rush you out of here. Give me a call a little later when it's not so hectic around here. I haven't seen you in a while. I kind of miss your ugly mug." He smiled, sipped the last of his coffee, then rose from the table, signaling to Jake that it was time to leave.

* * * *

Maggie knew she would get what she wanted if only she persisted. Her persistence paid off, and today was the big day. At least she hoped he would keep his promise. She was relieved she never had to use the bed slat, but she figured she would keep the option open as a backup plan. Since the offer had been made the night before, she found it hard to sleep. She tried to convince herself not to get her hopes up too high, as things might not go exactly how she planned.

But she couldn't help herself. Her hopes were high as she imaged the opportunity had finally risen to leave her prison (or was it a cage?) She wasn't sure whether her plan would work, but at least it was an opportunity. And opportunities have a way of fueling hope.

* * * *

Jake swung open the glass doors of Wilson's Hardware. He still had many questions, and he assumed Frank would be the man who could supply the answers. He had been unprepared for their last encounter, but this time he had a long list of questions for him. And if Frank refused to answer them, he was fully prepared to whip out his badge and bring him down to the station.

He found an attractive woman wearing an orange-colored apron with the company logo faintly painted on front and asked her where he could find Frank.

"Frank's on vacation. He won't be back for a while. Is there something I can help you with?" She smiled through glossy lips, as her white teeth chewed on a piece of gum.

"I'm just an old friend of his. I just thought I'd stop in and say, 'Hi.' But I guess he's not around. You know where I can find him?"

The woman hesitated for a moment, and her eyes scanned over his body from head to toe. "Well," she said, recapturing eye contact, "actually, he's at my place," she said proudly.

Jake eyed the woman's long blonde hair and petite figure. At a distance, she would easily pass for Maggie. "How is he? I've been a little worried about him lately."

"Yeah, I know what you mean," she smacked. "What with the mood swings and all. Sometimes he can be a little scary. But I think he's okay. If you want, I'll tell him you were asking for him. What was your name, again?"

"Billy. Billy Martin. And yours?"

She looked him over once more, then said, "Crystal. Crystal Bernheart. But most people just call me 'Miss Legs.'" And with that, she lifted her orange apron to uncover two shapely legs, which she displayed for him. She smiled, then walked slowly away, checking over her shoulder to see if Jake was watching her.

He turned and laughed to himself. *Billy Martin?* he thought. *That's the best you can come up with? Billy Martin?* As he walked toward his truck, he removed a piece of paper from his front pocket, scrawling the name "Crystal Bernheart" in wavy letters, using his hand for a desk.

He wondered whether she had given her real name, and figured it would be known as soon as he looked it up to get her address. The next stop on his journey was Frank's apartment, and if he weren't there, he would try Miss Leg's place. But first, there was one more stop he had to make.

Jake pulled into the driveway and parked behind Maggie's SUV. He thought about parking down the street to be less conspicuous, then brushed the thought away. He jumped from the car and opened the door for King to follow. He then raced around the house to the back door. Extracting a hammer from his coat pocket, he tapped the window of the door, smashing the glass. Reaching gingerly inside, he unlocked the door.

He entered through the kitchen, noting the sink full of dishes. He continued to the bedroom, where her cosmetics cluttered her dresser, and her drawers were full of clothes. It did not look like the house of someone who was planning on taking a long trip. He felt a little guilty as he searched through her private things, opening one drawer after another, searching for clues. His heart skipped a beat as he opened the last one, revealing a diary similar to the one at the store.

At first, he thought someone had moved the diary to a new location, but upon opening the cover, he discovered that Maggie had kept a separate journal unbeknownst to him—a journal to her mother. He flipped through the pages, each containing the salutation, "Dear Mom."

The pages were filled with more intimate details of Maggie's life, in her own thoughts and words. The content was more personal in nature than the one written to her father, and seemed to dwell more on her feelings and concerns about her personal life than her business. He decided to flip to the end of the book and read forward.

Dear Mom,

I feel it's my fault she's dead. I should have done more. I should have seen the signs. I should have been there for her instead of being so caught up with my own problems. Problems that are so minor and stupid compared to what she must have been going through. She had no one to turn to, no one who would help her. She must have felt terribly alone. I feel that way sometimes, too. I guess I shouldn't.

Sometimes Frank really drives me crazy, but I keep hoping someday he'll grow up. And then there's Jake. I thought we were moving in the right direction, but now I don't know. He's so involved in his work, and so bothered by his past, that I don't think he has it in him to begin a new relationship. Even Hank has been acting strange lately. I can't figure out what's gotten into him. I'm confused, Mom. It wasn't the first time, but today when he called me by your name it gave me the creeps. He was holding me and whispering for me not to worry. Then he said I would never be hurt again. He kept gripping me tighter and tighter. Then he said he loved me and he called me 'Allison.' And when I looked up at him, he wiped my tears and I thought he would correct himself and laugh it off like he usually did. But instead, he took my chin and held my face and he tried to kiss me—not as a father would, but as a lover. He even called me Allison again, and said he would never leave me again. He said he would protect me until his dying day.

Jake did not need to read any further. He couldn't read any further, as his attention was diverted by an old, familiar heartbeat. He could almost feel the boy's presence. He could almost see his little hand reaching out to him. He expected the evil thought to rapidly dissolve once Worm finally appeared. Instead, as their minds touched, he received a violent shock, physically and mentally. And he realized that he had finally put it all together. It wasn't himself who was the guilty party, and it wasn't even Frank. He closed the journal on his lap and placed in on the nightstand.

He sped off down the road with King at his side, mentally untangling all of the loose ends in his memory and melting them together, forming one long chain of incredible strength. Hank had always loved Sam's wife. His whole life revolved around his best friend's family. Many times, while sitting with Hank over a few beers, he heard endless praise of his beloved Allison. One night, Hank confessed that he had pulled over the drunk driver that killed Allison. He administered a field test and determined that the driver—a friend of his from the VFW—was sober enough to make it home. Moments later, that driver sped through a stop sign and plowed into the driver's side of Allison's car. Jake could only imagine the guilt that must have weighed heavily upon Hank's conscience all these years.

He recalled other conversations he had with Hank over the years, oftentimes sitting on the back porch of his house, or in the living room of the Cape Cod, and always surrounded by several empty beer cans. The reference his mother made to Hank's old partner jogged his memory of a time when Hank had confided the story to him. His partner was a baby-faced young rookie, just weeks into his first duty on the force. Hank was assigned to him, to show him the ropes. During their first week together, the kid got shot by a man holding up a convenience store. Hank had sent the boy in to get some coffee while he stayed in the car. He heard the gunshot, and was able to get the robber as he left the store. By the time he got to the kid, though, it was too late. He held the kid in his arms and felt the life drain from his body. He felt guilty for not watching out for the boy, and it didn't help when the boy's mother slapped him at the funeral. Jake remembered the sly grin on Hank's face when he told him that the robber was found hanging in his jail cell the next morning.

That conversation spawned another memory that was eerily similar to the first. He remembered Hank telling him about a similar fresh-faced nineteen-year-old boy who just came over from Vietnam. Hank was razzing him about his scuffed shoes as the two of them strolled downtown one day. He pointed to a shoeshine boy on the sidewalk and began talking with a young lady nearby. A few minutes into their conversation, they were forced to the ground as the bomb inside the shoeshine box killed both the young boy and his buddy.

Jake took the corner too wide and spun off the road, sending a spray of sand from his tires as he wrestled to keep the vehicle on the road. He imagined the suffering Hank must have experienced after such painful experiences. He imagined that after Allison and Sam died, Maggie was the only person left who mattered to him. Hank made Sam a promise on his deathbed that he would protect his daughter, and he would fulfill that promise no matter what the price. Only he went a little too far.

He had access to the journal. He had access to the evidence room. Everything seemed to point in that direction no matter how badly Jake wished it weren't true. Did Hank have it in him to eliminate so many people for the sake of his treasured little girl? He had the badge at his disposal. He had experience with crime scenes and knew all the little mistakes criminals tended to leave behind. He could not believe what he was thinking. Hank was no murderer. He loved Maggie just as everyone did. Did he love her enough to kidnap her and lock her away in a little glass bubble to protect her from all the evils of society? Jake's foot pressed harder on the accelerator. As he approached the house, he truly hoped he wouldn't find what he feared.

Chapter 36

Whipping into the driveway, Jake noticed that Hank wasn't home. At least, his car was gone. He swung open the door and allowed King to follow. The dog ran immediately to the garage door as if he were expecting Jake to let him in. Jake peered into the dark garage, seeing the covered old clunker resting in its usual spot. The tarp that covered the rusty machine had been partially pulled back to reveal the trunk of the car. He hesitated for a moment, looking casually over his shoulders, then tested the door.

It opened easily, gliding on the runners over his head. He raised it high enough to duck under and King was the first to enter. He walked slowly toward the car and tested the trunk, discovering it was locked. He pulled the tarp back a little further as a curious wave of recognition came over him. He found a late model Chevy underneath, with dark tinted windows and no license plates either on the front or the back. He took a small step back to encompass the whole car, using what little light he had. He felt as though he had seen the car before, but he couldn't remember where or when. He forced himself to concentrate and it suddenly came to him. He remembered the dark tinted windows zooming past him that day in the parking lot of the pet store. He recalled the huge car with missing plates roaring past him and squealing around the building. It was the same car parked next to the barn that day so many years ago. It was the same car driven by the same man: Hank.

The memory lingered as he turned his attention to the low, throaty growling coming from the rear of the garage. The growling stopped, and was replaced by irritating digging noises, as if King were trying to bury a bone in the cement floor of the garage. From where he stood, Jake could see only the top half of King's tail, waving at him in front of the hood like a hitchhiker flagging down a ride. He called out to the dog as he made his way around to the front of the vehicle. The dog promptly stopped and responded with a low-keyed bark. The bark turned to a throaty whine as Jake reached the dog's side. Checking the wall for any damage done by the dog's claws, Jake found the door. He wondered why Hank had chosen that location to build an addition to his house, and he tried to remember whether Hank had even mentioned that he was doing so. He thought for certain that Hank would have recruited his skills. He shook his head curiously for a moment as his mind reeled. He looked to the dog, whose eyes were riveted to the door, his ears standing on end.

* * * *

Maggie's hands were shaking as uncontrollably as her knees and legs. She told herself to calm down. She could do this…it was the only way…there was no other choice…he gave her no other choice. He had lied to her. There would be no trip to the store. It was just another one of his drunken promises. Christmas was just four days away, and she was not about to spend the holiday locked away in some cell, the prisoner to a madman. She took several deep breaths, cautioning herself that she would have just one chance. It was too late to back out now. Either she would have to continue with the plan, or he'd see what she was up to and he just might kill her. She felt her heart pounding loud and fast, and she could almost hear her pulse from her wrist close to her ear.

She held her breath, listening for his movements. She didn't hear a sound, and slowly lowered her arms to give them a rest from their tense position over her head. Suddenly, she heard the noise again—faint and muted, but he was definitely out there. And she was ready. She would not chicken out this time. She would do it, or die trying.

* * * *

Jake focused on the dog, and listened intently to the series of whines and moans that emanated from him. It was a familiar sound, yet one that he had heard only once before—back when the dog had found little Tommy Patterson in the woods. Whatever was on the other side of that door, King obviously thought it deserved Jake's attention.

Jake stepped closer and found the door was locked. He noticed a heavy sliding bolt lock mounted near the top of the door, and he slid the bolt easily from its track. Without a key, the knob still would not turn. He thought about turning away. Whatever was behind that door, he wasn't sure he wanted to know. That's when he noticed the small, hinged, metal plate at the bottom of the door. Two metal pins fastened the kick plate closed, and they slid out easily as well. The lid lifted slowly, as if it were sealed by a pressurized vacuum, and found a metal shelf. A light streamed into the dim garage through the small window in the room on the other side. Bending slightly at the knees, pushing King's head away, Jake peered through the window and was amazed at what he saw.

Hank had done an excellent job remodeling the room. It seemed like the perfect guest bedroom with all of the necessities. It appeared as though it had been used recently. As he closed the window, King nudged his way in front of him and Jake conceded to let the animal sniff around a little. The dog stuck his nose through the opening, then let out a bark. A voice from the room on the other side startled him, and he jumped a little when he heard Maggie's voice say, "King?"

They stared at each other through the narrow opening in the door, and neither one said a word at first. Maggie tentatively reached through the opening and touched Jake's face. Her eyes welled up with tears, and she smiled in relief. She released the broken bed slat from her hand, and it dropped to the floor.

"Are you okay?" he asked, frantically.

She nodded her head and bit her bottom lip. She took a deep breath as she tried to compose herself long enough to say, "Get me out of here."

He instructed her to stand away from the door, and he tried forcing the door open with both his foot and his body. He extracted the revolver from his holster and fired several shots into the doorknob. Finding a crow bar on the floor nearby, he pried open the door and ran directly to Maggie standing in the corner of the room. He gathered her in his arms and held her trembling body close to his for a few moments. Then he gently pushed her away to look at her face. He kissed her softly and told her she would be okay.

"Where's Hank?" he asked, as King barked loudly. They followed the dog's line of vision to the silhouette of Hank framed by the open door. He stood with a stern expression on his face, a hint of disappointment in his eyes, and a revolver in his hand, pointed directly at the two of them.

Jake stepped in front of Maggie and put his hands down to his sides, feeling the revolver tucked beneath his shirt under his arm. There was silence as the two men faced each other. Jake stared into the eyes of his father and all his questions were answered. He saw the man's stoic expression, his arm holding the gun steady and rigid. A thousand questions formed in his mind, but he found the courage to ask just one.

"Why?" He believed he already knew the answer, but he needed to hear the words. He wanted to hear the man say it was all a mistake. Maggie was only his guest. He wanted to hear his pleas of innocence. He wanted to hear that, behind those black eyes was the man he once knew and loved as his friend, as his partner, and as his father. He asked the question again. "Why?"

A strange look passed over Hank's face. His arm seemed to waver a bit, then corrected itself sharply. He began to speak, then changed his mind and motioned for them to sit down, waving the gun toward the bed. Hank rubbed his forehead slightly, then shook his head.

"I knew you were getting close. But I really thought I'd have more time. One more day and we would've been outta here. I had us all packed and ready. I just had to take care of some last-minute details. I really thought you'd be outta here, too, Jake, what with you losing your mind and all. I mean, your theory about roosters and animal revolts? Where do you come up with this stuff? I didn't want to do it, but you made it so easy, I couldn't let the opportunity pass to get you off my trail. If you only stayed out of it...I wouldn't have had to put all that stuff in your attic. If you got any closer, I was prepared to use it against you. It's a shame we couldn't have worked together, Jake. It really is."

Maggie found herself mesmerized by Hank's willingness to talk. After all the pleading on her part, to give her the smallest morsel of explanation, he never conceded. She didn't understand half of what he said, but she had grown used to his nonsensical rambling. She noticed the steady eye contact between the two men, and was surprised to see Jake so calm. She hoped he had a plan.

Jake listened intently as his question was answered. He had to keep the man talking, and he waited for the opportunity to present itself. A man as disturbed as Hank usually makes a mistake along the way, and he was just waiting for that mistake. All he needed was the right question at the right moment.

Jake saw the man losing his train of thought, as if he were coming out of a momentary lapse of self-awareness. Hank stopped speaking, and he stopped pacing, but the gun remained steady in its position. Jake briefly pondered how to get him back on track, then decided the beginning was a good place to start. Hank seemed to want to tell him. He seemed to be very proud of what he had done, and it seemed like he wanted to boast about it. Jake was ready and willing to comply.

"Why Sheila Bennett?"

Hank's face registered confusion at first, then a curious look of pride formed on his face. "You're good, Jake. I always knew you'd be a good detective. Sheila Bennett deserved it. Of course, it didn't go exactly as planned. She wasn't supposed to be killed by the rabid squirrel I put in her car—just bitten enough times that she'd get nice and infected the way that boy did. You know the one I mean, Maggie?" He looked to Maggie for the first time, and Maggie simply stared at him, bewildered by the conversation.

"You were really on a roll about that woman's irresponsibility. I couldn't just let her get away with upsetting you the way she did. Not after all you went through with Rocky. You didn't need any more stress in your life. The death of Sam's bird set this whole thing into motion, you know. I couldn't do anything about helping you punish some faceless bird killer, but I could do something about the ones with faces and names."

Jake prodded him a bit further since he seemed to be on a roll. "And you needed to take care of Dick Williams for the same reason?"

"That took a bit more planning and creativity," Hank said boastfully. "But yeah, he screwed up my Maggie's life a bit by getting her all upset about those poor horses. It really wasn't so hard after I got him up to the old mansion. We used to go there as kids. The man gave me a little bit of a hard time, not wanting to cooperate. It was really his fault that it had to end like that, but I had to find some way to cover up those rope burns on his neck. The same thing kinda happened to poor Fred Wilkins and old man Haggerty. Remember them, Allison? They weren't too cooperative, either, and things just got out of hand. It doesn't matter, though. They were all pond scum, anyway."

He seemed almost brimming with pride as he divulged all he did for his loved one. Surely she would realize just how much he loved her, he thought. Jake felt Maggie's hand slip slowly under his arm, grabbing him tightly. He didn't look at her, but squeezed her hand slightly before gently moving it away. He also noticed that Hank just called her "Allison." Was it a Freudian slip? Or had he completely lost touch with reality?

"It wasn't easy sometimes," he said wistfully, "but I did it. I did it all for you, dear. It especially wasn't easy with Stacey. It was the toughest assignment I've ever had, but she left me no choice. An order's an order. That was the last straw, though. I realized the job was getting too overwhelming, and I was getting too careless. That's why I brought you here. A safe environment is a good environment. Allison always instructed potential pet owners with that advice. Never sent them away without giving them that lecture. She always made sure her pets were comfortable and happy to the best of her ability. Safe and protected from harm. Loved and cared for. Loved in return with no strings attached."

Jake saw a brief, distant look pass over Hank's face—so brief that he might have missed the whole thing if it hadn't been for inside knowledge. Jake took advantage of that one fleeting moment to try a different approach. If Hank were teetering between reality and fantasy, maybe a push would send him over the edge.

"I understand your frustration in trying to do the right thing," he said. "It must have been an incredible strain trying to keep her safe and sound. You must love her very much to only want the best for her. You thought the only way to ensure that she was safe and happy was to keep her locked away so no one could hurt her. But look at her, Hank. She's not happy. She's scared to death, and she's slowly dying inside. She is too much of a free spirit to ever be happy being caged, you know that. If you truly love her, let her go. Let your Allison go, Hank. Let her go."

Hank seemed to consider the proposal without saying a word. His arm and the gun slowly lowered to his side, and the expression on his face softened along with the look in his eyes. He looked straight into the eyes of the open-mouthed girl who sat on the bed shaking with confusion and fear.

"I've always loved you, Allison," Hank said with a trembling voice. "I loved you from the moment I saw you. You are the most beautiful, wonderful woman I've ever known. I only wanted to make you happy. You left me once, and I found you again. I want you to stay. I can't let you go. Please understand it's not safe out there for you. You don't have to give me anything in return. Just be with me and let me keep all the ugliness of the world from spoiling your sweet beauty."

Jake slowly reached for his gun, never diverting his eyes. Carefully, he folded his arms to hide his hand under his jacket. The motion wasn't slow enough, as Hank suddenly snapped the gun up and pointed it directly at him, his finger poised on the trigger.

"Hold it, Jake. You think I don't know what you're up to? You think I'm about as crazy as you are? Or do you just think I'm stupid? You want her for yourself, don't you? You don't think I'm dumb enough to not see what's going on. You want me to let her go so you can have her. I didn't want it to come to this, but you give me no choice. Just by you being here, you're upsetting her. Can't you see how she's shaking? I have to get you out of here. I have to make sure you don't bother us again. I'm truly sorry, Jake."

Jake let his eyes wander for a moment as he noticed a flicker of light out of the corner of his eye. He peered out the door and watched as Bean appeared in front of the parked car with his gun drawn. His eyes followed to the floor, where King sat patiently at Hank's feet.

"*Sprung!*" he shouted, "*SPRUNG!!*"

The dog rose onto his hind legs, wrapping his arms around Hank's body. Startled, Hank was knocked off-balance, and his gun went off. King let out a loud cry and fell to the floor. The gun dropped from Hank's hand and he bent down to pick it up, raising his eyes to find Jake standing with his gun drawn and pointed directly at him. A bewildered Bean rushed to the opposite side of the room and stood with his gun wavering between the two of them, unsure of what was happening.

King's labored panting could be heard above the hush in the room. A pool of blood slowly stained the carpet beneath him. Jake was aware of each person in the room, including a frightened little boy with a rooster under his arm. Jake glanced down at Maggie and whispered for her to stand with Bean.

"I have to know one more thing, Hank. And I want the truth. What happened between you and Ida's husband so long ago? Was it an accident, or were you doing your duty even way back then?"

Hank looked at him through dark, round eyes. He appeared confused by the line of questioning.

"You remember," Jake continued. "Back about twenty years or so…a night in a barn…a blow to a man's skull with a shovel…ring a bell?"

Hank stood slowly, his face reflecting the forgotten memory of an event so long ago—a secret event shared by only two people. He didn't say a word as he slowly realized that the man knew. Slowly, he put the pieces together, and he recognized who the man must be. He seemed reluctant at first, then gave Jake a sly smile.

"Things just got out of control," he said. "The man wouldn't listen to reason. I had no other choice but to eliminate his existence on this planet. He didn't deserve to live. He was a cruel son of a bitch, Jake. He was your father, right, Jake?"

Jake nodded his head slowly, realizing the old man had gotten the point.

"Ida was a dear friend of mine," he continued. "She didn't deserve getting the crap beat out of her by some asshole on a daily basis. You didn't deserve what he did to you, either. He was a lowlife sack of shit, and deserved every ounce of the beating I gave him. It would have been easy if you had just stayed in bed and not startled that goddamn rooster into crowing at a crucial moment. Just as I was in mid-swing, that damn bird started crowing, and he almost got me killed. Fortunately, I was able to beat the life out of the old man anyway. All's well that ends well, I say. Sometimes you gotta take the law into your own hands, Jake. A lesson learned early, and a lesson learned well."

Jake saw no need to continue the discussion. He learned all he wanted, and there were no more loose ends to tie. The nightmare was over. He could feel Worm slowly disappearing, and he heard his laughter fade away into his soul. The boy had been vindicated. Justice had been served.

Hank winced a bit before meeting his eyes. "It's time to do your job, son," he said, smiling slightly. Jake hesitated for a moment, eyeing Bean on the other side of the room and making sure Maggie was safe. Hank made a sudden lunge for the gun on the floor. In one quick movement, he stretched out fully as he fell, reaching out with his hand past the dog's still body. Jake was startled as he heard both Maggie and Bean scream out his name. He watched as Hank grabbed his gun, and time seemed to stand still. His revolver was still aimed at Hank's body, and he saw the determined expression on the old man's face. Jake pulled the trigger. Hank did not seem surprised. He grimaced slightly and fell to the floor, holding a hand over his bloody chest.

An eerie silence fell over the small room. Jake calmly lowered his smoking gun and turned to look at Maggie. When he finally caught her eye, he instructed Bean to call for an ambulance. He then knelt between the two bodies on the floor. He kicked the gun away from Hank and looked into his eyes.

"I guess your job is over," Hank said to him, his breathing labored and irregular.

"It didn't have to end like this," Jake said, turning his attention to the weakening body of King and rubbing the dog's head. He turned to Hank and examined the wound caused by his own bullet.

"I don't know whether Ida told you, Hank, but I feel you deserve to know." He paused for a moment, looking up at Maggie as he gripped Hank's hand. "I'm your son, Hank. I'm the product of a brief affair you had with Ida many years ago."

Hank's eyes grew wide, and he raised his hand to Jake's face. His expression wavered from brief recognition to remorseful sorrow. His grip on Jake's hand loosened. He then closed his eyes and drew one final, labored breath.

Jake felt a hand on his shoulder and turned to see Maggie kneeling beside him. She bit her bottom lip as tears slowly ran down her cheeks. Their eyes locked on each other for moral support and they knew there was no need for words. Bean announced that an ambulance was on its way. He then turned to Jake with his gun still drawn, pointed toward the floor.

"Give me your gun, Jake," Bean ordered, still unsure of what had just occurred. Jake slowly turned his gun around and handed it to Bean.

"What the hell happened here?" Bean asked excitedly. "I got a call that shots were fired, and next thing I know you two are having a showdown. Will someone please tell me what's going on?"

"I'll give a full report at the station," replied Jake.

Jake and Maggie watched silently as Hank was loaded into a body bag. Jake released his hold on her to check on King, who was being carried out as well. King's wound looked far worse than it was. He would be all right. The dog was a hero. He had saved both Jake's and Maggie's lives.

"So…where do we go from here?" Jake said, turning to Maggie to touch her hair as they sat in the back of Bean's cruiser.

Stealing a look into the rear view mirror, he saw there was not a glimpse of the boy who sometimes looked back. He also saw, as he looked into her eyes, that he was finally free to love her. He kissed her to seal the promise of their future together.

EPILOGUE

Five months later

It was a perfect spring day. The air was warm and a cool, gentle breeze made the newly formed leaves on the trees sway gracefully in the sun. The brightly colored flowers dotted the rolling hills behind them as they lay on a plaid blanket, talking softly and holding hands. Their conversation was free and open, and it centered mostly on their trials of the past and their dreams of the future. They spoke at length of the plans for their wedding day. She wanted a formal and elaborate wedding, complete with a horse-drawn carriage ride from the chapel and a ceremony held on a gazebo overlooking the water. He preferred something more subdued, but listened to her plans just the same.

He fed her ripe, red strawberries, picked fresh that afternoon from a small farm down the road. Her laughter filled his heart with warmth, and he thought that he would have felt undeserving of that kind of emotion not long ago. But as he watched her animated expression and dancing eyes, he knew those feelings were gone forever. Everything may not be right with the world, he thought. But here, on this hill, sitting on a blanket with the girl he loved, he had found his heaven.

King, who chose that moment to straddle her legs and lick whipped cream from her fingers, interrupted Maggie in the middle of her speech. In an angry voice, Jake told the dog to back off. He grabbed the first thing he saw and tossed an oatmeal cookie to the grass nearby.

"Hey! That's my cookie!" she protested. "You always did like that dog best!"

"Yeah, well, he is a better kisser than you," he said with a sly grin. She slapped his shoulder teasingly, and he gave her a kiss.

"Now, back to business," she said. "We have to settle all these plans while I can still fit into my mother's wedding dress."

"Why? You're not planning on ballooning up on me anytime soon, are you?"

"Well now, I guess that depends on how soon you want to change dirty diapers."

They laughed together, and Jake's thoughts turned to his mother. Just when he had finally begun to feel close to her, she passed away. He was with her, holding her hand, when she took her last breath. He supposed he should consider himself lucky that she was able to find him and say good-bye before it was too late. Though he only knew her a short while, he found that he missed her.

With both his mother and father gone, Jake found himself truly alone in the world, were it not for Maggie. In Maggie, he recognized the wonderful opportunity to begin a new life and start a new family of his own. The prospect of being a member of a loving, caring family for the first time in his life was simply overwhelming.

Jake felt an elbow to his ribs, and realized he hadn't been paying attention to Maggie's words. "Are you listening to me?" she said with a frown. "It's getting late. Maybe we should go."

Jake looked into her eyes and kissed her gently. He held up his index finger and said, "One minute. There's something I have to do." She watched him strangely as he rose from the blanket and walked away into the field. There were moments in their relationship when he could tell that she was still struggling to figure him out. He was sure, however, that eventually she would learn to not only live with his quirkiness, but love him for it.

Jake hiked far into the tall grass with King at his side, into the empty field ahead. He turned to look over his shoulder and watched as Maggie lifted a flower to her nose and he smiled. He bent slightly at the waist and, using both hands, lifted the invisible pane of glass in front of him. He felt an icy wind hit his face as he peered through to the other side.

"Come on in," he said, and reached out his hand.

There was a twinkle in his eyes as he allowed the shivering little boy to join him on the beautiful spring day. He turned to face Maggie and the picture he had created. He was finally free.

And so was Worm.

0-595-66332-X